My Life and Times

An Autobiography

George M. Hartung

Order this book online at www.trafford.com/08-1553
or email orders@trafford.com

Most Trafford titles are also available at major online book retailers.

Note for Librarians: A cataloguing record for this book is available from Library
and Archives Canada at www.collectionscanada.ca/amicus/index-e.html

Printed in Victoria, BC, Canada.

ISBN: 978-1-4269-0003-7

*We at Trafford believe that it is the responsibility of us all, as both individuals
and corporations, to make choices that are environmentally and socially sound.
You, in turn, are supporting this responsible conduct each time you purchase a
Trafford book, or make use of our publishing services. To find out how you are
helping, please visit www.trafford.com/responsiblepublishing.html*

*Our mission is to efficiently provide the world's finest, most comprehensive
book publishing service, enabling every author to experience success.
To find out how to publish your book, your way, and have it available
worldwide, visit us online at www.trafford.com/10510*

Trafford
PUBLISHING®   www.trafford.com

North America & international
toll-free: 1 888 232 4444 (USA & Canada)
phone: 250 383 6864 ♦ fax: 250 383 6804 ♦ email: info@trafford.com

The United Kingdom & Europe
phone: +44 (0)1865 487 395 ♦ local rate: 0845 230 9601
facsimile: +44 (0)1865 481 507 ♦ email: info.uk@trafford.com

10 9 8 7 6 5 4 3 2 1

1

Millvale and Creighton

The sixth of January, 1926, must have been a time of excitement and anticipation. Little George, Jr. was on the way through the birth process. Of course, at that time, without the cat scans now available, no one knew whether it would be George or Georgina. Somehow, in all the excitement, my parents did succeed in getting to a hospital in Pittsburgh, Pa. While I was there, I knew nothing of all the events. I was assured by my parents, however, that I arrived at about 7 a.m. on January 7, 1926. As far as I know, I arrived about on time. I recall my Mother telling me I weighed about 7 ½ pounds, or a tad less. My parents also told me that I was born in, I believe, Presbyterian Hospital in Pittsburgh.

I mention that I am assured of the above events because I learned some years later, when I first sought a U.S. passport, that the government has no record of my birth. It seems that at the time I was born, births in the cities of Pittsburgh and Philadelphia were duly recorded in the health department of the respective cities. For whatever reason, it seems that at that time births outside the two cities were recorded by the Pennsylvania Health Department. And there lies the root of the confusion over the matter of my birth. I was born in the Presbyterian Hospital which was in the City of Pittsburgh. We lived in the town of Millvale, a suburb of Pittsburgh which abuts Pittsburgh. It seems unusual that I could have slipped through the cracks of the government. But there it was. When I applied for a passport in June of 1951 I was unable to obtain a copy of a birth certificate. The Commonwealth didn't know I existed.

My parents, being resourceful, easily solved the problem. My parents knew that I was baptized on my first Easter. They knew also, of course, that my Dad had baptized me. I recall sitting down with Dad and making the calculations to determine when Easter fell in 1926. After figuring out the date, my Dad duly filled out a birth certificate, nunc pro tunc, certifying as to my birth and baptism. (Subsequently, I wondered whether there was a copyright date on the birth certificate. While I do not recall clearly, I seem to remember that there was a copyright date sometime later than 1926. Whatever the facts, armed with this birth certificate, the Government of the United States of America was satisfied that I was indeed born in the United States and, further, that I was born on January 7, 1926, and issued my first passport.

I was doubly blessed by Dad's resourcefulness. It didn't occur to me at the then age of 25 that it would be important years later that for Social Security purposes to settle on a date which the United States would accept for determining when I reached the magic age for social security benefits.

I have also reflected a number of times on the incongruity of the problem of determining my date and place of birth for a U.S. passport. After all, some years earlier, when I attained age 18, and the government was in dire need of more bodies for the armed services, it accepted without question my own certification as to my date and place of birth - and promptly inducted me into the U.S. Navy!!

Although I was never led to believe that there was anything other than unbounded enthusiasm over my birth, I have at times wondered if there was a bit of disappointment over the exact date. After all, if I had waited just one day, my Dad and I would have been able to share the same birth date - January 8.

I seem to recall my Mother telling me she and I spent the first week of my life in the hospital. At least a one week stay was the routine hospital stay in 1926. In any event, both of us obviously survived the hospital routine and duly left to our home in Millvale.

Millvale was Dad's second pastorate in the Methodist Episcopal

Church. He had served College Hill, a suburb of Beaver Falls for one year. The Bishop of either the Pittsburgh Conference or Western Pennsylvania Conference (I'm not sure which at this time), then appointed Dad to Millvale. I understand that it was regarded as a rather choice appointment for a young pastor. I believe that the Bishop may have been Adna Wright Leonard. I do know that Bishop Leonard was serving just a few years later. Also, he was serving the conference in which Washington D.C. was located when President Roosevelt appointed him to some special post in the Second World War. The Bishop was killed in a plane crash while on a trip in this service.

While Bishops in the Methodist Church make the appointments, appointments at this time are often made with the understanding of the congregations, the Church leaders, etc. At the time I was born the Bishops could, and did, make appointments in a very autocratic way. (Perhaps that is the better way, even if some modifications have crept into the practice in more recent years.)

Dad was appointed to Millvale before I was born. I don't know where Dad lived before he and Mother were married. I was told, however, that the Church in Millvale did not own a parsonage. By the time I was born, my parents lived in the Mazer apartments. They were located next to the Church.

My Dad received a new appointment when I was just little more than one and one half years of age. So I have no recollection of Millvale when we lived there. It was, though, with some anticipation and apprehension, that when I was just twenty two years of age and by which time I held what was then known as a Local Preacher's License, that I was asked to fill the pulpit of Millvale one summer Sunday morning of 1948. I have no idea whether I did a credible job. I recall two biased attendees assured me I had done well. One of the attendees was Stella Gidding, who had been very active in the Church at Millvale, a person who had been very supportive of Dad and good friends with both him and my Mother. The other attendee was Lois, to whom I was then engaged. (As I say, I have no credible reports on the quality of my efforts.) I did serve a number of Churches that summer, and I recall that one of the Churches thought I was older than I was and that I had completed ministerial training and inquired about my being appointed to their Church.)

While in Millvale, and perhaps before he and Mother were married and when he had a bit more time for some outside activities than later, he served as the Scoutmaster of a local troop of Boy Scouts. I have always been very proud of my Dad for taking on that kind of job.

Millvale also was the scene of an event that gave us a lifelong story and source of comment. There was a couple, parishioners, who invited Dad to dinner—before he and Mother were married. When Dad arrived he found that he was seated with the husband and that the wife felt her place was to serve as cook and waitress. Dad reported that the table was laden with an overwhelming number of foods—meats, vegetables, sauces, dressings, etc. etc. The wife tried to interest Dad in I guess nearly all, if not all of the dishes. The husband's name was Jake. With each food offering, the woman would say, "Reverend, don't know if you will like this, but Jake likes it"!! From then on, that was a favorite comment at our table any time a new or different kind of food appeared at the table!!

Years after living in Millvale, and while I was at Allegheny College, I developed a friendship which brought warm feelings for the time in Millvale. A fraternity brother at Allegheny whom I especially liked, Jim Reetz, told me that his Dad was a banker in Millvale and that his Dad had known mine years earlier. When I asked Dad about it he remembered Mr. Reetz well and spoke warmly of his acquaintance. Mr. Reetz was not a member of the Church Dad served, but somehow they had become acquainted. As I reflect upon it, it may be that Dad and Mr. Reetz had known each other through Masons. Dad joined the Masons at some point in time. Don't know how active he was, but I do recall that there were evenings when Dad was not home for dinner and I was told that he was at Masons. I believe that Dad was a Thirty Third Fourth degree Mason, whatever that may mean.

Dad served four years in Millvale. I think it was a happy pastorate for Dad. It was followed by a one year appointment which was apparently an anomaly among his appointments. I have no idea how it came to pass that he was appointed to Creighton. I do know that Mother was disappointed and upset over the appointment. Dad never said that much about it. But Mother spoke of it as the most awful thing that happened to them. I never heard them speak of anyone from the community. I never heard how it was that Dad was sent off to what for them was Lower Slobovia for a year. I suspect that Mother worked as strongly as she could to get a move for Dad after a year there. Just how it was accomplished, I don't know, but it was. We never spoke of Creighton at home, except when my mother brought it up in hushed tones of grief. I don't even remember any mention being made of the parsonage in Creighton, or even whether there was a parsonage. As I say, the whole event was painful - too painful to dwell upon.

2

Blawknox

During the years I was growing up ministers in the Methodist Episcopal Church were moved fairly frequently. And so it was that in, I believe, 1929, after a four year pastorate in Millvale, that the Bishop decided that it was time to move from Creighton.

As nearly as I have been able to figure out, the frequent moving routine was part of the evolving legacy of John Wesley. John Wesley was, in many ways, as nearly as I can determine, an evangelist and itinerant minister. I gather he spent much of his ministry on the road. I gather also that only over a period of time did ministries for a fixed term come into play. All assignments are for one year. There may be successive terms for an individual pastorate, but each assignment is for one year.

The next assignment for Dad was to Blawknox, a steel mill town located on the Allegheny River. It was an upriver move from Millvale of about five or ten miles. The parsonage was located on Freeport Road, the main street through the town. I recall Freeport Road being paved. Based upon a picture taken of me when I was about two years old, it appears that at that time the Road was paved only on one side.

As with many of the steel towns on the Allegheny and Monongahela River, the mill was built along the river. Some distance above the mill would be the main streets through the towns. And then the balance of the towns would be built on to the top of the hill at the top of the river valley.

The Church in Blawknox was built about half way between the river and Freeport Road. The public school, on the other hand, was built near the top of the hill. This meant a climb of 148 steps for me up to school. I recall that number because of the groans from my mother the one or two times that she walked up to school.

Blawknox also had a County "Workhouse". The Workhouse was, and perhaps still is, a prison. I remember it being referred to frequently, but knew very little about it.

The parsonage was a very old house. I never thought about it when we lived there. I heard my parents talk about it, however, and later on when I saw the house, I realized that it was indeed an old house. It was a rather long narrow house. On the main floor there was a living room in the front of the house, then behind it the dining room and then a kitchen behind this the living room. I remember many comments on how high the ceilings were in the house. From the comments I heard about the ceilings, I would be inclined to think that the ceilings on the first floor were somewhere between ten and twelve feet above floor level.

Thinking back on the sequence of events, I think we must have moved to Blawknox in the early fall of 1929. I say this because I know that we moved from Blawknox after I finished first grade, I know that we lived there for six years (a long pastorate, at that time) and we moved to Derry in the fall of 1935. I think I am correct on dates also because of an event that relates to my brother, Richard. Richard was born on June 14, 1928. As we said when he was growing up and as I think he really believed in his early years, everybody puts out flags to celebrate my brother's birthday.

I remember over the years hearing the story of an event that occurred when we lived in Blawknox -- an event at a Quarterly Conference - and the event involving my brother. The Methodist Episcopal Church had quarterly conferences. I think in Wesley's day they were probably held every three months. Today, and when I was growing up I think they were held perhaps only once or twice each year. The Quarterly Conference is a meeting of the Church leaders with the District Superintendent to review the affairs of the Church. I remember that on a number of occasions that the meetings were held in the evening and my Mother and Dad would invite the District Superintendent, known as the D.S., to dinner at our house before the meeting. The event to which I refer now must have occurred in the fall of 1929 when my brother was about fifteen or sixteen months of age. Dinner was proceeding well, I guess, until for some reason my brother suddenly, and without warning threw a teaspoon across the table. The spoon barely missed the D.S. Predictably, I think, my Mother was mortified. No sense of my Dad's reaction. The D.S., a Dr. Trosh who must have been born as an old person, simply looked up and said "Well, at least the older boy seems to know how to behave." The story of this event was repeated many many times as we were growing up. I suspect Richard grew very tired of being reminded of it.

My Mother also felt that stuffed olives added a nice touch to dinner. She apparently served them more than once when Dr. Trosh was at our place for dinner. He dragged out more than once a story about a newlywed woman who went to the grocery store to buy stuffed olives. Being a young bride she couldn't remember the name for stuffed olives. So she asked the grocer for olives with the little red tail light. Mother told me later, that after a couple of times with this story she simply stopped serving stuffed olives when Dr. Trosh was going to be at our place for dinner.

Our yard was large enough that Dad was able to have a veggie garden. Being part farmer, my Dad planted every possible space in veggies which we could enjoy all summer long. The only veggies I particularly remember ere the green onions and the tomatoes. The tomatoes were a special treat. I remember many times going out in to the garden with a salt shaker, picking an onion and then after that eating a red ripe tomato. I always found this such a treat! We also found growing as a weed in the yard something we called "sour grass". We would pick it and eat it often. Really liked the sour taste.

We got our fist dog when we were living in Blawknox—a Cocker Spaniel which we named Bobbie. I remember Bobbie very well. He was a pretty dog. Unfortunately, however, as I think is the case with many cocker's, he could be very cross. I remember being bitten a couple of times. And so, I didn't have as good a relationship with him as I guess I had hoped for. Bobbie left us when we left Blawknox. Don't know just how long he lived with us.

Bobby created another embarrassing moment for my Mother. The person living on one side of our house was a family by the name of Holden. I played some with their son Bobby. Seems that on one occasion, there was a lot of commotion in the back yard. My Mother looked out and saw there was some commotion between Bobby Holden and either me or my brother. Bobby the dog was in the same area. I assume my Mother thought that dog Bobby was the cause of the commotion. In any event, she pulled open the back door and in a loud voice shouted "Bobby, stop that." My Mother's remark was intended for the dog, she told me, but Bobby Holden thought it was directed to him and he ran off home crying. Another bad moment for Mother who wanted to enjoy good relations with the neighbors. Bobby was the source of another upsetting event in the Hartung house hold. Perhaps it was that the depression had hit and things were getting tighter. Anyway, Dad told all of us that he thought that we might start having some cornmeal mush for dinner. He added, parenthetically, that if there was mush left over that we could give the rest of the food to Bobby. I'm not sure exactly what Dad intended by introducing the idea of cornmeal mush for the dog. It took my mother only a short amount of time to tell Dad that we were not going to eat corn meal much for dinner so that there would be mush for Bobby!!

On the other side of our house lived the Walzers. I think Betty Walser, a daughter, must have been nine or ten partway through our stay in Blawknox. I recall her being a very nice kind girl who I think baby sat my brother and me.

Another thing I remember about Blawknox was that my parents or my Mother (I think the latter) bought me a black toy cat and a big boy doll. I didn't care one way or the other about the cat, but I thoroughly hated a boy doll. All the time I was growing up Mother kept talking about the boy doll. And I all the time showed no interest in the doll. I don't have any reason to think that I ever convinced my Mother that I hated that doll. I must have been two or three years old when my Mother had a picture taken of me pulling my new wagon, with the cat and doll in the wagon. She always liked that picture. I still have it, but keep it as a memento of the time.

One of the parishioners in Blawknox whom I remember (one of the few I remember) was Mrs. Bain. I remember her only because she stopped by every so often and if it was evening she would have the biggest flashlight I had ever seen. I was just entranced by the flashlight. Seems that she walked home and had the light to better see her way.

When we lived in Blawknox Dad bought a 1929 Chevy. I am sure the purchase date was late in the model year—probably early fall. We didn't buy very many cars while I was growing up, but I recall my Mother saying that my Dad always bought a new car in the summer because he wanted to show off his car in the next family reunion, which would occur in July or August. I remember, too, watching Dad take care of car maintenance. I can remember him changing spark plugs, changing the oil, etc. All the sorts of thing which people could do easily then but things which have become almost too complex to handled now.

Because of my birth date, and because January 1 was the cutoff birth date for starting school, I was older than most in my school class. In any event, I was duly enrolled in the Blawknox public school. I think my Mother probably went to school with me the first day. She probably hiked up the 148 steps up to the schoolhouse.

There were some good things about school and some things not so good. My teacher was Miss Wertz. Turned out that in a few years she and my parents began talking about relatives and I found out the Miss Wertz was a second cousin. The only kids I remember from school were two boys with whom I had an altercation. There was Jack Kissel. For Christmas in first grade I received a nice pocket watch. I think Jack must have decided he liked the watch and would like to have it. He grabbed it in some way and succeeded in breaking the chain or some part of the watch. The other boy I remember was a Peter something— the last name began with a B. By hindsight, I think Peter was a slow learner and a problem. I have the sense that he was he was repeating first grade - at least that was my sense of it.

School must have gone well for me. I recall that I got all A's during the year. I also recall my Mother telling me that one night toward the end of first grade I woke up, and was crying. My Mother tells me that I was crying because first grade was nearly finished. My anxiety was because I was afraid that I would pass into second grade and that worried me greatly because I had decided that second grade would be very hard - too hard for me!

Since the ceilings were so high in Blawknox we could have very large Christmas trees. I remember one Christmas having one of the frights of my life. I had slipped in behind the Christmas tree the one year. I was the only one in the room. I shouldn't have been where I was. But much worse, I had fiddled around and the tree started to tip over. I recall holding on with all my strength and just barely keeping the tree from falling. Never told anyone about this. But I never again tried this stunt which almost created a crisis for me.

It was unusual that we would be in the same town for six years. So it was not too unusual that we would move after six years. Conference after my first grade was in June. This was about the only time when I was growing up that the Annual Conference was held in the summer. Other times it was held at the end of September, then moves came very early in October, and the P.K.'s (preacher's kids) would have to start in a new school about a month after the school year had started

Blawknox and maybe Creighton were the "Walters Chapel" years. At some point Dad was assigned a "second charge" - i.e. a second church to handle. It was then out in the country from Blawknox and Harmerville (a coal town) was a little country chapel. Dad served the congregation for about seven or eight years. I always thought of it as a nice country Church. I guess the Church was barely surviving when Dad was assigned there. The first Sunday there were only about five or six parishioners, all, I think, members of the same family!! Dad apparently thrived in this environment. And as was fairly typical in his pastorates, the congregation grew in size while he was there. I understand that the last Sunday he served Walters Chapel every seat was full and people were sitting on chairs in the aisles.

The Church did not have a basement when Dad went there. But a basement was built during his ministry. Perhaps because a depression was going on during a portion of the time he was there, the parishioners built the basement largely with volunteer labor. I recall that teams of horses were used in the excavation and hauling of dirt.

The chapel had big cake dinners, or something like that. I recall the only one of the events I think I attended. There was a very special cake to be awarded. All participants walked in a circle while the music played. The winner was the one walking around the circle in front of the broom handle pointed toward the circle, when the music stopped playing. Lo and behold, I was the winner.

I remember only a couple of things about the cake award. I remember walking in the circle, I remember winning, and taking the cake home. I also remember overhearing two women, who probably didn't know who I was, commenting to themselves about how awful that that little kid won the cake rather than some older person. The tragedy of the whole event, however, was that we took the cake home; carefully put the cake on a stand in the kitchen to eat the next day. When we looked the next day, ants had invaded the cake and were marching on one side and out the other. Don't recall if any of the cake was edible, but I do recall being very disappointed about the whole event.

After six years in one charge, it was of course not too unusual that we would probably be moving.

3

Verona

The Methodist Conference in which Dad served held its only summertime annual conference sessions during my growing up years in June of 1933. Other than for this annual summertime conference the powers that be seemed utterly insensitive to the complications in the lives of young students created by holding the annual conference in late September. With the Annual Conference held in late September those ministers appointed to new charges would begin their new pastorate in early October (the first Sunday after the Annual Conference) and the families would move in the second week of October. For students this meant changing schools just over a month after school began - with all the complications that such timing brought with it.

I have no recollection discussing with Mother and or Dad the possibility of a move. Certainly, since we had been in Blawknox for six years, it would not have been a surprise for Dad to be assigned to a new Church. At that time, as I recall, few ministries lasted six years. Perhaps Dad and the Bishop or D.S. had even discussed options.

In any event, Dad was moved—and so was the rest of the family— to Verona. It was not a long distance move. Verona is not a long way up the Allegheny River from Blawknox—perhaps three or four miles. But it is a distance up river and on the other side of the Allegheny River. Dad did not serve at Walters Chapel after we moved to Verona...

The parsonage was typical of housing provided at that time for ministers. It was an older house which the church had acquired from a well to do parishioner who had lived in the house but who had built a new place and moved into it. It was a three story house built on a large lot. The Church rented out the first floor and then provided the second and third stories for the minister and his family. I remember the address as being 734 Bruno Street - Bruno was not paved, but oiled. There was a very large front yard and vacant property at the intersection of Bruno Street and Center Street. Bruno was level and Center Street ran up and down the hill on which the town was built.

My brother and I had a very large room on the third floor. I suspect that it was intended or used as a game room for a prior user. Mother and Dad had a good sized bedroom, also on the third floor. I think there may have been just two bedrooms on the third floor. Dad had his office on the second floor. There was also a bedroom on the second floor, as well as kitchen, dining room and living room.

I suspect that from energy consumption standpoint the house was very inefficient. Coal was cheap, relatively speaking, however. We always burned what was called run of mine coal. I think it is just what is left over after the good stuff is separated off.

June of 1933 was the depth of the depression. During a part of the two years we lived in Verona my cousin Viola, Uncle Clarence and Aunt Mamie's oldest child came to live with us for a time. She was able to get some kind of job in Verona or in the area - perhaps as a domestic. Probably there was no work for her in the country where the family lived.

An area that I think may have been the northeast part of the property, on the downhill side, but not a part of the parsonage, had been excavated to a grade perhaps ten or twelve feet below the rest of the grade in our yard. A man by the name of Costa had built a house there. He lived there by himself as I recall. I have no idea whether he was married, had family, or whatever. He apparently did not take kindly to the idea of the minister's kids and their friends wandering down over the hillside by his house. I think perhaps he had chased us out of his property at one point.

In any event, my brother and I supposed some of our friends found it a challenge to go down into Mr. Costa's property to look around. We devised a system for one person to be a lookout. If Mr. Costa showed up, or I think if we thought he was coming, the lookout or any of us who saw Mr. Costa would shout "Costa Drill" whereupon all of us would high tail it out of his property.

The "oil" on Bruno Street was actually, I think, oil and slag from the steel mill. If it was, it was waste product from the mill. Today it probably would be regarded as absolutely wrong environmentally to spread the slag on the street. But then was then and now is now.

Verona is a steel mill town, built on the banks of the Allegheny River. As with many of the steel mill towns along the Allegheny and Monongahela Rivers, the mill was built along the river. The Allegheny and Monongahela rivers have cut fairly deep valleys so that the towns were built on fairly steep hills. Verona was no exception.

In any event, my brother and I soon discovered that Bruno Street was filled with small pieces of pig iron. We also soon discovered that it was fairly easy to dig out quite a few pieces of pig iron. During the depression there were junk dealers who frequently drove up and down streets buying junk. They would buy the pig iron from us. The dealer would weigh our pig iron in his hands and then offer us one or two cents, which we were glad to have. Soon I decided that we should be able to make a bit more if we put together a big gunny sack of pig iron. I recall that we put together what we thought was a big sack and when the dealer next came down the street we offered it for sale. Instead of offering perhaps a quarter he offered us only ten cents. We were disappointed, but we didn't have any other buyer so we sold. After that we only sold smaller handfuls, figuring that we could earn more that way!!!

Money was in very short supply as we grew up. We didn't understand much about the depression, but we knew there wasn't much money around. Somehow somebody came around - at least I think that must have been the way it worked - who talked us into trying to sell magazines. It was a chance to earn money!!! I think I went to a couple of doors and didn't make a sale. My brother, Richard, went to one door and was chased away by an irate woman. That ended my brother's efforts at selling magazine subscriptions. Without him, I, too, lost any interest in trying to sell magazines.

Our school was located just about two or three blocks from us. I think it must have been an elementary school with the first six grades in the building. I remember that my second grade teacher was a Miss Coulter. I remember she was young and I thought very pretty. Don't remember much about her teaching. I do recall, however, that one day she apparently fell down a flight of stairs, perhaps from the second floor. I don't recall whether we heard her fall, or whether she didn't return to the room promptly as she had said she would. In any event one of the more brave boys of the class wandered down the hall to where the teacher was lying He came back and said her eyes were closed. I have no idea how long she lay there or how she was picked up. I suspect she had suffered a concussion.

I remember Miss Coulter was at home recovering for some time. Much to the embarrassment of my brother and me, our parents announced one evening that we were going to Miss Coulter's home to visit her. I remember going to the house. I think my brother and I were probably too tongue tied to say much of anything. But anyway, my parents were satisfied that we had done our courteous duty to demonstrate our concern for the teacher and how much we thought of her.

There was a second school building next door to the elementary school. It may have been the junior high or even the whole high school. Verona was not such a large town. Two buildings probably would have been very sufficient for all the classes all the way through high school.

One of my vivid memories about my school experience in Verona was that one day the teacher asked me to accompany a student who had done something bad and for which he was being sent to the school principal. I recall being nervous about the whole thing. I recall also, that I was so nervous that when I got to the principal's office I just barged in and started talking, even though the principal had somebody at his desk. The principal looked at me and said, "What do you say?" I really didn't know until he told me to apologize for the interruption. Somehow, I survived this traumatic event.

I don't remember very much about the balance of second grade. By the time I was in third grade the course offering was expanded. I particularly remember studying geography. I was fascinated by the study of various parts of the world. I can still remember, for example, a photograph that showed a man in some tropical area climbing up a coconut tree. I think that my interest in travel and seeing the world was influenced significantly by the third grade geography class.

As I have mentioned earlier, Mother was very interested in our progress through school. She also wanted to keep a record of all our accomplishments in school. As a part of this process, Mother kept a book for both Richard and me, which recorded events from each year. Mother always wanted to get each of our teachers to put a note in this book regarding us as a student in her class. I just groaned at being involved in the process. I was sort of embarrassed by all the attention. But Mother persisted in her efforts. I don't know that she continued all the way through high school, but certainly the book went through elementary school, and perhaps junior high school.

It was while we were in Verona that I first learned about Carnegie libraries. Verona did not have a library. But the next town upriver, Oakmont, which was just a short distance, did have one. I was a rather voracious reader by the second or third grade. Trips to the library were big events. Can't remember the titles of the books, except that there were a series about twins. I have no recollection how many of the "twin" books were in the library, but I think I read all of them. I think I also read Robinson Crusoe and Swiss Family Robinson

It was also while we lived in Verona that I began collecting stamps. Captain Ivory (I think that was the name) had a fifteen minute radio program, probably Monday through Friday. Naturally, Ivory soap was the sponsor of the program. Very soon I acquired a stamp album and started collecting stamps. I suspect that with wrappers from Ivory soap one could get some special deals. I really don't recall that part of it. I just know that I enjoyed collecting stamps. I learned about where so many countries were, looked at the pictures of rulers on the stamps, etc. I also learned about "first day cover" and sent off for and received all of the stamps in a series of famous Americans I think I still have those covers at home - somewhere.

Stamp collecting was an interest that I carried all the way through high school. It was an interest that I have often thought I should revive - but haven't so far.

I continued taking piano lessons, which I had begun while we lived in Blawknox. I remember that for a time at least we continued taking lessons from Miss Sugden, the teacher when we lived in Blawknox. I remember that Dad drove us to Miss Sugden's for the lessons. Don't recall too much about the trips to her place except for some of the winter drives. Dad was a very good driver. He knew how to negotiate hills, often without chains. I recall that we had a steep hill, I think probably going to Miss Sugden's. One time when we went there had been quite a snowfall and I thought, right or wrong, that the streets would be very slippery. I recall being so frightened to go up or down the hill that time. But Dad, as usual, successfully negotiated the slope.

My parents made a change in piano teachers while we lived in Verona. I don't recall why. I suspect that perhaps Miss Sugden charged a bit more than some other teachers. In any event, the new teacher was a man teacher. I recall he was strong on having us play scales, etc. It was probably good to strengthen our fingers and give us better finger and hand control. I recall not liking him as much. I must have shown something less than the interest I had earlier. There was a change in teachers or perhaps there was a gap in our lessons. In any event, I recall that at some point my Mother said she sensed that I didn't care as much for the man teacher. I don't recall saying anything like that, but I guess she was very perceptive.

Mother was very intelligent, very perceptive, very committed to her family. She had what I think was a terrible conflict within herself which resulted in her imposing on herself and the rest of us what I think were unreasonable limitations on activities. Mother was very proud and pleased to be married to a minister. She wanted to do everything possible to make Dad's work more successful. She wanted to be certain that she did nothing that would offend or upset parishioners. This led to some rather bizarre limitations or least that is my perception, on things we could do or not do.

I knew, for example, that Halloween was a great time for trick or treating. But Mother was very concerned that if my brother and I went out trick or treating it might in some way offend some parishioners or, I guess people who knew parishioners. I think she felt that if we went some places, or perhaps did not go other places, people would be offended. Therefore, with one or two very minor exceptions, neither my brother nor I were permitted to go out trick or treating.

This concern for how certain activities would be perceived by parishioners carried over to the subject of birthday parties. I never had a birthday party when I was growing up. Mother was afraid that by omission or commission, by inviting or failing to invite the child of certain parishioners there would be a parishioner upset by reason of inclusion or exclusion. Only after Mom and I were married did I have my first birthday party.

Mom and I moved to Chicago after I finished law school. During that time, as my birthday was approaching, Mother decided we should invite friends for a birthday party for me. At that time Mom was not aware I had never had a birthday party. The party was a great success. After the event I thanked Mom for it and told her it was the first birthday party I had ever had. She couldn't believe it. We didn't always have birthday parties after that, but my birthday was probably recognized more than would have been the case.

There was one exception to the no birthday party rule when my brother and I were growing up. For some reason my brother had a birthday party when we lived in Verona. At that time there was a man who had a radio program, Monday. to Friday, aimed at children. It was possible for parents, or others to write in a message for the birthday child. The message would be read over the radio.

When my brother was probably six years old, in June of 1934, Mother decided that Richard could have a birthday party. Several of his friends were invited. During the party we had to turn on the radio to listen to the program for children. The announcer suddenly said "Well here's an unusual location for birthday presents. It says that if Richard will go out in the yard to the Mulberry tree he will find a present. Well, the table cleared in about two seconds as we all roared outside. Sure enough, up one of the two mulberry trees in our yard, but at a height Richard could reach, was a present. At this time I don't think either he or I can recall what the present was. But it was an unusual way of celebrating Richard's birthday.

One, if not the only tenant on the first floor of the parsonage during the time we were in Verona, was Mr. and Mrs. Ruse. They were an older couple. He was a mortician. I don't know where he had done business before they came to Verona. As I say, they were older, had no children, but had a small dog - I think perhaps a Pekinese, of which they were very fond. Mr. Ruse's business apparently did not prosper. Perhaps it was the depression; perhaps he was a bit old to start over again in his business. I remember the Ruse's very favorably. I liked him. He was always very kind to Richard and me. He must have suffered some terrible depression from the lack of business. I remember that he committed suicide. It was very shocking to our whole family. It's the first time I can ever recall having heard about someone committing suicide. Mrs. Ruse moved soon after her husband's death. I have no idea where she went. The whole event made an indelible impression on me however.

We had a number of friends in Verona. They were not friends of one another, however, so when we played with friends it would be one group or another. There were two boys—one was named Wooding. His father owned a hardware store in Verona. Then there was a boy whose father was a doctor. I was never real comfortable with the boys. The Doctor's son especially always seemed to me to think he was a bit superior to us. One of the Christmas's we lived in Verona I received a new coat. It was the style of leather jacket that was popular at the time. I remember the boys were over to look at our Christmas presents. The boy whose father was a doctor looked at my new coat. He sort of turned his nose up and said, "This is not really leather, it's naugahide." I'm sure my parents got the best they could afford. I was very proud and pleased with the new coat. But my friend's comment really hurt me. I have never forgotten it.

The Wooding boy was the victim of an auto accident. I recall that in the winter of probably 1934-1935 his parents and the family were going to, I think, Florida. The car rolled off the road, turned over and rolled down the hill. The boy was killed. I think he was either an only child or only son. I'm sure his parents took it very hard. Probably thirty to forty years later, Mom and I were visiting along the Allegheny River, looking over towns I had lived in. I suggested we visit the hardware man, Mr. Wooding. He was still in business, but I think about ready for retirement. He was just so pleased we had stopped by and it gave me a very good feeling that we had taken the time and made the effort to look him up.

The Rearick boys were also friends. Older boy had a terrible temper and would go into rages. I always felt a bit uneasy around him. The father of another boy, whose name I cannot now recall, (it may have been Henderson.) had been in the service in the First World War. The family was parishioners. The wife had been a nurse. Apparently the father had been gassed in the war and suffered some long term problems. I don't think he was employed while we lived in Verona. Don't know if this was because of a service disability or just the economy. I recall them fairly well. He was the first person I had known who had suffered gas poisoning in the First World War.

The First World War was still fresh enough in peoples minds that Armistice Day was well recognized. It was a school holiday. There were big, well attended parades. I remember going to downtown Pittsburgh for one of the parades. It was perhaps the first time I had seen a band parading and I was really taken with the performance of the band especially with the bass drum).

One of what I regard by hindsight as one of the funniest things occurred in Verona. There was a girl who sat next to me, either behind, in front or alongside, in class, in perhaps third grade who asked me if I would like to go with her, and perhaps another friend or two to a movie after school. Don't recall what prompted her (I think her name may have been Jean Kerr) to ask. Further, I don't know what possessed my parents to agree. After all, during the time I was growing up, about the only movies approved by my parents were ones that were well rated in Parents Magazine. (This movie definitely would NOT have been recommended for children.) Anyway, as I recall we went right from school. Have no idea who paid for my admission. (At this time I seldom had any money, let alone have money to carry in my pocket)

I still remember some parts of the movie. There was, I think, a bank robbery or something like that. There was a wild car chase, and I don't recall what all. I was fascinated by the whole thing. When the film ended, we just all stayed in the theatric and pretty soon the film began to roll again. By this time it must have been getting a bit late. Certainly, it must have been dinner time. In any event, suddenly my Dad showed up and said something about going home. I said, as I recall my parents telling the story, "Dad, you are just in time. The movie's just starting again." Whereupon my Dad said we were leaving - NOW!! So much for the movie's second run.

Mother never learned to drive a car. Events lead me to believe that my parents had discussed the subject. Whether they both agreed it would be good for her to learn, or whether the initiative came from one of them, I'll never know. What I do know is that my Dad picked Highland Park as the place to "try to teach my Mother' to drive. Well—I still remember that leaving Highland Park on the way to Verona involved driving downhill, fairly sharp turns around a very winding road where a driver would suddenly come upon another car coming in the opposite direction.

From the description I recall hearing about the event from my Mother, over the years, the location was absolutely the last place where a teacher would take a new driver to learn how to handle a car. I have pondered many times over the years the question: Did Dad just make an innocent mistake in trying to teach my Mother to learn at this location—or-was Dad not interested in having Mother drive the car. Perhaps I have just let my imagination go into free fall. Whatever the answer to my question and pondering, my Mother never learned to drive. And by 1955 when Dad had a heart attack when they were at Chautauqua, it was a definite disadvantage for her to be unable to drive.

There was one event about which I recall only the slightest mention. It was something which, by hindsight I think may have been very divisive between Dad and the powers that be in the Verona church. I think the event was driven on Dad's side in part at least by economics and on the Church's side by Church pride on the other side.

There was a small community, village, or whatever, by the name of Rosedale. It was located along the Allegheny River between Verona and Aspinwall, but on the Verona side of the Allegheny River.

Dad's salary was never a subject of discussion at home. Comments were made, sometimes after the events which gave me some insight into the very low salary Dad received. After all it was the depth of the depression. That said, I learned at some point that Dad's salary was $100 per month when we lived in Verona. And at that time there was no such thing as a car allowance, no such thing as medical insurance, no reimbursable expense for car operation, no phone allowance even though the bulk of our telephone calls would have been related to Dad's job.

During the time I as growing up, physicians did not charge ministers for services to the minister and his family. The services were just as a professional courtesy, Perhaps that is still the case. Anyway, most times there was a doctor in the congregation, and sometimes a dentist. In such event, it was a foregone conclusion that we would use the services of the member physician or dentist.

I almost never had any significant health problems when I was growing up—measles, chicken pox, etc., but nothing serious. With one exception. I developed a very bad cough and cold, when we lived in Verona, which turned into pneumonia. This was before antibiotics, sulfa drugs, or any of those medicines which have made such a difference in health care.

I can still recall when my pneumonia was the worst that my parents set up my bed in the dining room. With sheets they built sort of a tent over my bed. Then somehow they got the teakettle to steam sent under the "tent". Something, I think perhaps camphor was worked into the steamer. I remember being very sick but not liking it at all.

And then there were the mustard plasters. Mustard was spread on one side of a soft cloth. Then that cloth would be fastened on the inside of the pajamas, at chest height so that the "plaster" would be plastered up against the chest of the ill person. The odor was awful as I recall. Maybe it sped up the healing process because of the smell!

Returning to the subject of Rosedale-I gleaned from comments my mother dropped at one time, that if Rosedale would have been joined as a second charge at Verona, Dad would have earned an additional $500 per year. It seems that the parishioners at Verona were very upset with Dad that he would try for that. They felt that Dad should spend all his time on the affairs of the Church in Verona. I recall that in 1933 or 1934 my parents experimented with a party phone line service. Very quickly I understand, and I can understand why, a party phone line was not acceptable for a minister whose communications would often be privileged.

We stayed in Verona for only two years. I never did understand why we moved after just two years. By hindsight I surmise that there was some joint dissatisfaction between Dad and the parishioners. Perhaps there was mutual upset over the Rosedale effort by Dad. I never heard Dad say anything to support that. It's only intuition that leads me to this feeling. What the real facts may be, the Annual Conference in 1935 was held at the end of September, just about a month after school had begun and when the announcements were read, Dad was assigned to Derry.

During the time I was growing up, the Bishop was able for the most part to act like a little dictator on Church matters. He (it was always a man) made the decisions on when and where ministers were moved. I do think that the Bishops did their best in trying, in most situations, to fairly deal with the needs of the Church and the ministers.

I think there must have often been discussions between the Bishop and individual ministers and the District Superintendents, about what would be best, but this was not always the case.

Richard and I started going to the closing service of the Conference at an early age and so we were at the service closing the 1935 Conference. I can still remember the D.S. (District Superintendent) motioning to Dad to come up to him in front before the service began. I recall Dad looking a bit shocked and whispering to Mother that he was going to be reassigned. Dad never said, but I have to think that was the first clue of a move.

I'm sure there were things that caused distress within the Church, and the Conference, but things seemed to hold together. During the time I was growing up, and it may still be the case, at the close of the last service of the Annual Conference, the congregation sings as the closing hymn, Blest Be the Tie That Binds!! I have always thought that there must always be ministers and their families who have a bit of a time choking through that hymn, he knowing that he's been forced to move on to a new charge or stay when he wanted to move..

I never really understood Dad's feeling about leaving Verona. He just never discussed it with Richard and me. I think, though, by hindsight, that Verona was perhaps the least successful of Dad's ministries. I don't know what he felt when he learned we were going to Derry. For me it was a wonderful move. The move opened the door on the most enjoyable years of my growing up.

4

Derry

When the appointments were read at the Annual Conference at the last session on probably the last Sunday of September in 1935 I learned that we would be leaving Verona and moving to Derry. Don't recall whether I said, "Where in the world is Derry". But certainly I had no idea where the place might be. I suppose I probably thought little about it. After all, my life had been made up of a number of moves, and this was simply one more.

As it turned out, the move to Derry was wonderful to me—and I think to the whole family. Derry was and is today a little town of about three thousand people, located about 50 miles east of Pittsburgh. It lies at the foot of Laurel Ridge, about five miles from Latrobe, the most significant nearby town, probably, and about seven miles from Blairsville.

The move occurred, predictably, about nine days after the appointments were read. Predictably, also, moving was a long day of work—much more so for my parents, especially my Dad, than for my brother and me. I assume that we must have gotten to bed a bit late the night of the move. Or perhaps it was just that Mother and Dad didn't know the school hours in Derry.

The school we attended when we first moved to Derry was the third ward school. The building was brick, had four classrooms for six grades and a fire escape I remember very well - it was a tube, big enough to accommodate students and teachers, running from the second to the first floors. I always wanted to go down in the fire escape, but unfortunately we never had a fire drill while I was in the school. (The school is no longer in existence. It was torn down a number of years ago!!)

There were four teachers - Miss Henderson, Miss Love, Mrs. Welch and Miss Ballentine. And as luck or misfortune would have it, all four of them were members of the Methodist Church. (I don't too much recall, but suspect that the Church membership of the teachers may have put a bit of stress on me, although I don't really recall if that was the case.)

Mr. Walter Giesy lived across the street from us. He was the Derry reporter for the Latrobe Bulletin, the local newspaper. Part of his job was to meet and contact all the passenger trains arriving in Derry. At that time train travel was still the most common way for people to travel from one city to another. Mr. Giesy overused certain stock phrases. Passengers returning to Derry from Pittsburgh had been to "the smoky city": passengers returning from Johnstown were coming back "from the flood city" etc. Mr. Giesy was really very kind to me. More about him later in this journal, though.

I suspect we were late getting to bed after a long day. Dad would be going to school with Richard and me, and I suspect that he figured we could sleep in a bit the morning after the move and still get to school on time. We got to school a little before 9 a.m. which he assumed was the starting time. To his surprise, he learned school began at 8:30— oops! Everybody is going to have to start their day a bit earlier than anticipated.

My brother and I soon developed close friendships in Derry. I think especially of Joe and Floyd Hysong, brothers, Larry and Mary Ruffner, twins, Tom Greubel, Kenny Lowman, Jimmy Caldwell, Elmer Valko. Joe and Floyd's Mother was a widow; Mr. Ruffner worked for the Pennsy (Pennsylvania Railroad), Mr. Greubel was the postmaster for Derry and as a sideline hobby and business raised dahlias, and sold chicken chicks. It was the depth of the depression when we moved to Derry and I'm not certain whether Messrs. Lowman and Valko were employed.

My brother and I were immediately taken with Derry. Among other things there were such wonderful play areas. Just across the creek which ran along side the Church and Parsonage was the "Mossy" (more formally known as the Moss holder.) Don't know where the name Mossholder came from although I suspect there was a lot of moss on the hill. Then there was the creek that ran along our house. Sadly some raw sewage ran into the creek from time to time and even though Westinghouse at its tile insulation facility in Derry ran tile coloring waste right into the creek, a few blocks from where we lived. It colored waters from the dyes used in the plant. The creek was a great place to float boards or sticks which we christened with boat names. Then, too, perhaps half a mile from where we lived, was the local cemetery with all kinds of hills to run around on.

The main line of the Pennsy ran right through town, and there was a bridge over the tracks which rather divided the town into two parts. All the locomotives at the time were steam powered, with coal as the fuel. We often stopped on the bridge to watch the locomotive pass under. Derry was on a slight grade, and so all the freight trains went slowly through town on their way up to Byrd crossing.

The slow moving trains on the grade up to the Byrd's crossing provided an opportunity for another croup of citizens during the depressions years. It afforded the hoboes who were riding the rails an opportunity to hop on and off the trains. These were the days long before the container cars. Box cars, flat cars, etc. were used by hoboes to travel from one point to another.

The hoboes who got off the train on the grind up to the crossing walked the streets of town and stopped at houses, begging for food. The minister's house was a likely point for a hand out. Indeed, we had a chalk X on the side of the house for much of the time we lived in Derry - a signal that this was a good house to get something to eat.

And indeed, Dad did take care of the hoboes. I think that most men (they were all men as far as I recall) did get a jelly sandwich or something like that. In the summertime, though when our veggie garden was producing, men would be provided a whole plate with all kinds of cooked warm veggies, etc.—probably one of the few cooked meals they got at the time.

I recall Dad talking one time about a black man who came to the door. He asked Dad for some money, saying that he wanted to get some milk for his ulcers. Well, Dad would not give money. But he called a local grocer whom he know and arranged for the man to get a quart of milk. The man said he would pay Dad back, as soon as he got some work. Dad figured that would never happen. But a couple of weeks later the man came to door. He thanked Dad for the milk, said he had gotten some work in Latrobe-five miles distant. He had walked all the way back to Derry from Latrobe to pay Dad back. Our faith in humankind got a real boost from that act.

I mentioned before the veggie garden we had in Derry. It was quite good sized and provided us with a lot of food. Spading a good sized garden as we had in Derry can be quite a challenge. But a member of the Church, Mr. Hughes, who was a farmer, came to plow the garden each spring. I have to think he had done this for a number of years. Anyway, the first year this plowing was to happen Mr. Hughes said he would be over a certain morning. Mr. Hughes lived on his farm which was probably a mile and a half or two miles from the Church. I can still remember on the appointed plowing morning hearing Dad hop out of bed and say to my Mother, Jim golly's neds (a favorite expression of Dad) Hughes is here already. It was, as I recall, only about a 7 a.m., which meant that since Mr. Hughes would have had to get up, get dressed, etc., feed the stock, hitch up the team and drive them to our house. He had probably gotten up sometime between 3 and 4 a.m. Mr. Hughes also brought manure to spread on the garden. Quite a parishioner!! And Mr. Hughes was active in the Church. I think perhaps he was a Trustee or on the Official Board, etc.

I learned a great deal about veggie gardening during the time we lived in Derry - spading, raking, planting, weeding, watering, harvesting. Dad took care of my full learning experience. Including teaching me how to dig and fill a wintertime food storage area. Also got to help with canning, especially tomatoes but also beans, corn, peas, etc.

At the back of the yard there was a hen house. I quickly became interested in having chickens. During our first spring in Derry one of the parishioners kindly gave me a hen with her brood of chicks. Dad thought it would be a good idea to get a few additional chicks. I think there were only 10 or 12 with the hen when we got her. So we bought ten chicks from Mr. Greubel, nest door. Ten cents per chick.

The first night I went with Dad to the hen house, after dark, and tucked the chicks under the hen, along, of course with the rest of the chicks. To our surprise, I found next morning that the hen had kicked all the new chick out from under her and these little ones were huddled in the cold. So we had to rig up a box with a light in the basement, and feed and water to try to raise them. It was not a very successful operation. Only four of the chicks survived to adulthood. And of all things, all four of them were roosters!! Bad luck for a boy trying to build up a flock of hens to get eggs to sell.

Within a year of the time we moved to Derry, I had my chickens and went into the business of selling eggs. I had perhaps half a dozen customers, including Mother and Dad. I had enough customers that it was a real challenge to provide each of the customers with a dozen eggs each week. Sometimes, with the Kestners, who lived up toward the Mossy and got their eggs on Saturday, I would have to go back Sunday with one or two eggs to fill out the dozen.

Mother taught me single entry bookkeeping so I could keep an accurate record of my business. Mother and Dad paid me for the eggs I provided to them. Only fair, since I had to buy all the feed, the scratch, oyster shells, etc. I bought the feed at McBroom's grain and feed store a few blocks from home. I went up to the store, pulling my wagon, on the Saturdays mornings when I needed supplies.

Rats and mice can be a real problem. My problem was made easier by two things. First of all, I stored the mash and grain in metal garbage cans. But then there was a special helper—a skunk which lived, I think, under the hen house. The skunk kept the hen house a bit odiferous but it also kept the mice and rats away. Once somebody must have trapped or done something to get rid of the skunk. The rats and mice promptly came back—until a new skunk took up residence!!

One of the things needed in a hen house is straw or some similar produce on the floor of the henhouse. By I think the second fall, our neighbor, Mr. Giese showed me how to save money. We had a huge sycamore tree in our back yard with tons of leaves. Mr. Giese said to save the feed bags after they were emptied and then in the fall fill them with leaves. Sure enough, it worked like a charm. I think Mr. Giese helped me fill a few bags, but then it was my job.

My brother, Richard, Decided he would like to get in the chicken business also. How to separate the chicks — his and mine. Well I had new Red New Hampshires. We got him dome White Rocks. Somewhere I also got two pairs of bantam chicks. A pair of Buff Cochins and a pair of Golden Seabrights. The Seabright rooster ran that henhouse!! Don't know that the banties laid much in the way of eggs but they were a decorative addition to the henhouse.

My brother's chicken business was rather short-lived. One of the jobs in having a henhouse is cleaning the henhouse each week. Cleaning most of the henhouse was not much of a problem for Richard, but he just couldn't handle cleaning the roosts. I protested that it wasn't fair for me to have to clean the roosts all the time. So it was decided that Richard would go out of business and I would handle the whole chicken business.

I guess that Dad believed in teaching me the whole business. Some of my chickens I sold live weight - roosters, old hens, etc. But sometimes my customers wanted them slaughtered. Well, I never had to use the hatchet, but Dad did insist that I hold the feet while he whacked off the head. Like I say, I learned the whole business.

There is one event I clearly recall which is only tangentially related to the chicken business. One afternoon, for a reason that is lost in the mists of time, I recall that one of the teachers; I think Miss Henderson said that for something I had done or failed to do I would have to stay after school, as punishment, a certain amount of time. With a straight face I told Miss Henderson it would work a real hardship if I had to stay. I told her that it was my job to feed the chickens as soon as I got home, and if I had t stay my chickens would be neglected. I seem to recall her saying that my petition was imaginative but that it didn't change her position.

In Derry, we had a dog, named Topsy. She was mostly terrier but I'm sure she was a curbstone terrier. I will never know why we didn't have her spayed. But we didn't. Every time she came in heat all the dogs from the neighborhood invaded our place. We tried putting up chicken wire, fencing, and all sorts of things to keep the dogs out. But nothing much worked, and Topsy had a bunch of litters. We never had puppies around the place, however. I don't know why, but as I have gotten older I have had a suspicion. I think that as Dad grew up on a farm he was accustomed to getting rid of pups. That's just a suspicion, but I think a correct one.

Topsy was a nice dog. Much better than the Cocker Spaniel, Bobby, which we had had in Blawknox. Topsy was friendly, and didn't snap like Bobby. As with all of our dogs, or I guess both of them, no dog made a move with us. When we moved the dog found a new home in the area.

By the time I was in Fourth grade, which grade I was in when we moved to Derry, my parents (mostly my Mother I think) decided that school was not a challenge for me and that I was getting bored. So she worked out an arrangement for me to skip fifth grade. With an early January birth date, I was always one of the oldest students in class in the first three or four grades. Anyway, the grade skipping was very hard on me. The work wasn't hard, but living with the kids was very difficult. Even some of my close friends made comments and did other things that made the change hard on me. But perhaps it was the best thing.

Since after two years in Derry, I had finished the sixth grade, it was time to move on to Junior High School. Derry had the 6-2-4 system at the time. So for seventh and eighth grade I had a longer walk to school. Don't know if it was the second ward school or not. But it was a longer walk. But there as in all the public schools I attended, I came home for lunch. None of the schools had a lunch room.

The seventh grade teachers were Miss Young and Miss Yealy (known as "swifty" to the students.) The two teachers were good friends and did a lot of domestic gaveling each summer. I always thought they were good teachers. At that time, as I understood, it there was the class for brighter students and the class for slower students. Nothing much was said about it, but I think we all understood how it worked. I always ended up in the upper class.

The nickname "swifty" for Miss Yealy came about because of how fast she was with the paddle. At that time, corporal punishment was regularly administered. I remember in fifth grade the teacher always took the students in the coat room. The rest of us would be very quiet but would count the number of whacks with the paddle. I think there was a benefit to the corporal punishments. I have always felt that the concern of some people over the paddling was overdone.

While we lived in Derry I continued with my piano lessons. As I think I mentioned before, I started taking piano lessons about the time I started to school. In Derry, we had a Miss Drips. I think she may have been a parishioner in the Church. It was a long walk to the place. All the way out to about the high school, but I made the trip weekly. The only time I recall feeling particularly bad about taking piano lessons was when it prevented me from learning how to play basketball.

During the time we were in Derry the school got some money, I suspect from one of the federal programs of the time, to build a gymnasium. When I was in I think eighth grade the opportunity arose for boys to come to school in the evening, perhaps once a week, and learn about basketball. Unfortunately, that night conflicted with my piano lesson day. It wasn't so bad until the warm spring evenings, when I had to walk to Miss Drip's place, go past the high school, and with the windows open hear my friends playing basketball.

While we lived in Derry, I got in to Boy Scouts. (At that time, age 12 was the beginning date.) There were two troops in town, troop one and troop three. I got into troop three. We had our meetings in a building not too far from where we lived. I really enjoyed scouts and thrived. Mother insisted that I have a full uniform - about the only scout with a full uniform. With the full uniform I remember being in the front of a parade. Anyway, I went through tenderfoot, second class and first class ranks while in Derry. And of great importance to me, I got to go to Camp Wesco one year. (We were in the Westmorland, Fayette Council of Scouts (named for the two counties, Westmorland and Fayette from which scouts came going to that camp.) It was a wonderful camp; I learned a lot, really advanced in scouting, etc. It had a pool, took scouts from quite an area, and had a good staff, etc. (much better than Camp Laurel Mt. which was the Duquesne camp where I went when we lived in Duquesne.

I remember the campfires at Wesco, my parents driving over for one or two of the campfires, my excitement about going away to camp for a week - the first time I had been away from home without family. I think if I could have gone to Camp Wasco, or a similar quality camp, other years I might have made Eagle. But in Duquesne there was no pool where I could learn go swim enough to get the swimming merit badge and the lifesaving merit badge. The one year I went there Joe Hysong also went to Camp Wesco. I have often wondered how his Mother managed for him to get there because I don't think that it was in the financial scheme of things for his Mother.

Scouting provided my first real opportunity to see the great out of doors. Perhaps these experiences contributed to my attraction to mountains and things like hiking and camping. I remember being very impressed on hikes we took to the stone quarry. The stone quarry was probably two or three miles out from Derry. It was a hike up into the hills to get there. I don't recall that the quarry was being worked at the time. Perhaps it was just that in the depression there wasn't much call for stone. In any event from the upper side of the quarry it was possible to look down into the valley and see Derry, the Westinghouse factory, and the surrounding countryside all spread out before us. It was from there that I learned first and how much faster sight travels than sound. I remember watching steam rise from the factory and only seconds later the sound caught up to me. I remember, too, going on scout hikes and cooking my lunch. I recall one time taking bacon and eggs and cooking over an open fire. The eggs burned a bit and I think the bacon was a bit raw (perhaps it's a wonder I didn't get trichinosis. I was really enchanted being outdoors in the hills, hiking, building a fire, cooking, eating, etc.

One requirement for I think first class scout was to do a fourteen mile hike. One summer day, a day which I think was much warmer than we imagined it would be. Another scout and I (I think it was Joe Hysong, but am not sure) set out on a hike to a fire lookout which was on top of one of the ridges that make up Laurel ridge. I recall that from some point in the Derry area it was possible in the distance to see the lookout. We didn't have a map, and our understanding of just where the lookout was located was perhaps a bit sketchy. Anyway, we proceed, unconcerned about the shortcomings of our knowledge of the trails. We made it to the lookout, perhaps a bit later than we had intended. It was very hot and we were very short of water. We found a pool of water from a spring by the fireplace. The water was very cold and I was very thirsty. So I took many many big mouthfuls of water. We went up the steps to the top of the lookout. Shortly after getting to the top I developed the worst case of stomach cramps I think I have ever experienced. I think it must have been the cold water in a hot body. I remember feeling so bad that I guess I didn't care whether I lived or died. After a time the cramps disappeared. I learned a lesson the hard way about not gorging on anything liquid cold when very hot.

After lunch we started back toward Derry. It seemed much hotter than in the morning and it probably was. There seemed to be some splits in the trail which we did not recall. After some hit and miss we did arrive home late in the afternoon. We were so tired, but so proud that we at our ages had successfully negotiated this big hike and passed one of the Scout requirements.

We left Derry just after I started ninth grade, so I wasn't dating girls or anything like that while there. I do recall one girl, Leandre Heacox, whom I thought was a real nice girl. I think she may have felt the same about me.

When we lived in Derry, there were still four living veterans of the Civil War. Probably partly because of that, we always had a big parade in Derry on Memorial Day. The four civil War veterans always rode in cars near the head the parade. The parade began somewhere across town, I suspect near the High School, then wound all through town, over the railroad bridge, past our place and on up to the cemetery, where there was an appropriate ceremony. One of the parts of the service at the cemetery involved a recitation of the Gettysburg address. Pattsi Buckeye, a high school teacher and the football coach, always recited the address. One time he couldn't remember his lines. But from the back of the crowd came Delly Vitale's voice with the prompt. Delly taught eight grade, was a good teacher, an old maid and not at all afraid to speak up. I don't know if there was anybody else in the crowd who could have given the prompt or who would have had the courage to speak up the way she did. I always thought that Miss Vitale was a good teacher. I got a lot out of her classes.

Another thing we did in Derry was learning swimming, or perhaps improve on the little swimming skills we had. We went to Ridgeview to take lessons. The pool was in a resort village located about 2 ½ miles from Derry. Dad gave us a ride there, but my brother and I had to walk back. I can still remember how hot it was in midsummer in mid to late afternoon to walk about 2 ½ miles in the sun with very little shade!

We did have a family crisis while we lived in Derry, although at the time I don't think I fully realized the severity of the crisis. All the time I was growing up my Mother had suffered from sinus problems. I recall her going to the doctor from time to time. While I recall her referring to it as sinus problems I think it was quite a bit more serious than just minor sinus problems.

In I think nineteen thirty seven Mother had a mastoidectomy at Allegheny General Hospital. I recall hearing that Dr. Bodkin, the local general practitioner, and member of the Church, was a bit put out that Mother didn't have him do the surgery. For the sake of all of us I am glad she did not have him do the work. Anyway, I recall that Dad on an almost daily basis made the near fifty mile each way trip to the hospital. What I did not know at the time, and what my brother and I were never told, was that at the time of the surgery the doctors discovered that my Mother suffered from breast cancer. So while she was in the hospital she had a mastectomy. I remember hearing people saying that my Mother was very low for a time in the hospital. I don't think I knew that meant she was near death's door. I learned at some point, I think some time later, that my Mother had deferred the surgery for some time, until my brother and I were a bit older. I guess the mortality rate at the time was a bit high.

It took Mother quite a time to recover from the surgery. We had a young woman - I think just out of high school, and I think a woman from Peanut, a little burg on the outskirts of Derry named for the size of coal dug from the mine near Peanut. I don't think she stayed overnight, but she was there each day for several weeks, I think.

It was during this time that my brother and I learned much of the fine art of house cleaning. Each Saturday morning it was my job to vacuum the house and do other things I do not now recall. I don't know what all of my brother's duties were, but I do recall that dusting was one of them.

When I sometimes hear parents today express the view that their children who are about the same ages as my brother and me during this period, are not old enough to do housework, I just shake my head. The experiences did not harm us a bit and we learned some skills that have held me in good stead over the years.

During the time in Derry I pursued hobbies from earlier years and also picked up some new ones. Stamp collecting, which I had started doing in Verona was something I was very interested in. I recall learning about "first day covers", and proceeded to get such covers for all the stamps in the series honoring outstanding Americans. I think I still have the collection. I think we continued to follow Captain Ivory (I think what was the name) who ran a stamp collectors fifteen minute radio program. (His sponsor was Proctor and Gamble.) I also began to do business with H.E. Harris Company, a Boston company selling stamps. Money was in very short supply, but whenever I had a few cents I would buy another pack of stamps.

Harris put out a catalog, which of course was sent to me. I recall that it had a listing for several thousands of stamps and I don't know what all. I looked and looked at that page in the catalog, trying to think of some way I might possible get the five dollars, or was it four, at which the package was offered.

I came up with the idea of asking Grandpa Callow for the money. I mentioned it to my Mother, who very firmly told me in no uncertain times that I should never even think about asking Grandpa for something like that. Four or five dollars was a lot of money, but I guess, also that mooching for a gift was not considered good form.

Another hobby I developed was chemistry - chemistry sets, that is. At the time it was possible to buy sets with all kinds of chemicals. It was good fun working the experiments. At one point I got what was billed as a formula for gun powder. I tried it, although I recall my Mother was not at all enthusiastic about it. Fortunately, or unfortunately, I could never make the gun powder explode.

My Mother generally measured her works quite carefully. One time though, she did not and it came back to bite her. There was a parishioner in the church by the name of Mrs. Irwin. She was poor as a church mouse, but a very good hearted woman and always had the welfare of the minister and his family in her mind. She did the housekeeping for two bachelor brothers (I think their name was something like Lunnen, who lived on second or Third Avenue (the street on our side of the railroad tracks). She lived just across the creek from us, so she walked past our house a couple of times each day.) Being short of cash, Mrs. Irwin maintained a garden. I think she grew a fair amount of her food. One spring she grew a new species of pea where the pod was tender enough to eat and it was not necessary to hull the peas. She gave us a batch of them, which Mother cooked for dinner. Mother did not much care for them and offered the opinion that they tasted like horse food.

A few days later Mrs. Irwin stopped by and in the course of conversation with Mother asked how we liked the peas. My Mother was forever afraid of offending a parishioner, or somebody else, and she had an expression which she overtaxed. She would say, "It's very nice". So on this occasion, in response to Mrs. Irwin's inquiry, my Mother said, "they were very nice". My brother remembered Mother's comments about the peas and her comments to Mrs. Irwin's inquiry and my Mother's response. Richard promptly added, "Mother says they taste like horse food." I remember Mother turning all shades of the rainbow and stumbling through that comment. It turned into a long time family joke.

Dad was also known as the marrying parson when we lived in Derry. There were four protestant churches and a Roman Catholic Church - Methodist, Presbyterian, Lutheran and I think Episcopal. I don't recall many Church weddings when we lived in Derry, but I recall many weddings conducted in the living room of the parsonage. Many of the weddings were ones where the couple just stopped by and wanted to get married—right then. Well, during the depression, a wedding fee was a wedding fee. More than once I can recall that Dad was not home when the couple stopped by, generally with their two witnesses. Mother would explain that the minister was out just then, but that if they would be seated, she was sure he would be back soon. One occasion I recall my Mother calling me, telling me that a couple wanted to get married, and I should very quickly run to one or two places where she thought he might be. I was to let him know that he should get home right away for a wedding. One time, when I think I was probably twelve a couple stopped by and did not have any witnesses. My Mother would always fill in. Well, Dad looked at me, and told me I could serve as a witness - and so I did. Over the years I've hoped that that couple never had need to dig up the witnesses and learn that I was only about twelve when I got pressed into service.

I don't remember the name of but one of the other ministers in Derry. But I do recall that was the minister of the Presbyterian Church was named Reverend Crummy. I don't know that I every met the minister with that wonderful name, but I did get to know and dislike his son, who was several years older than I. My dislike for him arose because of what he did to a friend of mine and me at the tennis court at the YMCA.

There was a large YMCA in Derry, or at least it seemed large to me. I think that perhaps it was in some way tied to the Railroad, or the Railroad may have been a good supporter. Anyway, I learned a bit about tennis in Derry. A friend of mine, or perhaps my brother played I think it's called a set of tennis. We were about to playa a second set when the Crummy young man came by and told us we would have to surrender the court to him and his friend because a person was not allowed to play second sets. Well, I was cowed by some one older. But I never got over feeling he had taken advantage of me.

Derry was a town of about three thousand and an awful lot of those people seemed to be parishioners at the Methodist Church. There was Dr. Bodkin whom I have mentioned, Dr. Smith, a dentist, Mr. Kunzs, the barber, Mr. Edsel, who owned the paint store. Then there were two counselors at Camp Wasco, "Dip" Bryson whose father was the chief of police in Derry, and Holmes Yealy, whose Dad was I think in the choir at Church. "Dip and Holmes were both Eagle Scouts and boys to whom I really looked up. Mrs. Trogler was the organist at Church. I can't recall much more about her. Then Mrs. Spear and older woman, and her daughter, who I think was a bit handicapped, were the custodians.

There was one other event of significance to us which I haven't dealt with. That was the purchase of a new car. Dad started driving as I understand it in the very early 1920's. I think he bought his first car at that time. In 1929 he bought a Chevy which served as the family car until 1937. At that time cars were, or often were, shipped in rail box cars - four autos to a box car. Dad decided first to buy a 1936 car. He was a little disappointed because he really wanted a new car. Anyway, I understand that Mother told him to go ahead and buy a new car. The dealership was just about three blocks down the street which came into town and past the Church. So when my brother and I knew we were getting a new car we watched the new cars come in to town, being driven from the railroad to the dealer's. Our car had something less than a mile on it when Dad took possession. That would be our car until 1948, and little did I imagine it would be the car on which I would learn go drive.

As I recall, there was a membership roll of about 700 at the church. Dad was very well liked at the Church. I heard one man say that he had never heard anyone who had a bad word to say about Dad.

Dad worked very hard in Derry, as at other places. He was in the pulpit every Sunday except when we were on vacation. He spent about three afternoons each week calling on the parishioners, attended all the board meetings, etc. etc. When I see today how many churches the size of the Church in Derry think they need at least two ministers, I wonder how Dad held it all together. But he did and thrived on it.

I think everyone in town expected that Dad would stay at least a year longer in Derry than we did. But as I understand it, My Mother especially was concerned that the Derry schools might not be as good as they could be. She thought it would be better to go to a school in a larger town or city. I never really did hear all the details. But in an event we moved, and my brother and I were very unhappy with the event.

Vacations

During the time I was growing up we spent our summer vacations with my Callow Grandparents, in Evanston, Ill. I have no idea whether there was some sort of an understanding when Mother and Dad were married that this is the way it would work out. But given how anxious my Grandparents and I assume my parents were to see all of us at least once a year, this is way things worked out. It's about a 500 miles from Pittsburgh to Evanston. When we were growing up, getting from here to there, 500 miles, took a lot longer than it does today. When my brother and I were very young there was almost no plane service, busses were not very comfortable for a 500 mile trip, and train or car was the best way, if one had a car to get between the two points. And we always had a car when my brother and I were growing up.

Dad had gone to Allegheny College, in Meadville, Pa., and then he had gone to Garrett Divinity School, a part of Northwestern University, in Evanston. Mother went to Northwestern University. Dad was graduated from Allegheny College in I think 1918, after completing his service in the Army in the First World War. I'm not sure what year Mother graduated from Northwestern, but I think it probably was about 1921 or 1922. They were married in May of 1924.

I came along on January 7, 1926, and was given my Dad's name, with, of course, a junior on the end of it, or as my Mother often pointed out, I was really George III because my grandfather Hartung was also George Michael. Brother Richard came along on June 14, 1928, Flag Day. All the time we were growing up we insisted at home that people were putting out their flags to recognize my brother's birthday.

Dad's vacation was almost always in August. So our trips to Evanston were almost always in August. I don't know when we first drove out to Evanston, but I suspect that it was in about 1929 or 1930. I suspect that it was 1930. Dad and Mother bought a new car in the late summer of 1929. This was always a bit of a sore point, I thought with my Mother. The Hartung family reunion was always held in about August, which at that time would have been the end of the car model year. I recall my Mother saying that Dad didn't buy a new car until August because he wanted to be able to drive a new car to the family reunion. Vanity, vanity!! I think Mother would have preferred to have a new car to go to Evanston. So it is in this convoluted way that I arrive at the time of the first driving trip to Evanston. I don't ever recall any discussion about trips to Evanston before I arrived on the scene.

A five hundred mile auto trip was a big deal in the late '20's and early 30's. Some of the road had not been paved. I recall there generally were one or more detours on the way - and of course those detours were almost always on dirt roads. And August was a hot time to travel and there was no air conditioning. It was always a two day trip to Evanston. We might have been able to make it in one long day - Dad did it with Aunt Lilly and Uncle Nick in either 1933 or 1934. But Dad always had some last minute things to do on the Monday after his last day in the pulpit before vacation. We didn't generally get away until late morning or early afternoon.

Aunt Lilly and Uncle Nick went with Dad to Evanston one of the two years the Chicago World's Fair was on. There were twin towers at the Fair, with a track at about midway on the 200 foot high tower on which cars went around. Uncle Nick wanted to take Richard and me for a ride on the tower train. My Mother said no. It's just too high and too dangerous!!

During the depression years we almost always overnighted in guest homes. During the depression many people along the main routes would try to earn some money by renting out rooms for travelers. I remember well the search for the overnight stay. Some towns were regarded more favorably than others. We always avoided Van Wert because they charged more for their rooms than in other towns. It was generally dark by the time we stopped to look. Being summertime, it meant it was late for my brother and me. I recall being very anxious to get to bed.

Getting a good price for rooms was more important that getting to a destination earlier. Dad would always to in to check out the rooms and their prices and then come back to report to Mother. I remember one time when I was particularly tired and very anxious to get to bed. Dad came back to the car and reported to Mother that the rate for two rooms would be $2.75. Even more I remember Mother saying that she thought we could do better. So we headed on. And that price would have been for two rooms!! On the second day we generally arrived in mid to late afternoon. I remember how anxious my brother and I would get once we got on Sheridan Road in northern Chicago, because by then it would just be a short time to Grandma and Grandpa's.

As I said, a trip of 500 miles was not something one did every day of the week. I recall one time when we were stopped for a red light at the intersection where we turned on to Sheridan Road, the policeman on the corner stopped other traffic and motioned for us to go thorough. The only thing we could figure was that he saw a Pennsylvania license plate and thought that a long distance driver as that was entitled to some special treatment.

Grandma and Grandpa Callow lived at 720 Foster Street in Evanston. Grandpa had founded the Evanston Business College sometime between 1910 and 1911. Foster Street is just about three blocks west of the Northwestern University Campus. Grandma was a business woman in her own right. Their house on Foster Street was a three story house - a big house with lots of bedrooms. Since the house was so close to Northwestern University she ran quite a business renting out rooms to college professors and other people of that kind.

Since there were few if any roomers in the summer, in August, there was always space for us. My brother and I shared a room and our parents had a room.

We were always very glad to see our Grandparents, and vice versa. We were the only grandsons, and until the mid '30's there was only one granddaughter, so we were special to them. Grandpa was still running the school when we first started going to Evanston, although he was just about at his retirement age.

For my brother and me being in Evanston meant seeing Grandparents, Uncle Bill and Aunt Jane (later Lee) and Uncle Alva and Aunt Elsie (later Aunt Cora and another Aunt. We generally would go frequently for swimming in Lake Michigan which was just on the east side of Northwestern, and a fairly short walk for us. Then there was a lagoon where we could go, float boats, etc. Mother and Dad would also line up tours for us, such as to a packing plant (Swift and Armour) and others were all located in Chicago at the time. Then there were the tours to museums, etc.

There was at least one aspect of the trip to Evanston which neither my brother nor I enjoyed. Mother always wanted to get together with "girls", women with whom she had gone to Northwestern. Getting together with them meant a very boring afternoon, for my brother and me, when it was warm and sunny outside. Then the "girl's" children would always be there. Everyone had to ooh and ahh over how the children had grown. The children would have to line up back to back to compare heights, etc. And then the seemingly endless boring conversation!!

We did take a couple of trips out from Evanston during the time I was growing up. One trip was up to Wisconsin. Grandma and Grandpa had both grown up in southwestern Wisconsin, near Mineral Point, Dodgeville and Cobb. I remember on the trip to Wisconsin visiting the farm of my Great Uncle Grant. We were there during threshing season. At that time, generally one farmer in the area would own a threshing machine. Other farmers in the area would use the machine, for some share of the crop. All the participating farmers would participate in each of the threshing session.

It was very exciting to me to see the threshing operation. I can still recall my Uncle Grant being up on the equipment forking wheat into the machine. I recall my Dad marveling at the work Uncle Grant was doing. Uncle Grant must have been about 65 at the time and as Dad said he was doing one of the hardest jobs in the operation. I remember, too, walking around the barn area. I remember one of the help who was milking a cow paused a moment to shoot a squirt of milk directly in to the mouth of a cat. It was such a smooth process that I am sure he and the cat did this frequently. I remember all the farmers would be served lunch in the dining room of the home where the threshing was going on. Even at about nine or ten years of age I was amazed at the quantity of food that would disappear inside the working men. There seemed to be no end to the corn on the cob.

On perhaps this Wisconsin trip, or perhaps on another trip we stayed overnight with Great Grandmother Cynthia. I think, as I recall it, that when my great grandfather Callow died he married Cynthia. She was a very nice woman but very deaf. Don't know whether they had hearing aids at the time, but she had one of those horns which a person held up to their ear so they could hear someone speaking to them. Perhaps one of the most interesting things was when we got up the next morning and noticed that Great Grandma Cynthia or at least we assumed it was she had washed the license plate on our very dusty car so that the Pennsylvania license plate would show. We figured that Great Grandma Cynthia did not have many visitors and she wanted everyone in town to know she had guests from a long ways off. Cobb was then a metropolis of about 210 people, mostly located on one street so I assume everybody knew most everybody in town.

On another vacation trip we went to Williams Bay, Wisconsin. It's a large bay Lake Geneva. We just stayed, I think, for two or three days. But Dad got us some fishing tackle and we fished and caught lots of fish. They were all small crappies. But we cleaned them and had them for dinner that night.

On I think one of the two trips that I mention where, we went to Waterloo Iowa, to visit my Uncle and Aunt. The most memorable part of this trip was the arrival in town of the Ringling Brothers Barnum and Bailey circus. We all got up early in the morning—at least Dad, my brother and me and Uncle Howard (or was it Uncle Walter?) to see the Circus parade to the big tent. It was so exciting to see all the elephants being let through the town, and the lion cages full of lions, etc. I remember also being to the area where they were putting up the big top. I was so impressed to see the huge log stakes for the tent being driven into the ground by a power driven sledge. I'm not sure if we went to the circus today it would be anything like it was then. Seeing the parade and seeing the big top going up was enough.

On this trip to Iowa we also went to see the Little Brown Church in the Wildwood. I remember going in to the chapel and being very impressed. This is the Church we sing about!! Years later when Lois, Richard and Kirk were driving to the Midwest we made a special point to visit the chapel again.

Grandma and Grandpa visited us a couple of times when I was growing up. Grandpa did not much like driving to Pittsburgh. He didn't like the hills. He had grown up in flat Wisconsin and lived in flat Illinois that was much more to his liking. One time Grandpa did drive us to Evanston.

I recall also one vacation incident that occurred just after we moved to Verona. It occurred at the beginning of Dad's ministry there, and was probably an indicator of what the pastorate might be like. When we moved to Verona, the members of official Board decided that Dad should have only two weeks vacation because we had just moved there in June. (Never mind that Dad hadn't had a vacation since the prior August). So Grandpa drove to Verona and drove us to Evanston. I remember that we stopped the second day and had breakfast in YMCA where we had bacon for breakfast!!

Grandma and Grandpa started sometime in I think the mid to late 30's to go south in the winter. They would leave Evanston after Christmas, go to Florida and return in March. By that time Grandpa was driving a Packard so they traveled comfortably

We went out to Evanston at Christmas time one year. I remember going by train. I remember we packed our lunch in a shoe box - hard boiled eggs included. It was very exciting to make that big train trip. It was my first long train trip!

There's one other thing about our vacation trips which I recall and which began either while we were in Verona or very soon after we went to Derry. I learned very early how to read highway maps. And then when it came to our trips to Evanston I examined the map and tried to figure out a different routing. Anyway, I would look at the map and suggest maybe more on Route 22, or perhaps more on route 6 or whatever. Dad was very patient with me and think made a few adjustments to our routing.

I recall feeling very badly when we left Derry. I really liked the town, had so many good friends there, etc. And my following description of Duquesne will dwell in part about how badly things did turn out in Duquesne. Dad certainly did not have to leave Derry. Indeed, people were surprised and sorry to see us move. I seem to recall Mother say in later years that it was a mistake to leave Derry and go to Duquesne.

5

Duquesne

Duquesne at the time we lived there was a City of perhaps fifteen or twenty thousand people, located on the Monongahela River about fifteen miles or less from Downtown Pittsburgh. It was a heavy industry town—a steel town. I understood at the time we moved there that about forty percent of the population was foreign born - largely eastern European - Poland, Yugoslavia, etc. Much unlike Derry which was more rural in nature with relatively few foreign born.

Things went badly the first day after we moved. The school differences were significant. In Derry we started studying Algebra in the ninth grade, so I had had only a bit of it before moving. Duquesne started algebra in the middle of the eighth grade. Duquesne started the study of Latin in the middle of the eighth grade - again a change from Derry where study of Latin began in the ninth grade.

Dad went with me to the junior high school to arrange for the transfer. We met with Mr. Magee, the principal. (His parents lived next door to us in Duquesne. I recall them as a very friendly older couple.) Mr. Magee gave me a choice - I could just tough it out with Algebra and Latin, or I could drop back to the eighth grade. Clearly, it was no choice for me. How could I be expected to drop back to the eighth grade?

I never understood why my parents, with their intense interest in our education never suggested engaging a tutor to help me catch up. I never thought of such a thing. So from then on, math was tough for me. I never really did come to grips with some of the theory. Latin was a different thing. I could pick up on that, although Bessie Kratzer, the Latin teacher had a real problem - I think a psychological problem which made her very difficult for everyone. If anything she was a bit easier on me, perhaps because of Dad.

I quickly picked up with Scouts. The Methodist Church was the sponsor of the troop, or at least the weekly meetings were held at the Church. Then as might be expected, I was promptly involved in Sunday school and in the Epworth League program at Church. After perhaps three years in Duquesne I became bored with Sunday School. I suggested to my parents that I might drop out. Well, that just wasn't going to happen as I knew all too well, Dad knew also, that it wouldn't be wise to let me fester in Sunday School. So, marvelously, it was decided that the Sunday School needed a treasurer, and who better than I to occupy that position. So on Sunday morning, I was busy counting collections from Sunday school, keeping the records, etc. And no more attending Sunday School sessions!!

One of the toughest things about the move, though, was that there were almost no kids living near us. There was one boy who lived across the street. He was difficult to know. Just a strange kid. Then there were two boys who lived a few blocks from us - Bob Aton and Bill Swanson. They and their families belonged to the Church. I liked them both very much. A problem was that they were cousins and had always lived next do to each other. So I was always sort of a fifth wheel when with them.

For the first time I was in a school which had both a gym and a swimming pool. Duquesne always had a very good basketball team. The phys-ed teacher was also the basketball coach. So the only thing we did in gym was play basketball. I assumed that the thinking was that if all the boys played basketball in gym some new talent could be developed – a mistake, as far as I was concerned. Unfortunately, I knew nothing about basketball and the teacher saw no reason or need to teach me anything about the game. Gym was always a bad time for me. There I was, no real idea of how basketball worked, but stuck in a situation where the only thing we did was to play basketball. One time

I made a basket from some distance out. Everyone was so shocked that the game just about came to a halt. On of the fellows did congratulate me, however!!

Most of the kids in school came from a different background than I had grown up in. So for that additional reason I found it very hard to make friends. Maybe this was my fault, but I think the system was very difficult. With the passage of time I did make some good friends. I remember Mike Miklos especially. He decided fairly early he wanted to be a Dr. I have many times wished that I had made contact with him in later years. Then there was Ted Mizik. Great guy!!

At home, Mother was ill and spent a great deal of her time in bed. Migraine headaches were the principal problem that I knew of, but I'm fairly certain that after effects of her major surgery a couple of years earlier dogged her.

Because of Mother's health we had a cleaning woman come in perhaps one day each week. Her name was Lena. She lived in the neighborhood, and was a good hearted hard worker. Unfortunately for her, she suffered from epilepsy. I wasn't filled in on this. So I was rather shaken the first time I saw her writhing on the kitchen floor with one of her seizures. As I recall Dad was at work when this happened and I assume Mother was in bed. So the whole event was more difficult than it would have been, I think, if I had been informed and given some suggestions early on.

I think that it was when I was in ninth grade that I got a bicycle. I had wanted one for a long time and was just delighted with it. By today's standards it was very heavy - a steel bicycle with coaster bakes, and no gearing system (actually I think gears didn't hit the scene for about fifteen years after that.) But I was very soon pedaling all over the place. It was somewhere between three and five miles to the Allegheny County airport. I really liked going out there and watching the plane traffic. But on Saturday, or other non school days trips of ten to twenty five miles or so was a fairly regular event. Unfortunately, I never did find a friend or friends to go with.

Cycling on the high ways at that time may not have been as risky as today. There were a lot fewer cars on the roads and the speeds were much less than today. But on the other hand most of the highways were narrow two lane roads.

While we lived in Duquesne brother Richard learned to play the organ. He and I had both started taking piano lessons by the time we started school or sooner. I enjoyed playing the piano, but was not as proficient as my brother. He quickly developed a real interest in playing the organ.

It was only natural, I think, that my brother advanced to the pipe organ. All the Churches which Dad served had pipe organs. In Duquesne the organist was Mrs. Osborne. She was an excellent organist, albeit with idiosyncrasies. She was also a strong supporter of Dad. For example, she very much hoped that Dad would stay in Duquesne, rather than being moved. Somehow on the new minister's first Sunday (in the Methodist Church when a minister is appointed to a new charge he never returns to the pulpit from which he is being moved. There is generally about a ten day gap between the end of conference and the move. So the new minister always goes to his new charge the first Sunday after Conference.) So anyway, when the new minister came (his first Sunday in the new charge) there was suddenly during a hymn, I think, a "power failure" and the congregation had to sing a cappella. I don't think anyone knew for sure just what happened, but our family suspected that Mrs. Osborne caused the "power failure". Anyway she was a very good organist and a good teacher. Richard learned a great deal from her.

I did have occasion to give my brother a start one time when he was practicing the organ The Church and the parsonage were one building. I discovered early on that I could go from the parsonage to the Church in the area above the ceilings of Church and parsonage. It was not a recommended route and I never told anyone that I had discovered it. I would occasionally up there, although I don't think my parents ever knew it. One time when I did it my brother was practicing the organ.

I slipped up to the ceiling area, above the sanctuary and opened one of the small windows from which I could watch my brother. When he paused I said in a soft voice "whoo." My brother stopped playing, looked a round, then started up, not realizing that the whoo was my voice. Richard stopped playing after a minute or so, and I again whoo. Richard looked around and then nervously went on playing the organ. He stopped soon and checked again. About the third or fourth time this happened, my brother shut off the organ and took a fast exit. I never told him about this little escapade of mine which caused him such concern, until many, many years later. I have laughed about it over the years, but I don't think that Richard ever saw the humor!!

With the passage of time in Duquesne, I didn't care any more for the city than I had at first, but I did become a lot more involved in various activities. I was extremely busy when in senior high school. I went out for the school paper and year book. My writing for the newspaper was different than most copy we staffers produced. I wrote editorials. I must have done some of the writing before the War broke out. One or more of the editorials I recall were very critical of Roosevelt's actions with the British - such as lend lease etc. I expressed the view that the President was taking steps that most surely would result in our country being dragged in to the war. I recall being very upset when the Superintendent of schools for Duquesne put the red pencil to one whole editorial. He wrote margin notes in which he suggested I read some book related to opposition to the Civil War. I was so angry that I considered resigning from the newspaper staff - but I didn't.

As we got to the end of our junior year in high school it became necessary to select the editor for the paper for our senior year. I don't know whether I was anxious to get that job, but I suppose that I must have had some feelings on the subject. There was one other student - Ollie Suthard or Sutherlin who I always thought was well liked and regarded. I didn't much care for him. I always thought he was a smiling smooth talker and didn't much care for him. I felt also he was a bit of an egotist.

Well when nominations were asked for the position of editor both Ollie and I were nominated. I figured that that sweet talker Ollie probably would be selected. And I am sure he felt that way. To my surprise I won. The job involved not only the monthly newspaper but also the annual. So when I got that job I knew I had taken on a lot of work.

The Latin Club was a natural organization to join for a person continuing with the study of Latin. And my Latin teacher, Laura G. Pound made sure I became involved. I always felt that Miss Pound was a very good Latin teacher. But she did favor boys over girls; so much so that I think she was sometimes not fair to girls. Anyway, I got along with her very well. The Latin Club did not involve a lot of work, but we did have at least monthly meeting. I can't recall now exactly what we did at the meetings, but I think she probably taught us about the different styles of the Greek arches - Doric, Ionic and Corinthian. I think we must have done a play or dome thing one time. The reason I think that is because I now recall a very good violinist in my class, Frank Yaroshuk, who would when we were talking about some events, which must have included fire, would start playing "I don't want to set the world on fire, I just want to set a fire in your heart".

Then there was the school orchestra. Somehow Maude Witherspoon, the director of the high school orchestra and director of music for the school, asked me if I would like to learn how to play the bass fiddle. Maude (always Miss Witherspoon to us students) knew my parents, she studied at Northwestern University, where Mother went to school, and knew that if I would be a part of the bass fiddle business I would pay attention and learn.) So learn I did - probably not very well to anyone who was really skilled. But I did take lessons from her and play in the high school orchestra. The school had one other bass fiddle and a very nice fellow by the name of Jennery Falvo. We filled that department in the school orchestra. It was good training and I did enjoy it. I did take the instrument back and forth from school once or twice a week. We lived two or three blocks from school. Especially in the winter when the streets were snowy and icy I had quite a time getting the instrument back and forth from school given the hill between home and school. .

Then the math teacher, Mr. Mellon, organized a swing band and asked me if I would be willing to join the band. Maude hadn't taught me how to slap bass. With her I always used the bow. But one didn't use the bow in a swing band. We practiced at least one evening per week. I think we got together right after school. Then we played for the school dances (not the prom but just after school dances.)

Mr. Mellon always tried to liven up band practices by singing a few numbers. One of his favorites was "I can't dance, got ants in my pants." He did the solo part. Great fun!!

I have never been real well coordinated for athletic activities. But I decided I wanted to do something. So I joined the volley ball team. Mr. Mellon was the coach (math teacher and band director). I think because of scheduling problems we had team practice very early in the morning—before school. I think we must have started at about 7:30 a.m. Another complication in my schedule. I did play in a number of interschool meets. I got a real good feeling riding a school bus to a game in another town. Just sort of an ego booster for me, even though I knew that I was not a very good player.

And then there was the Boy Scouts. I had joined the Scouts and was in Troop 3 when we lived in Derry. I think our Scoutmaster in Duquesne was a Bob Schaeffer. I enjoyed Scouts very much. At least some of the meetings we played a few games. The game I really remember was Capture the flag. We always played in a darkened scout hall which made for a lot of fun but also, I am sure to the outsider, a very confusing thing. Then there was Camp Wesco. This was the camp for the Westmoreland and Fayette counties Council. It was a very well run camp. There was tight discipline and a very good program. One of the things I really remember about Camp Wesco was the swimming. It was a good concrete pool, lanes, etc. - an excellent place for teaching and working on some merit badges - or at least I have always felt it would be.

There were two eagle scouts in Troop 1 in Derry - Holmes Yealy, Jr. and Dip Bryson. Holmes Yealy's Dad was active in the Church in Derry, and Dip Bryson's Dad was police chief in Derry. (never did learn Dip's real first name.) I really looked up to and admired them.

Unfortunately I only went one year to camp Wesco. The next year we moved to Duquesne. Duquesne had its own camp. I think there may have been two troops in Duquesne, or perhaps only one. But the Scouts in Duquesne had acquired some property and developed a camp which was named Laurel Mountain. The camp was too small to have a very good program. It did not have a cool. Instead, swimming was done in a creek that ran along or through the camp property. I always felt that if there had been a good pool at the Duquesne Scout camp I might have earned my Swimming and Life Saving Merit badges. I earned about a dozen or so merit badges while in scouting, and some of them, like Pioneering and First Aid, were hard ones to earn. But I just didn't have a way of learning enough about swimming to earn Swimming and Life Saving merit badges. I have always felt that if I had been able to get those two merit badges I could have made Eagle.

There was one "bonus" to being in Scouts in Duquesne. We had the opportunity, along with scouts from many other troops in many other towns to serve as ushers at the football games of the University of Pittsburgh. The team had enjoyed top national ratings in the late 30's and perhaps early 40's. There was a change in the coaching staff, I guess, and the team didn't do as well in the 40's but it was still a thrill to see the games in return for ushering. On cold days, though, I remember it was very cold because we just weren't dressed will enough in our uniforms. But we were willing to pay the price to see the games. I guess I probably ushered for two or perhaps three games each of two or three years.

During the time we were in Duquesne I also had the opportunity to serve as a camp counselor. The Methodist Church sponsored a summer camp, Camp Epworth Woods, which I think was operated primarily to provide camping experiences for young folks living in some of the poorer areas of Pittsburgh. Anyway, Dad knew about the camp and I think in large part because of his acquaintances I got a job here. The Director of the Camp was a Paul Slater. He was an educator, probably in one of the schools in the region. He served as Director for several years and I always thought he did a good job.

I think that by today's camping standards the camp was a big primitive. We lived in tents, and the Counselors lived and slept in the tent with his or her campers. I enjoyed it very much and learned a lot. There was quite a bit of learning on the job. It was wartime and getting young men was not easy. So I suppose I had a better opportunity than I would have had in peacetime. The camp was located not far from Mars, Pa. where Aunt Mary, Uncle Frank and Aunt Lucille and their families lives, although I did not see them during the summer. The evenings, after we had the kids in bed were most enjoyable. The counselors got together in the main hall. I remember a number of great people serving as counselors and then especially I remember a lot of very attractive women counselors. The women were a little older than the male counselors because the draft did not take the women. Ordinarily, the women probably would have looked down at us male counselors as "kids". Bit since it was wartime and all the men their age were in the service they couldn't be too choosy.

I remember walking a mile or so, each way, on some evenings to get a hamburger at a little shop out from camp, in the evening after we had the kids down. And I enjoyed the camp scene. The events, such as hobo hikes (where each group wanders around to find designated items to put into a big "stew" at the end), singing after each meals, campfires, etc.

Probably by the junior year of high school, but certainly by the senior year all of the fellows began thinking about the likelihood that we would be facing the military draft before too long. I think it was probably during my senior year that I learned about the ASTP program. This was a program the Army had by which men who qualified could apply to be put into the ASTP program which would involve some college training related to some of the Army needs. It founded like something worth pursuing so I took and passed the Army test for the program. I don't know whether I really thought that I would get into the program, but I think it was in the back of my mind that if the war was still on it was something I was going to try to pursue. More on this little twist later.

In the fall of I believe 1942, I suggested to Dad that I would like to learn to drive a car (I was 16.). Dad looked a bit shocked by the suggestion. I told him that I thought there would be a benefit if I knew how to drive. I told him that gas rationing was in, the things might get even tougher on the gasoline front. I'm sure there were other reasons I gave to Dad the details of which I do not know recall. After some thought, and perhaps after a discussion with Mom, he decided that perhaps it would be ok. At that time, the minimum age for a driver's license was 16, so as far as the Commonwealth was concerned I was old enough to drive a car.

At that time I don't think there were driver training courses. In any event, the subject never came up. I just assumed, and I think Dad did also, that he would be the one to teach me how to drive. And so it was. And I always felt very fortunate. Dad was always an excellent driver and also a very good teacher. He was very patient with me and put up, I am sure with a number of jerky starts with the stick shift.

At the time, Dad still owned his 1937 Chevrolet. There was no such thing as automatic transmissions. Living in a city as hilly as Duquesne, and learning in the fall and early winter, Dad taught me how to start up very gradually if the street was slippery. He taught me how to start and stop in such a way as to create a bit of bouncing action to work out of a slippery spot etc.

Down near the edge of town there was a large open field. I think it was probably an area that had had a fairly deep valley which had been filled with slag from the steel mill and then leveled, compacted etc. We would drive around this field, starting and stopping, turning, reversing, etc. Dad also did a superb job in teaching me how to parallel park. I've always felt I do an excellent job in parking and I learned it form Dad. Well, after perhaps a month of instruction we went to the license office so I could take the test and, if I passed, get a license. I as very glad to pass on the first try.

Getting a license did not mean that I would be doing a lot of driving. Nor did it change the fact that we would continue as a one car family. As a minister, Dad had a C gas rationing card. Most everybody got only an A card which entitled a person to I think it was three gallons per month. (It might have been three gallons per week, but I don't think so.) With the C card Dad could purchased enough gas to drive, on average, as I recall it, about 2000 miles per quarter, which was much more generous than the allowance for most drivers.

Dad showed a lot of courage in the driving he allowed me to do. I recall that in about January or February after I got a license, after perhaps a couple of months, he agreed to let me drive with Mother and my brother to downtown Pittsburgh. I'm really not sure that I had enough skills to drive a car, on my own, to downtown Pittsburgh. But I did, and managed to do it without having an accident. I do recall, though that I think I inadvertently drive through one red light. Fortunately, traffic was light and the speeds were much slower than today.

Then came the time for the senior prom. Dad agreed that I could drive the car for the event. I invited Alice Morgan as my date. She was a then a junior in high school. I knew her pretty well, because she played in the school orchestra. She had to check with her parents, and they agreed it was ok, and they would get her a formal for the occasion. The dance was held in the high school gym. Then, after that, those who wished could go to a nightclub in East McKeesport to a night club where we would have a late dinner, dance to a live band, etc. I recall the price was $3.00, which I think was for the two of us.

Mike Miklos and Ted Mizik, both very good friends of mine, decided that we would all like to go to the dinner outing after the dance. I know I didn't' dance well (I do a little better now, but not too much. I can't image how we were out so late, but I seem to recall that it was about 2 a.m. when Alice got in to her house - probably about as late as I had ever been up. I didn't think a whole lot about who I invited to the dance, vis a vis the Church girls. I didn't date much at all and didn't think about it, and I doubt it would have made a difference to me anyway. But I did learn later, in a round about way, that there were some girls from the Church (I remember Nancy Brumbaugh, Lois Burton, Margery Whittaker) who had really hoped that I would ask one of them. Ah, yes, being a PK carried a price!

Well, in due time I came to the end of high school. We got out the Echo, the annual in which I was listed as the busiest person in school. As usual, in the baccalaureate and Commencement programs, a number of students gave speeches in the baccalaureate and commencement programs. I remember that I had a talk on our class motto - Ad Aspera Per Aspera - To the Stars Through Difficulties. I remember very little about the programs except that Maude Witherspoon got very upset with all the students in a practice session, when the students started stamping their feet to the music of the William Tell Overture. And I have no recollection as to who spoke at the programs or what they said.

Somewhere I suppose I might have a copy of my talk, but I really don't know. I do remember after Commencement walking around, probably with my parents, feeling a bit at loose ends. I do remember it was a very pleasant late spring evening. Especially with all the things I had going on in the senior year I just couldn't get used to the idea of having some unplanned time.

Not too long after high school graduation I headed off for my second year as a Counselor at Camp Epworth Woods. Quite a few of the staff were new. The first summer my special friend was Jeannie Winterseen. I don't think I ever saw her after the end of camp. The second year, my special friend or summer girl friend was Doty Datt. I recall she was a couple of years older than I and was a student at Muskingum College. I think I saw here once or twice after that, but the special friendship was just for the summer.

I was 17 during this summer, and known that I was probably going to face the draft before long. I recall speaking to Paul Slater, the camp director about the possibility of him getting a deferment for me for the summer of 1944 so I could be a Counselor. I knew that was not going to come to pass and Mr. Slater assured me he had no power with Draft boards.

There are a couple of miscellaneous things which I realize I have not commented upon. One was stamp collecting. I started collecting stamps when I was in Verona, and in about second or third grade. I always enjoyed it very much and have thought many times that I would like to take up the hobby again. But that never came to pass. I recall that in my senior year I would on some Saturdays take the street car to downtown Pittsburgh and stop at Rosenbaum's department store to look at stamps. It had the best stamp store in downtown Pittsburgh as far as I knew. There was a fellow who ran it was very patient in talking to me - especially since my purchases could never have been more than $1.00 or $2.00

Especially during the senor year in high school, my parents and I turned my attention to where I might go to college. It was always assumed that I would go to college. What I didn't really comprehend at the time was that for all practical purposes the only school to which I would go was Allegheny College, in Meadville. It was a Methodist-related school. And I don't know that we talked about it at the time, but at some point I learned that the College gave some significant discount to children of Methodist ministers. We never discussed this. But I can understand now, that given the meager salary paid to Methodist Ministers, at least at that time, my going there was the only option. I went some place in Pittsburgh, spoke with an admissions officer and then took some kind of test and was admitted. College admissions certainly did not involve anything like the testing, applying, etc. that goes on today. But in any event I knew by sometime in the spring of 1943 I would be going to Allegheny in the fall.

There was one thing of appeal to Duquesne - Kennywood Park. It was an amusement park on the edge of the downriver side of Duquesne. It was and still is the major amusement park in the area. We didn't go there often, but when we did it was always a lot of fun. I remember one summer when I went there I noticed my high school English teacher operating one of the real exciting roller coasters - Mr. Barber. He was a very favorite teacher of mine. He did such a great job in introducing us to Shakespeare that I have always enjoyed the author.

6

Allegheny - First Year

In early September, 1943, we loaded up the 1937 Chevy with all of my things for my first year at Allegheny College and Dad, Mother and I headed to Meadville. We drove up Highway 19, which was then the main highway from Pittsburgh to Erie. Since there was no freeway or interstate program I would guess it probably took the better part of three hours for the drive. I think I was probably filled with a bit of apprehension over the whole thing, although I don't at this time really recall.

In 1943 nearly all of the men on campus were freshmen, since upperclassmen were almost all in the military services. The customary freshmen men's dormitory, Caflisch Hall, served as housing, I believe, for an army military unit in school training at Allegheny. The percentage of women students may have exceeded the college dormitory housing for women. The fraternity houses were largely vacant since the men were mostly in service.

The College had arranged for several of the fraternity houses to be used for freshmen housing for men and women. I was provided housing in the Delta Tau Delta fraternity house. We had one "real live" Tau Delt in the house, an upperclassmen who was 4F. I think there were probably about 20 or 25 of us housed in this fraternity house. My roommate was Edgar ("Eef") Ward, from Erie. The College had all of us eat at Brooks Hall, the college food service area.

Allegheny is a Methodist-related college - the relationship today is not nearly as strong as it once was. During my freshman year twice weekly chapel attendance was required. And attendance was kept!!

I really was a bit at sea in the whole process. And by present day standards did not have the faculty support in class and course selection. When I started College I had no idea what my major would be, which I think in most cases should be the way it is now.

My first year courses were largely ones that were required for graduation. There was English (required), History (required), some sort of an introduction to Science, (one of the required courses,) and Spanish, and I think one other course. My College advisor was the College librarian and English professor, who was kiddingly referred to as Elephant Ears. I can recall only one actual meeting among the professor and his advisees.

The meeting was painful and boring. PM, his initials and one of his nicknames, told us he wanted to read poetry to us which he though was wonderful. Most of us groaned but suffered through the meeting. As I say, I don't recall much other contact with my advisor.

I fairly quickly became involved in the drama productions. I don't recall the name of the play that we did, but I found it an interesting program.

Perhaps it was because enrollment was down during the War years, but we had very good professors the first year. Dr. Reed was the English professor - brilliant man and excellent lecturer. He had been in a serious auto accident a few years earlier which left him with a very pronounced stutter. His lectures were so well done that after a very short time we didn't notice the stutter. Then there was Dr. Cares, a fairly young history professor who, again, was an excellent lecturer. Spanish was taught by Dr. Blair Hanson. That class was a bit of an agony for me. The good professor wanted us to all learn and sing songs in Spanish. There were only three of us men in the class - one, Malcolm Young had an excellent voice and then there were the other two of us. It was obviously always possible to know when the men were singing and the limitations on my voice skills I felt were always very plain. I'm sure there was another course, but at this time I cannot recall what it was. As is readily apparent, there was nothing daring or dramatic in my first year course selections.

Since there were few men and many women, we men were an attractive commodity, I think. I was shy enough then that I didn't socialize as much as I might have. Fairly early on, however, I met Lois Eichenberg and Barb Dietterich. One of the other men in the class was Don Ludwig. As the year progresses I dated Lois a few times, and on at least a couple of occasions had double dates with Barb and Don and Lois and me. Little did I know what lay ahead from these friendships.

During the first year, women were rather tightly regulated as to evenings out. I think they had to be back in the dorm by 9 p.m., except for one or two nights per week they could be out until 11, and I think once or twice a month could be out until midnight – whoopee!! And girls had to check out and in on a register at the entrance to Brooks Hall. Nobody had a car to drive at school, so we walked on dates, and for that matter on everything else.

College brought a lot of changes in my life, even in ordinary day to day things. There was, for example the matter of laundry. Can't just put it in the family clothes bin. I recall that I found a woman to do my shirts. The rest of my laundry was handled in some other way, but I can't now recall just what. I know that a number of people had laundry boxes which they mailed home each week, and then a few days later received the box back with clean clothes. The boxes were hard sided, probably of a stiff cardboard, or perhaps even a plastic, although plastic was still a new product.

Then there was the matter of fraternities and sororities. Allegheny had six or seven of each. The sororities did not, and even now do not have their own houses. But the fraternities had houses. At that time most men joined a fraternity. By hindsight I think I was a bit naïve about the whole process. Also, as I reflect back upon fraternities, a fair number of the men had father's who were in a particular fraternity. I think there probably was, and maybe is today, a "legacy" system by which certain men join the fraternity their father was in. Others had some sort of connection. I had no connections and knew very little about the whole process. In any event, I pledged Theta Chi. It did not have a long history at Allegheny, but was a good fraternity. During the first year I think there were only about two members actually living on campus. One was Paul Beaver, and the other was Jim Rhinesmith. Jim started out with some science major, but fairly early on he changed to pre-Theo and so he had an exemption from the military. I don't recall that I ever know why Paul was on campus, rather than being in the Service. Allegheny did not operate our fraternity house, but for some reason we had access to the house. The initiation, for example, was conducted in the house and we had a few meetings there. I recall that we had initiation procedures—little juvenile things, which had been a part of the system for ever, I guess. (This kind of initiation process disappeared from the scene everywhere when men came back from the Service and refused to put up with that kind of truck.) Our fraternity house was a grand big old house. It has since been torn down and the sight is occupied I think by a bank.

During the first year at Allegheny, I think all of us men knew that we were short term at Allegheny, at least during the War. When I turned 18, in January, 1944, I duly registered with the Draft Board. It was about at that time that Allegheny announced that if a person was able to continue in school until the either the 22nd of April of first of May, he could get credit for the whole college year. I hoped that I could make it until at last then. But I knew that the military was moving fairly rapidly in the build up of the armed forces.

I was surprised, however, when, within two months or less I received notice of call up. I applied for a deferment for long enough to allow me to complete the College year on the regular schedule. This deferment was denied. I was given only a two month deferment. This meant that I would be in the service by early May. All of us knew at the time that our fate was tied to the local draft board. As it turned out I received just enough deferment to get credit for the full college year.

I don't know activities I was involved in by the second semester at Allegheny. I know that I did some writing for the school newspaper. I think that basically life proceeded at a normal pace. All of us fellows knew that fairly soon we would face the draft but we went along without much of a sense of urgency. The college year was not quite what you would call a "normal" college year.

Sometime in April I received notice to report for my induction physical. I recall it was conducted in downtown Pittsburgh at some large center. There were a lot of us going through the physical on the day I went through. I recall moving from point to point and being checked out by a number of doctors or persons who preformed a part of the process. I recall very well coming to the end of the line and knowing that I had passed the physical exam. I think it was probably pretty hard to flunk the test. What I most remember about the process though was coming before a big fat sergeant at the end of the line.

At that time the newspapers were filled with articles saying that whenever possible the boys were being given their choice of the branch of service. So when I came before this sergeant at the end of the line I heard him ask me what branch of the service I preferred. I recall telling him the Army. I recall him also asking me why the Army. So I told him I had taken and passed the ASTAP test and would like to get in the Army, and get some college training (which was part of the ASTAP program). I can to this day clearly see and hear him as he picked up this big stamp and as he brought it down telling me that he thought I would look real good in a Navy uniform. (He handed me a card, or I received it shortly saying Navy or Marines. I was disappointed, but by hindsight I thanked my lucky stars.

The Army wiped out the ASTAP program in September of 1944. Those in the program were all sent overseas promptly, as I heard, and arrived in Europe just in time for the Battle of the Bulge (The last big push of the Germans at the end of 1944. A push designed to fail because Germany was really at the end of its line. But Hitler was not paying attention to his generals or anybody else and so Germany went on to a plan of destruction to the bitter end.

I recall after the War rooming for a year with Ed Ferguson, a fraternity brother who had been in the Battle of the Bulge. Fergie's eyesight was about the same as mine. He lost his glasses in the battle and had to crawl for several hours along on his belly because he didn't really know where he was. Fergie had a very bad nervous shake at the time. Today the military would put him into a rehab program, but it wasn't done at the time. His experience and all the other accounts of the Battle of the Bulge made me eternally grateful to that top Sergeant who I am sure never thought or knew or cared of my feelings on the subject.

The whole process moved very quickly after the physical. I wound up at Allegheny by the end of April and reported for duty in the Navy on May 10, 1944. I don't recall any special statement or recognition by Allegheny that I was going in to the Navy. This was just like what was happening most every day to other men in Allegheny.

I'm sure Mother and Dad drove up and brought me home from Allegheny. One year down and three to go - whenever.

7

Navy

May 10, 1944, is a date etched in my mind. It was the day I reported for service in the Navy. In some way I knew that I was to appear at the induction center in downtown Pittsburgh in the early evening.

When I got to the induction center I recall that a group of us who were going in to the Navy were seated in a room. I recall that a fellow stood before us and told us that he needed nine volunteers for the Marines. This was at a time when the Marines wee doing the landings and fighting on the island hopping in the Pacific. Like most everyone else, I kept my eyes glued to the floor. Finally, nine volunteers were lined up.

I took the trolley down to this induction center by myself. I had rather hoped that Dad, and perhaps Mother and Brother might to along because a lot of parents and families went down to see the recruits off. But Dad had some church meeting, Mother had a headache. So I headed out by myself.

Once it was settled as to who was going in to the Marines, the rest of us headed out to get the train that was taking us to USNTC Bainbridge. (U.S. Naval Training Center) I remember that it seemed most of the men had family along the way to the train waving their family members off. I remember feeling quite lonely going along by myself.

It was an overnight trip to Baltimore, Maryland, where we changed trains. I had something happen that I have never forgotten. We were at the platform in Baltimore for a short time. We all got off the train. While standing on the platform I saw a drinking fountain and decided to get a drink. I drank at a fountain which said Colored on it. I had never experienced this kind of segregation and only slowly came to the realization of the significance of the sign.

On arrival at Bainbridge we were processed and then issued uniforms. I recall learning at that time that replacements to our uniform were our responsibility but that our pay would include a nine dollar allowance, I think quarterly for clothing. Twelve dollars a quarter may not seem like much. But I recall that shoes cost $9, twelve dollars a quarter wasn't too niggardly. Our uniform included leggings, which we had to wear all during boot camp.

Boot camp lasted just about five or six weeks. A lot was crammed in to that time. We had to learn a lot about Navy discipline, saluting requirements, barracks etiquette, etc. Turn out time was 6 a.m. Most days the first order of business was to get out on the "grinder", a large track on which we had to jog. I recall it was while we were jogging that I learned of the allied landing at Normandy. Good news, but none of us knew exactly what would follow. Then there was the matter of getting all the vaccinations and shots the Navy required. I recall standing in a long line with corpsmen who administered the shots. At least once we got two shots at a time - one in each arm. We spent a fair amount of time on military drill. I also learned that laundry was something that everyone had to take care of for himself. There was no leave time during boot camp. It was a straight shot. I think the military was really hurried to build up the forces.

We got a leave, for about 10 days, I think, at the end of boot camp. Naturally, went to Pittsburgh. I think I took a trip to Allegheny for a visit - found it was very easy to hitchhike. I also had time for a few dates with Alice Morgan. I think by that time my parents had installed a service star in the window of our living room.

It was back to Bainbridge after my leave to see what the future held. I found that it was time for the Navy to decide what it wanted me to do. I don't know what choice I had, except that it there would be some training. Quickly a decision was made that I would be going to radioman school. As with most of us who came back from leave after boot camp there would be a three week wait. During this time, we would be assigned all the grungy kinds of work the Navy needed done. There was one horrible misfit which the people at the pool hall quickly realized. I was sent to be a pin setup man at the pool tables. Since I didn't have a clue about pool, I was sent to the bowling alley to set up pins (this was all before the days of automatic pin set up). This work lasted only a brief time which suited me just fine.

Then came KP. That I could not avoid. I learned that the mess hall for the section of the base where I was stationed served 6000 men in 1 ½ hours. I learned that I would be wakened at 4:30 or 5 a.m. to be on the line by 6 a.m. And except for a break of about an hour and a half I would be working until about two or three p.m. and then back for dinner. An exhausting grind! Bit finally the rest of the grungy work was done and I was sent to begin radioman school.

I found radioman school interesting. Also, the men in the program were fairly well educated, so had some interesting people around. At that time radiomen worked the "key", i.e. It was the dit da system rather than the electronic system in place today. It was a sixteen week program. To graduate from school a person had to achieve a minimum speed of 16 words per minute. During War time all dispatches were coded. A word was a 5 letter group of letters or digits. Sixteen words per minute meant eighty letters per minute, which means a fairly fast speed. Typing skills were required. Fortunately for me, Mother had taught me how to type when I was in high school. So I didn't have to do much typing school.

My skill with typing did result in one event I found very humorous. One day a petty officer came in to the classroom and announced that he needed the two best typers for a special project. Naturally, I did not raise my hand to volunteer, but others pointed to me and one other member of the class. So, the two of us went out to handle this special project. We found that the petty officer needed a little painting job, so the two of us each received paint brushes and a can of paint and were told which area to paint!

While we were in school we had weekend leaves for three weekends out of four. I took the opportunity to travel. I went to Washington DC several times - place I had never visited. I was just fascinated. At that time we could wander all over the capital building, look into the house and senate chambers, etc. with no security systems in place.

Naturally, Congress was not in session on the weekends but we saw where it all happens.

Then I also went to New York one weekend. Went with a classmate whose first name was Carl. He was from somewhere in the middle of Pa., told me he had lived as a hermit for eight months in a cave in Pennsylvania, etc. He was just a few years older than I and had traveled around some. He and I struck it off well and had a great time. We got free passes to a Broadway play. Tickets for the good plays had been handed out before I got to the USA Center which had the tickets. But just getting to see a Broadway play was great. On another weekend went to Rockefeller center and saw a performance by the Rockettes - fantastic.

During the War there was a wonderful USO organization which really helped out - even to the extent of sleeping accommodations. In Wash DC we could get a dormitory room for fifty cents (The "dorm room" I had was a school room which had been converted for the summer into a dorm for servicemen. With our pay of $55 per month as a seaman second class it was possible to do a lot for not very much money).

During the War I experienced another side of discrimination that I had never encountered. One time Ray Stahl (a student from Allegheny who was also at Bainbridge) was going to Wash. DC. My friend Carl lined up a niece of his as a date either for me or Ray. The evening did not work out well. Carl's niece was not at all friendly and we took her home early. It turned out, as I found out later from Carl, that his niece was Catholic. Somehow she apparently knew that Ray and I were Protestant. At that time the Catholic Church apparently frowned on socialization of their members with Protestants!!

Radioman school proved too tough for a couple of the class members. Sitting four hours straight and copying code was just more than they could stand emotionally. But aside from them, our class graduated, advanced to Seaman first class and wore a right arm patch as radioman striker (striking for 3rd class petty officer.)

Unlike the Army where groups of men stick together, the Navy is made up of specialists - radiomen, gunner, signalman, etc. So when we finished school only four of us were sent to the same location. I was sent to NAAS (Naval Auxiliary Air Station) Mayport, east of Jacksonville,

Fla. It was a small station. One of its principal purposes was to serve as a port for aircraft carriers of the Atlantic fleet.

During most of my schooling I had been learning to copy "fox" circuits. These were encoded broadcasts from one of the naval facilities. Here at Mayport I actually had to transmit and receive on a ship-shore frequency, with ships of the fleet. I found that there was quite a variance in the skills of the radiomen. I don't know that my skills were that outstanding, but certainly better than some. I remember one night working ship chore when I just could not "read" the sender. I spoke to the first class Petty .Officer in charge and told him my problem. He listened, agreed the sending was terrible and told me to send the radioman a QQQ. (The Navy had and may still have a whole book of Q signals, each with a special meaning. Well I had newer hear of QQQ and couldn't find it in the book. I asked what it meant and the 1st class said, "It means you have bird shit on your antenna". About the lowest message you can send to someone,

There was one special benefit of being sent to Mayport. Grandma Callow knew a second cousin, I think it was, who lived with her family in Jacksonville. Very soon I had an invitation to spend Christmas day with them. It was my first Christmas away from home and a very nice treat. The cousin and her husband had one child, as I recall, a girl three or four years old.

I don't recall spending more time with this family. But the wife's parents, whom my Callow Grandparents knew, lived in Jacksonville also. I was invited to their place and had a standing invitation to spend time off at their place. They were a very nice couple. Her name was Shirley Burns. I do recall, also, that they had a daughter in her late teens - a very attractive girl. If I hadn't been so shy at the time I probably would have become better acquainted.

It was a new experience for me to spend the winter in an area with the climate of Florida. And at the time Florida's population was less than 2 million. By today's standards the state was undeveloped.

In March I received orders to report for duty at St. Simon's Island NAS. (Naval Air Station). Only one of my radio school classmates went on this transfer. St. Simon's Island was different than Mayport in that there was a large school facility at that base. Radar was still new, and top secret. The Navy trained and educated officers on radar.

My work at St. Simon's Island was not a whole lot different than Mayport except that we had some electronic equipment for handling many of the dispatches which we earlier would have handled by the fox circuits, by mail, or something less "advanced" than radio with the key. We had a radio on the radio shack so occasionally could listen to a.m. broadcasts The local station in Brunswick Georgia., which was the closest town, came on at 7a.m. It began each day's programming with Dixie. On occasion I would turn the radio on full blast with the windows open so people walking by could hear Dixie.

I continued my practice of traveling in the area when I had a day or two off. Savannah was 80 miles to the North and a favorite city of mine. I also got up to Charleston S.C. which I always enjoyed. And once or twice I got to Atlanta. At that time Atlanta was a city of only 200,000 to 300,000 population. Stone Mt. was walking distance out from the city. Both St. Simon's and Mayport were small bases by many standards. I never knew exactly, but I think there were less than one thousand enlisted people at either base.

In the summer of 1945 I figured I was about to be shipped out, probably to the Pacific. I had been ordered to have a dental check up which was a pretty good signal that a transfer was in the near term future. Then the atomic bombs were dropped and very shortly the war was over. Once the War was over it became a time of seeing how many points you had and how many points were required for discharge. One point was given for each month of service plus twelve points for being in the service. The number of points required for discharge changed from time to time. But by June of 1946 I knew I was about to get out.

I knew one of the Yeoman on the base quite well. My discharge base would ordinarily have been Washington, D.C. But I wanted to travel some on the way home. So I worked it out with the Yeoman to set up my papers for discharge in Jacksonville. This way I would be closer to the area I wanted to visit plus would be paid five cents per mile for the trip home. A week or two before discharge I went to Atlanta and bought a set of civvies. I wanted to be able to wear my uniform with the gold discharge button while on the road and then wear my civvies in town.

So I was discharged in Jacksonville and then traveled by bus and hitching to New Orleans. Then I hitched up through Arkansas and Missouri and on to Evanston, Illinois, to visit my grandparents. While in Evanston I visited my Uncle Orville. This Uncle and his wife Aunt Pearl had always been favorites of mine. I was saddened when Aunt Pearl opened the door to their apartment and I saw my Uncle Orville suffering from Parkinson's disease. It was good to see them, though. I believe that my Grandma Callow was already suffering from cancer. Sad to see these changes. I knew though that they had lived good lives. And of course while n Evanston I spent time with Bill and Leetha. Nancy was still a young girl.

After a few days I headed for home. Took a bus to the east edge of Chicago and then hitched the rest of the way home, arriving in the latter part of June, and after having seen parts of the United States that nobody else in my family had seen.

When I got home I was surprised to find that my parents had bought me a dog. Gyp, as we called him was about a two month old Gordon Setter. Gyp was a beautiful dog, but I really had no use for him then. I was going to Allegheny in the fall, where I couldn't take the dog, and I just didn't have any place for him. But the story of Gyp will have to wait for a later chapter in this account. It was good to get home. I was glad that I had served my country (although I had no choice) but I was ready to get on with my life.

The balance of the summer of 1946 had some frustrations. I wanted to get some kind of a job, but doing it for short term just wasn't in the cards. So I signed up for what was known then as the 52-20 Club. Veterans who could not get a job could go to the government and receive twenty dollars per week for one year or until they got a job. I didn't like the idea of having to do this. But on the other hand I needed a bit of money. And it did last for only a couple of months until I started back at Allegheny College.

8

Allegheny College after the War

In September, 1946, I found myself at Allegheny College again. I think Mother and Dad must have driven me up to school, but I don't remember. What I do know is that Allegheny in the fall of 1946 was a much different place than it had been my first year. First of all, there were a lot more students than in 1943-1944. I was assured of admission to the school, having left only to go in to the Navy. But there was a scramble for admission by veterans who had not been in school before going in to the service.

Payment for College had gone through a sea change near the end of the war. Congress had passed an act with a long name - something like Servicemen's Rehabilitation Act or some such thing. The name quickly became "G. I. bill". Under the Act servicemen could get paid for their education based upon their time in the service. Every veteran was entitled to benefits for twelve months plus one additional month for each month the veteran had been in service. The months were actual months of schooling. There was no limit on the amount which the government would pay for tuition so long as the school was approved for payment by the government. (Most schools were approved.). Then each veteran was entitled to be reimbursed for up to five hundred so dollars ($500.00) per academic year for books and supplies. For single veterans there was a living expense of $65 per month (this amount was increased gradually over the years.) Payments to married veterans were more. I seem to recall $125 per month. Don't know if there was an additional amount if there were children. The plan literally made it possible for millions of servicemen to attend college - something which probably the majority simply could not have afforded.

In my case the bill covered three years at Allegheny College, although I consolidated it into two regular academic years plus two summers. It also paid for just over two and one half years of law school. I probably could not have gone to Michigan but on the GI bill. I remember Mother saying to me that she didn't think they would have been able to afford to pay for my schooling costs at Michigan. Most of us involved, and I think the population in general, believed that the Bill was a very wise use of tax revenues.

Living arrangements were much different at Allegheny College after the war. I moved right in to the Theta Chi, Beta Chi chapter. It was an older house, located on a large corner lot perhaps six or eight blocks from the campus. It served as the Theta Chi house for another thirty five or forty years, at which time the house was sold to a bank which constructed a new house at the corner. The fraternity acquired a new house closer to the Campus.

Most of my Brothers had been in the service. At the time I was inducted the number of men available to join had been reduced substantially by the draft. Most of my school age Brothers were not in school when I joined. I met most of my Brothers for the first time after the War.

The fraternity house had its own kitchen, so there was no more eating in a dorm dining room - or at least a large dorm. I also found out who would be my roommate at Allegheny. The rooms, or many of them, were rather small. So our room was where we kept our clothes, books etc. We all slept in a large dorm on the third floor of the House

My roommate the first year was Ed Ferguson, who I think was also a sophomore. Ed had been in the service for I think a bit longer than I. And, he had served in the Army and went through the Battle of the Bulge in late 1944 - the battle I probably would have been in if I had succeeded in getting in to the Army. It worked out ok with Fergie, as he was called, although Fergie had some problems. Today he would have been treated for post traumatic syndrome, but the military didn't spend much time or have much concern at that time for the mental welfare of veterans.

Fergie's eyesight was just about as bad as mine. On the battlefield, in the Battle of the Bulge he had lost his glasses and had had to crawl for several hours on his belly to get back to base. His nerves were really shot. Perhaps other events in the service contributed to his problems. If felt sorry for him but I don't think I spent a lot of time trying to help him on that score. We were always friends, but never became close friends. I roomed just one year with Fergie. The other year I roomed with Paul Welty and Ben Deutzer, both of whom I liked very much. Paul became an attorney and practiced in Herminie Pa. I saw Paul a number of times over the years. He passed away a few yeas ago. Ben I never did keep in touch with even though I liked him very much.

Staffing the fraternity proved to be a challenge. There was little unemployment so the choice was not the best. For example, we hired a cook by the name of Julius. He was German and told us he had run away from the German Navy in the First World War. Never verified it but suspect it was true. He cooked meals which he said "would schttick to our ribs". They were more meals designed for loggers than fairly sedentary students. He did not last a long time. After the first or second pay he bought a bottle of wine and was found sleeping in the back stairway with the half filled bottle. This did not set well with Reid Stormer, another Brother, who dismissed him on the spot.

We did hire a very nice "House Mother" whose name I can not now recall. She lived on the first floor and was with us for a year or two.

I served as the fraternity treasurer for a large part of my time at Allegheny, so had to take care of the books, make the bank deposits, etc.

I don't recall that we spent much time taking care of the yard, although we must have had someone mow the lawn. It always looked nice. Don't think we spent much time on landscape activities, however. The postwar years saw a lot of inflation, so we had to keep a close watch on our costs.

Then there was the matter of selecting my courses. And also thinking about a major. I thought that I would like to become a Dr. I don't really know what led me to that. But whatever, I signed up for chemistry and biology, among the other courses. I'm not sure how many hours I signed up for. I do know that most of the time after the War I signed up for about 18 credit hours to sort of speed up the schooling process. In this way I completed my work at Allegheny at the end of summer 1948, rather than June 1947, when I would have graduated if I had not been in the service. Again, I really did not have much of any counseling in my selections.

Very soon after school started, my fraternity decided we should have a party. One of my fraternity brothers was Gene McCoy - a really nice person. I think he was a junior. I think that in part because his brother Horace was a senior and Horace was the more senior of the two brothers. Gene was engaged at that time to Weegie McCoy (have no idea what her real first name was.) Gene and Weegie decided to try to fix all of us fellows up with dates. The two of them decided that I should date Barb Dietterich, whom I had dated in my freshmen year. But she decided she didn't want to do with me. She thought she would rather have a date with a sleepy bedroom eyed senior brother of mine. So Gene and Weegie decided they would get me a date with Lois Eichenberg. They asked her if that was ok (unknown to me) and she said sure, she knew me and liked me and that would be ok. I don't know why Don Ludwig wasn't involved in this but he wasn't. Of course Don was not in Theta Chi although I had tried in my freshman year to get him to join up with Theta Chi.

The first date with Lois went very well. I think it was the next week after that I called Lois for another date, this one a dance as I recall. This date went even better than the first. I recall that after the dance I walked her down to the Alumni Gardens. Only the second date but we ended the visit to the gardens and with what turned out to be our first kiss. After the dance I guess all the girls got together to compare their evening. Lois described her date with me and Barb Dietterich said, I was told, "my, he has changed since his first year." It was a grand evening for both Lois and me. As I reflect on the evening, I don't think either of us ever looked backward after that evening. I never had another date with Alice Morgan, although I did see her once, not to speak to, in downtown Pittsburgh.

My foray into science studies did not go as well as I had hoped. Dr. Cavelti, whom I had for chemistry, was an excellent teacher. I could never understand the theory of ionization, and the studies were hard for me. The biology professor was also excellent. I enjoyed the courses. My grades in both chemistry and biology were not A's. I think perhaps B's. But at that point I knew that given the intense competition for most graduate programs just after the War, and especially medical school, I would have little chance of being admitted. I didn't have any intense desire in regard to medicine anyway, so it was no problem to change my major.

I decided, therefore to change my major to economics with a minor in political science. I was more tuned to these areas, so it worked out well.

Overall, I don't think that the level of teaching in the immediate postwar years was as good as earlier, or perhaps as it is at the present time. There were some very good professors, as for example Dr. Edwards in certain economic courses. But the professor for my accounting course, for example was not very good - either in the contents of the course or in the way he presented it. Then there was Professor Kidd. He was strictly third class. Worse yet, he favored those who laughed at his sick jokes, who would talk about all sorts of things, etc. I knew enough about grades that some students received to know that those whom I knew were not very bright got better grades than those who studied and work on the courses more, but just left Kidd be.

I don't want to appear negative toward Allegheny. I always felt it ran a good academic program. But I recognize also that with the enormous flood of students after the War it must have been difficult staffing the academic positions.

It was a busy time at the fraternity, also. We had to put together a rush program and work on building up the membership. The whole rush process and induction process had changed very significantly. For example, until the end of the Second World War, those who pledged a fraternity had to spend time doing menial things and putting up with a lot of what I thought were demeaning nonsense items - part of what was known as the initiation process. Well, the whole world of the fraternities changed after the War. Servicemen coming back or beginning school had no time for some of what I will call the frivolity of the initiation process. The veterans simply said that they were there to get an education, they could just as well live in a dorm and would rather do so rather than put up with the frivolity. So the fraternity pledge and induction process became more businesslike. I for one favored the new system.

My brother graduated from high school in the class of '46 and so started school when I came back from the Navy. I didn't mention him at first to my brothers, but did so shortly. They jumped on this immediately, said they felt he was a legacy and wanted to get him in the fraternity. And so he became Theta Chi also. My brother and I did not overlap at Allegheny for any significant time.

School was a busy time for me after the War for at least two reasons. First of all I was carrying 18 or more hours most of the time. And I was busy courting Lois. She and I spent many evenings studying at the library. I assume that I must have headed for the library on toward 7 many evenings. The library closed at 9 p.m. so we would have a couple of hours together at the library many evenings.

After the library closed we would spend time together until she had to go back to the dorm. At that time the school was very strict about the hours of women students. Most nights they had to get back in their dorm by I think about 10 o'clock. Then once or twice a week they could stay out until 11 o'clock. Then I think there were just perhaps two evenings per month when the women students could stay out until midnight. The students had to sign out at a register at the entrance and exit and then had to sign in when they returned.

Lila Skinner was dean of women. She was a lovely person and Lois and I both thought a great deal of her. She was a very no nonsense person, however. She simply would not tolerate violation by the women students of the curfew hours. I don't recall any students expelled for violating the curfew, but I'm pretty sure that Miss Skinner would not have hesitated to do so if there were repeated violations.

I had written for the school paper and also was involved in dramatic productions my first year at Allegheny. I think I may have written after the war. I cannot now recall what other activities I was involved in. As I said, taking as many credit hours as I did, fraternity affairs and courting Lois kept me rather busy.

I found, as did other people, that hitchhiking after the war it was a lot more difficult than when I was in the service. A man in uniform during the war seldom waited very long for a pick up. After the War, though, there were longer waits.

When I was in school, there was another thing much different than today. Almost nobody had an automobile. Bill Thomas, a fraternity Brother, for example, had a car. But I think he was about the only one of my brothers who had a car while he was in school. Schools did not favor students having cars. I don't recall if Allegheny had a formal policy. But I recall that when I was in Law School at the University of Michigan, no student under the age of 25 was allowed to have a car on campus unless he or she suffered some disability, in which case he or she would get a special waiver. Then, too, in the late 40's the country was just coming out of a long depression, which lasted from 1929 until the War. Then during the War with rationing and shut down of a lot of civilian production. There just wasn't as much available for purchase.

Lois and I dated very steadily during the first year back from service. I think I fairly soon thought I had found the person I wanted to spent my life with, and I think Lois felt the same way. I do recall, though that I asked Lois something which, in hindsight was strange. At some point I asked Lois whether I thought she could be a Methodist. (She has been raised Lutheran.) She answered in the affirmative, but I then just sort of left things drop here.

We went to all the dances and other social activities at Allegheny. I don't recall us doing anything in town except, I think, perhaps for a movie now and then. In addition, most of us didn't have money to spend going out. And neither did Lois. She very much wanted to go to Allegheny. Even thought she was an only child, and her Dad had held a good job all through the depression and war, her parents did not really much favor college education. Her father was more supportive than her mother, but her mother saw little reason for Lois to be to school.

Because of her parents attitude and lack of support financially, Lois worked the first three years at Allegheny. She waited tables for I think three years, she worked for a photographer in town one or two afternoons each week and probably had other jobs. By her senior year she told her parents that she did not want to work and she wanted to have one year when she could be like most of the other students. Her folks finally got the message and said that would be ok.

Theta Chi had a tradition of a formal dance in the late spring each year. I can't now recall the name we gave to it. Any way, we of course went to it in the late spring of 1946. Had a live band at the house, etc. By that time Lois and I had been going very steady all year. I know there was speculation that I might "pin" Lois at the end of the evening. "Pinning" is where a fellow gives his girl his fraternity pin. Don't know exactly what it means - it's something between going steadily and being engaged without the formality of an engagement. Well, I knew I was going to pin Lois that evening. So at intermission, she and I went out in a borrowed car (I don't recall, but I think it must have been Bill Thomas' car.) We came back to the last half of the dance and Lois was sporting my pin.

There was also a tradition that the fraternity would serenade the girls in Brooks Hall (the main Women's dorm) for special events, like pinning. So a week or so after the event our fraternity serenaded the girls to recognize my pinning Lois and Lowell Thomas (yes, the name is correct) who had pinned Helen Merseberg, Lois roommate nearly all her time at Allegheny.

Commencement came at the end of May or the very first of June. It was as usual, a very festive affair. Lois parents were in attendance and I think perhaps another family member, but I'm not sure about that. So I had the opportunity to see a lot of the girls with whom I started school graduate.

Lois had lined up a job with the Pennsylvania Department of Public Assistance as a social worker in one of the Pittsburgh offices of the Department. I don't recall exactly when she lined up the job, but she started soon after school as I recall. I recall her supervisor was a Mrs. Ward, a woman who had been with the Department for a number of years. She and Lois got along very well.

Lois' "area", the place where the recipients lived, was on the north side of Pittsburgh. So, Lois spent part of her time in the office and part of the time on visits to her caseload. A couple of her fellow workers became very good friends and we kept in touch with them for a long time.

Meantime, I was back in Meadville for summer school. I recall attending the full summer to work off a number of hours. I'm pretty sure I got down to Pittsburgh a couple of times during the summer.

Hitching was harder, I as busy in school, and I didn't have enough money to spend on frequent bus trips.

In the fall, I headed back to Allegheny and had a very full load. Lois came up to Meadville two or three times for social events, so we got to see one another from time to time, and of course wrote letters frequently. By this year, my Brother was at Allegheny and living in Caflisch Hall, which was the men's freshmen dormitory. As I've mentioned earlier, he pledged Theta Chi and then was inducted. He did not live in the house during the time I was in school. He did live there in his latter years at Allegheny.

Sometime in my senior I made application to law school. I also took the first ever LSAT test (Law School Aptitude Test.) Although much of my efforts to get acceptance to Law School occurred during my senior year, I will include that part of my history in the chapter related to Law School.

By the end of the regular academic year I had completed all of my class work, and just had my Senior Thesis to do. I recall that my thesis related to the development and conduct of the ICC to the railroad industry. Late in the summer I was interviewed and passed. So, much as has been my history with schools, I graduated but did not participate in a Commencement exercise. There was no Commencement exercise at that time. (I also did not attend Commencement from the University of Michigan. It was so long afar exams and as I will tell later I had a job lined up out west and could just not wait around. So my High School Commencement is the only such program of which I have been a part.)

Since I was taking only one course, I had time to take a job for the summer. I worked for Retail Credit Company, in Pittsburgh. It was, or perhaps still is, a company which, among other things, does investigation and reports on applicants for insurance. I had to go in to the office each day to get my assignments and then go out in to the field to conduct my interviews and then back to the office to write them up. I was able to drive Dad's car. I learned my way around Pittsburgh as I had never before learned it because my assignments were all over the City.

In some ways it was unfortunate for my Dad that I used his car. He had in mind selling his car, or trading it in on a new car. At that time, right after the War there was a real shortage of cars and used cars brought a lot of money. I don't know how much Dad lost on the price because I used the car for a couple of months. In any event it was very generous of him and I appreciated it very much.

The job with Retail Credit Company was a lot of work for not much pay. But in the summer of '48 it was not easy to get a summer job. I had a couple of interviews, one I recall with Gulf Oil Company, and also with the Gas Company. I told both of them that I was going to school in the fall so they didn't hire me.

The actual work for Retail Credit Company was to make generally two or thee neighborhood stops to inquire about the habits and life style of the person applying for insurance (sort of a neighborhood snoop.) For all this work—the interviews and the one page form report I was paid, as I recall, eighty eight cents!! But it was a job!!

There is one thing which I have not really mentioned in detail before which I will cover here. It is about our dogs. When we lived in Blawknox, as I may have mentioned, we had a cocker spaniel named Bobby. He was a very pretty dog, but as I may have mentioned earlier, he had a short temper and would snap at us. I'm really not sure why my parents kept that dog with his biting habits, but they did I don't recall being sorry that he wasn't any longer with us. We did not have a dog in Verona, but in Derry we had Topsy. Topsy was a "curbstone setter" but mostly a fox terrier. She was a good dog, very friendly and we all liked her. I recall that she recognized the sound of Dad's car and would start running around when he heard Dad coming home. However, we never had her spayed. All the dogs in the neighborhood knew Topsy and we had a number of litters of puppies!!

Then when I got out of the service, I arrived at home to find as a present a Gordon Setter pup, which I named Gyp. He was a beautiful dog but I have no idea why my parents got him for me. They knew I was going to College and that I would not have a place to keep him at Allegheny.

Anyway, Gyp was with us during the summertime before I left for College, Gyp was big enough by the end of the summer, that he could put his paws up on the kitchen table to help himself to whatever looked and smelled good. Shortly after school started I received a special delivery letter from Dad. Dad was very upset. Gyp on Sunday had reached up on the Kitchen table, took off and started to each the pot roast which Dad had planned for our Sunday Dinner. In his agitation, Dad had broken his glasses. Yes, he was pretty steamed.

Dad wrote me a letter, sent it special delivery, in which he said that either I would have to take him to Allegheny, or he would have to go. And Dad wanted a response by return mail. Well, what could I do. Dad must have known the answer. But anyway, Dad found a good home for Gyp somewhere out in the country which was a place much more suitable for him. I really liked gyp, but his staying was not meant to be.

And so after completing Allegheny, and my job for Retail Credit, I turned my attention to Law School.

9

Law School - First Year

Sometime during my senior year at Allegheny I addressed the question of where I would want to go to Law School. As I saw it there were two major issues. The first was to select a very good school. The second was to decide in what part of the country I wanted to go to school, and generally, where I might want to practice law.

I had decided early on that I did not want to live in western Pennsylvania. The country itself is very pretty. But the coal mines with their big slag piles, the steel mills with the blast furnaces, Bessemer converters, and the open hearth mills, all belching smoke (with no filters or other smoke containment) created a blight on the area, in my opinion.

There was another problem, in my mind, in considering practicing in Pennsylvania. At that time (and perhaps it has not changed since then) was the archaic system Pennsylvania had for gaining admission to the practice of law. First of all, a person was required to engage a proctor, who must be a member of the Pennsylvania Bar, to work with the student during his or her three years in law school. I didn't really know any attorneys and Dad wasn't much help in this area, either. Then there was the requirement that after completing law school an applicant to the bar was required to work as an apprentice for some period of time before actually filing the application for the bar exam or taking the bar exam. I learned that some attorneys were compensated a nominal sum during the apprentice period, but many served without compensation. What would I use for money for groceries if I didn't get paid for my apprentice period. So, this system of Pennsylvania succeeded in further discouraging me from considering Pennsylvania as a place to practice law.

My Mother encouraged me to consider living in the area near Chicago and going to Northwestern. I think Dad sort of favored that, too. He had gone to Garrett Divinity School and I think liked the area. I didn't feel too much one way or the other at that time about the Chicago area.

So, with Pennsylvania an issue in mind and some sense of family thinking I set about deciding to which schools I would apply. I proceeded in what I think was a real sense of optimism about getting in to a good law school. I applied to four law schools - The University of Michigan, The University of Chicago, Northwestern University and University of Illinois. I favored the idea of Michigan both because it is a good Law School and because, unlike most law schools, it does not tend to concentrate on the laws of any jurisdiction. It regards itself as a National Law school, with the class members coming from nearly every state in the Union. Chicago had a very good school and so did Northwestern. So I was comfortable in making application to those schools. The University of Illinois was a last minute decision. Sort of, I guess, get a school that might not be as difficult but just file an application and then decide later about it.

To my utter amazement I promptly received acceptances from three schools—Michigan, Chicago and Northwestern. Wow!! I doubt I could get accepted in any of those three schools today. Perhaps I have become more conservative in my thinking and perhaps the competition has grown tougher. I don't know. All I knew as that I was very pleased. The University of Illinois obviously, I think, wanted to keep out-of-staters out of the school. I got a rejection from it because my grade point average was a small fraction of one letter grade or percent below its threshold for admission of a non-resident of Illinois.

Sometime in the summer of 1948, I think, I visited at last one of the schools to look things over. I went to Ann Arbor and was greeted very warmly by E. Blythe Stason, the Dean of the Law School. Because of the fringe of white hair on his bald pate he was known to the students as "Bubbles."

I also took the opportunity to look at the law school campus and was very impressed. An Alumnus of the school, Mr. Cook, who had a very successful practice in New York in corporate law had donated to the University of Michigan the money for the grand buildings of the school. A magnificent library, plus books containing the laws of the various states is on one side, the dining room and the lounge, with post office etc. is on another side, and then on the remaining two sides is the residential area known as the Lawyers Club. I was very very impressed by the surroundings.

I believe I did stop at the Northwestern University Law School, but have very little remembrance of it. I didn't stop at the University of Chicago. I think that overall, once I had been admitted to Michigan and then seen the law school campus I knew that was where I wanted to go to Law School.

I think that when I was in Ann Arbor in the summer I stopped at the Lawyer's Club and spoke to Inez Bozorth about getting in to the Lawyers Club. Miss Bozorth was a very prim, stern but friendly manager of the Lawyers Club. We had a nice visit. I can't remember whether she told me at that visit if I would be accepted into the Lawyers Club. It occurred then or very shortly thereafter. I know I returned home a very happy tamper as I thought about my future in Law School.

And so it was that on the appointed day in late September, 1948, I found my way to Ann Arbor. I went by train. I also took with me the steamer trunk which was Dad's and which I had used at Allegheny for at least the first year. At the time I started law school, the school would deliver a student's trunk to his room and then would store the trunk during the academic year. I doubt that system prevails today.

The Lawyers Club was chock-a-block full at the time. So, three of us were assigned to a room which in other times would have accommodated just two students. Dick Spaatz and Jim Mordy, my two roommates, were second year students. Dick was from Pittsburgh and Jim from some place in Kansas. They were both very nice fellows. I would have preferred to be teamed up with other first year law students, but that was not meant to be. Dick and Jim had both established friends during the first year with whom they were closer. I was sort of a fifth wheel, but I did make friends with other first year students in the same section of the dorm, and then with students in other sections of the dorm. The room was very nicely furnished. The furniture as very good — not cheap furniture.

One dined, not just ate at the law school. For dinner ties and jackets were required. And we were served by a wait staff. Breakfast and lunch were cafeteria style. The dining room is a beautiful building. All the buildings on the campus are built of Indiana Limestone. The gutters and downspouts of the building are lead. The dining room ceiling is very high - I think I heard 70 feet, but I think it may be somewhat less than that. There are a series of grand wooden beams a cross the ceiling of the dining room, with in bas relief a series of great jurists from earlier days. The food was excellent Guests were welcome for Saturday evening dinner. Lois was up for at least one weekend all thee of the years. She too was very impressed.

Classes were much larger than I had ever experienced before - fifty to upwards of a hundred students in each classroom. The professors all used the Socratic method of teaching. I had never experienced this before. Initially it was very difficult for me, but with time I got more in to the swing of it.

In prior schools the teachers had basically generally spewed out the subject, or at the very most would ask an occasional question. The whole purpose of the drill with the Socratic method is to teach the student to reason, to think about the issues, and to realize that often there is no clear answer. Just as in the practice of law, it becomes a matter of putting together the facts and then making a decision of whether there is a basis upon which your approach to the subject is one which a court might accept.

The classes in the first year were all or nearly all required. There were Contracts (a full year course), Property (one semester real property and personal property the second)., Criminal Law (a one semester course - which represented my whole exposure to the field of criminal law, except in the case of some areas as tax, securities, etc), Civil Procedure, and an introductory course on the study of law.. There may have been one other course, but as I write this I cannot remember what it was.

I always felt very fortunate to have been in Law School when I was. Many of our professors had been teaching for a long time - some nearing retirement - and they were mostly well recognized in their fields. I had Ralph Aigler for Property law, a well recognized authority and I always felt a good lecturer. J. B. Waite (known by the students as "Jabby"), a recognized authority in criminal law. Burke Shartell taught the introductory course. Professor William Wirt Blume taught us procedure. I always felt he was the weak spot in the faulty lineup. The "younger" professor was a Mr. Newman for contracts. He was probably in his early 40's, but he seemed young when compared to the others.

Law school was a lot of hard wok for me. The school generally said that a student should plan on about three hours of preparation for each hour of classroom instruction. I agree with that assessment. The preparation was different from prior schooling. For each class we would have as an assignment a number of law cases which we were expected to outline for our use in the class - 1. facts, 2. issues, resolution, of course, (the resolution was only, in the case of the law cases, how the court had decided the case.) In the classroom we would always be put to the test of challenging the reasoning of the course, questioning what other resolutions there might have been possible, etc. Some of my classmates bought what were called Hornbooks for various classes. The book outlined the cases, dealt with the facts, the issues presented, and the resolution of the cases. We were encouraged not to use the books. I did not buy the Hornbooks, but by hindsight I have often wished that I had.

In my first year in Law School, my room was located just opposite the residence of the President of the University. One event during the year brought to our attention a negative of that location. I think the event to which I refer occurred on homecoming weekend. It was a nice cool fall evening, the type of which we had a lot. Anyway, to get in to the spirit of things three or four of us bought a gallon jug of cider. We did not have refrigerators in our rooms, so we hung the jug out the window of our room, to keep the cider cool. The next morning we received a very stern call from Miss Bozorth informing us that the President of the University had noticed the jug hanging out the window. We were very upset and, Miss Bozorth said, we were to remove the jug IMMEDIATELY!! So much for what we thought was a good idea.

Fall brought the football season. And in Michigan at that time, and probably so today, the games were big events. The Law School was perhaps a mile or mile and a half from the stadium, so we always walked over and back for the stadium. I never ceased to thrill for the games.

First of all there was the mere size of the stadium. At the time I was there I think that it seated probably 80,000 to 90,000 people (it has been enlarged a number of times and I think now seats about 110,000 people. I had never seen or been in such a large stadium. But then when the Band took the field it was almost frenzy. At that time, and continuing at the present time, the Michigan band had a fast step. I think they march 100 steps per minute or perhaps faster. When that band, with probably 200 or so members took to the field there was sheer frenzy. Michigan always had a leader of the band (there's a proper term for that person, but I can't now think of it). He always had a very fancy outfit that really set him off. And then the band was extremely well coached and did some wonderful formations on the field.

The first year I was at Michigan it had a very good team. As a matter of fact it was in the Rose Bowl. For quite a number of years Fritz Crisler had been the Coach. He left the year or one year after that as Coach Benny Oosterbaan, as I recall, may have been the new coach. But most of the players had been coached under Crisler. So I saw a real winning team. The team in some later years, under Benny Oosterbaan did not do as well.

The last game for Michigan is always the Ohio State game. I can still remember that the weather was especially bad for one game. It was snowing, the wind was blowing and it was very cold. The only score of the game was a field goal, which Michigan kicked, and so it won the game 3-0. Some of my classmates went out to Pasadena for the game in the Rose Bowl. I had couldn't possibly have afforded to drive out, as some of my classmates did, and I don't think I would have tried for that game.

Come January and we all had to face the reality of the final exams. In Law School, our whole grade depended on how we did on that one test. There wee no mid-terms, no tests along the way, etc. And the classes were so large that even though there were some questions during class when you might be asked to reply, the teacher really had very little opportunity to judge the ability of the students. It is a system designed to put the maximum stress on students. I question the wisdom of running things that way, but no one has ever asked for my opinion.

Another thing about law school tests is that there are no plain right or wrong answers. We were never asked to spit out facts which we may have learned. All the exams were made up of responses to factual situations presented in the written material. There was no right or wrong answer. The questions were designed to test the reasoning skills of the student, although of course you were expected to bring in to your answer principals of law which we had been discussed the course of the year.

At the time I went to Law School, the LSAT tests had not been developed the way they are now. Other application considerations for some schools, such as essays, were not a part of the admission process. It was very common for the law school to flunk out about a third of the first year students. There was a saying that the professors told their students the first day to look to your right and then to your left, and tell them that one of you will not be here next year, I don't recall that having occurred to me, but here was brutal reduction in ranks by the second year.

I passed Criminal Law but with one of the poorest grades in all of law school. I just wasn't much interested in the subject and it was the first semester of the first year. I worried a great deal, but did pass.

Social life was not as developed in Law School as it was in College. I did join a fraternity, but we did not have a Chapter house and it was not something people got very excited about. We did have one big social event during the year. It was the Crease Ball, held in the spring. There was a rivalry between the Law School and Engineering school. As a part of his rivalry, the Engine School, as it was called had a Grease ball while the Law School had a Crease Ball.

While I was in Law School I was very fortunate to have transportation set up between Ann Arbor and Pittsburgh. Jack Yates, one of my classmates, who was from Hawaii, was dating a young woman whose home was in Pittsburgh. I became acquainted fairly soon with Jack after starting Law School. Another very good friend and classmate of mine, Tom McIntosh, generally rode with Jack.

Generally, this arrangement worked out fairly well. There was one problem which was of some significance at times. Jack's vision was not very good. But he would not wear glasses. He had read or heard somewhere that eyes would naturally strengthen and correct themselves if no glasses were worn. I never really bought on to this idea, but Jack did not seem about to change.

Generally, this driving without glasses routine did not present problems. Once, however, it did. As we were heading home, and going along the Ohio River Boulevard on the outskirts of the City of Pittsburgh, when the roads were a bit snowy and icy, I sensed that Jack was approaching a ninety degree turn a little fast for conditions. Sure enough, we clipped the other car going the other way. The whole thing unnerved Jack and he asked me if I would drive the rest of the way - actually nearly all of the way- instead of him being at the wheel. I was doubly glad to do so. It is the better part of 250 miles between Pittsburgh and Ann Arbor, so with no freeways it would take generally six or seven yours to make the trip.

Jack married Margie, I think Yates was the last name, about the time we finished law school, so the ride arrangement lasted just about all the time we were in law school.

By the second semester we did settle down somewhat to the routine, but it was still a stress filled time.

The second semester brought us another athletic event to watch - hockey. Michigan always had a good hockey team, which I found that I really enjoyed. Michigan attracted a lot of players from Canada where hockey is a huge sport, so we saw some very good games.

As we came into spring we would have some warm days. I'm getting a bit ahead of myself at this point, but in the second year I became acquainted with Joe Matsen, a classmate from Seattle, who has become a lifelong friend. It may have been the second year, but I recall one spring day when Joe and I went canoeing on the Huron River on the edge of Ann Arbor. Wish there had been more time to enjoy the activity, but things were too busy in law school to do too much of this.

As I was growing up I developed a real desire to work as National Park Service ranger during the summer. It turned out that my one roommate, Jim Mordy, had done this the year before. I asked him about the process. I've never known, but I think Jim was a political appointee.

He had worked at Rocky Mountain National Park, out from Denver. He suggested the form to fill out. I filled out applications to several of the parks. As I will tell in the next chapter, I was accepted at Crater Lake National Park. At the time there was an acting Chief Ranger who thought that the Park would benefit if there were people from the east who were accepted. Dewey Fitzgerald, the Acting Chef selected applicants from the east. So through this fluke I was accepted.

As we got to the end of the first year I started working on arranging for a car to drive west. But this will be covered in more detail in the next cheaper.

All my classmates and I persevered and got through the first year. There were a fair number of classmates who were not given the opportunity to return for the second and third years. I wasn't a top student, but I did succeed in making it through the first year. One down and two to go!!

10

Crater Lake

The day I received the notice that I had been accepted for a position as seasonal ranger at Crater Lake National Park for the summer of 1949 was one of the best days of my life. I had seen pictures of Crater Lake, knew it was in Oregon, but little else. The main thing, though, was that I was gong to fulfill an ambition dating back to the time when I was perhaps ten years old. I would have gone to any Park. I just wanted to be a ranger at a Park.

The letter advised me that I should report for duty by some date in June, 1949. (there was some flexibility on the date, but I had to be there by something like the fifteenth to twentieth of June). It also told me that I would be responsible for purchasing my own uniform, who the supplier of the uniform was, what my pay would be etc.

Just getting to the Park would be an adventure. At that point I had never been further west than Iowa. Amidst the need to keep up with law school classes I set about planning the trip and getting ready for the job. At that time, cars were still in very short supply because cars were not made during the war. I learned that it would be possible to line up a car to drive west from Detroit and deliver somewhere on the west coast. Fairly quickly I lined up an agency for whom I could drive a car to the west coast. I put an ad in the University of Michigan daily newspaper for persons who would be willing to go along and share expenses. Fairly quickly I lined up a young man and young woman and we settled on the departure date.

I also set about planning a route west. I knew that I wanted to visit Yellowstone Park and the Grand Tetons. Soon in the planning I also decided that the trip should also include a visit to Salt Lake City. I don't think I had to identify my two passengers to the agency for whom I would drive the car. Things were pretty loose at the time. I did find out, though when I picked up the car that I would be driving a Buick, probably a post war model, although I don't recall that detail. Further, I would deliver the car in San Francisco to Horse Trader Ed!!

As planned, the three of us set out and drove to South Dakota and then west with a stop at the Wall Drug store. Even then, it was a landmark for travelers going west. Either on this trip west or the next year I drove through the Black Hills. Unfortunately it was so late in the day that I couldn't see much of the Hills.

Yellowstone was a real thrill. Even though we were under a fairly tight schedule, we spent the whole day making the grand loop at Yellowstone - seeing geysers, hot springs, all kinds of wild animals. We were early enough in the season that the crowds were not bad. The next day we drove through Teton National Park. This was very shortly after the park boundaries had been expanded to their present size. I was just enthralled with the whole scene. It was the dream of a lifetime coming true.

The young man passenger left us before we got to Salt Lake City. I don't recall just where, but it was not far from where he lived. So then the two of us continued to Salt Lake City. Had a wonderful visit to the Tabernacle and a little visit around the city.

The drive west from Salt Lake City impressed me with the enormity of the area. Regardless of what it looked like, though, it continued to be exciting. As we progressed further, though, we did discover that one tire had a slow leak. The rate of leak increased as we drove along. Only after some time did we discover that there was no spare tire.

I remember driving through Sacramento before freeways, and driving right by the capitol. I recall also, that the closer we got to San Francisco the more frequently we had to stop to add air to the one tire. I recall also that as we started cross the Bay Bridge I crossed my fingers hoping we would not break down from a flat tire. I clearly remember driving down the ramp off the bridge, tire still with air in it. Then almost ahead of us I saw the sign for Horse Trader Ed! Good delivery!!

I never saw either of my passengers again, but we had a good trip. Then since it was an overnight bus trip to Medford, Oregon, I bid adieu to my woman passenger, and then later in the day got a bus for the overnight trip to Medford. Didn't have the time or money to spend on an overnight in San Francisco.

Once in Medford I got the bus which runs from Medford to Crater Lake. As we approached Crater Lake National Park, I recall being so impressed with all the Ponderosa Pines - the biggest trees I had ever seen and most beautiful trees. I have always liked the trees. When we to the South Entrance to the Park, I met Jim, a seasonal then already on duty. We became very good friends. When I got to the Park I Met the Acting Chief, Dewey Fitzgerald, whom I later learned was the one who selected me to be a ranger. I did not at that time meet Mr. Leavitt, the Superintendent of the park, a somewhat older gentleman whom I think was probably fairly close to retirement. I remember that first day hiking up to view the Lake. I recall getting out of breath on the fairly steep three mile uphill walk, and suddenly realizing that at over 6,000 feet elevation, I was being affected by the lower level of oxygen—another first experience.

The first week was training. I don't recall a lot of the detail, but I do recall that we had one day experience at fire fighting in a set fire. I quickly learned what hard and dirty work it is to be on a fire line.

After the week of instruction I learned that I would be assigned to the North Check Station. I learned also that the road on the north side was not yet open. Deep snow, perhaps fifteen or twenty feet blocked the way. The area was opened in just a very few days. I also met the other two men who would be at the North Check station. One was Jim Richards, from Warren Pennsylvania. We quickly became the best of friends, a friendship which continued for the balance of his life. The third fellow was from, I think, Alabama. He was a political appointee. He turned out to be a real complainer, constantly talked about how he was going to tell Daddy about how things were going, etc. etc. He didn't last but a couple of weeks and a third person was assigned to the station.

The three of us were responsible for manning the station seven days a week. Each of us worked forty hours. The station opened at 6 a.m. and closed at 10 p.m. There was just one ranger on duty for each watch, except for Sunday, the biggest traffic day, when the head of the check station drew the duty.

Certainly by today's standards, living conditions were a bit primitive. We had a wood shack to live in. There was no running water (We were supplied every few days with a couple of five gallon cans.) There was no electric power - we used Colman lanterns both at the Check Station and in the living quarters. There was a little outhouse a few feet from our living shack. The only phone at the station was in the check station itself. It was a phone where you spun the handle on the phone support to raise the operator who took your number. There was no radio or other means of communication.

None of the three of us had a car. The fellow who was assigned after the political appointee had a car, but neither Jim nor I nor I drove it. The check station is eight miles from the Rim of the Lake, and another six miles to the hotel and information center and three more miles to Headquarters for the Park. So we were a bit isolated. When we needed to take a shower, do any laundry, etc., we had to wend our way in to the Rim or Headquarters. This generally meant asking a Park visitor if they would give a ride in to an off duty ranger. People were always very helpful. We kept track of each day of visiting cars - by make of car and state of license (I think this second item was probably so that the Budget people could ask Congress for more money to support the Park.)

Included in the equipment at the station was a pistol, complete with a shoulder harness. I have no idea why. As far as I knew, none of even knew how to use the pistol. Plus I don't recall seeing any ammunition around. We had a safe in which to put the money and the District ranger picked it up a couple of times a week.

I've reflected a number of times about the living conditions, etc. It certainly was a far cry from what we observed in a visit to the Park in the summer of 2007. I think that in 1949 and 1950, early post war years, perhaps that the Park was just adjusting to significantly greater visits. I think probably that during the depression there were relatively few visitors, and before that even fewer. Car travel was just starting to build, the number of visitors increasing etc. None of this bothered me or Jim Richards. We were just enjoying the job and life very much.

Our work schedule was set up so that we actually had 72 consecutive hours off each week. On our last day of a work week we would have the 6 p.m. shift and on the first day back would draw the 2 p.m. shift.

And travel I did on my days off. I recall getting to Bend Oregon, Eugene Oregon, along the Oregon coast, etc. I think it was the second summer that I even succeeded in getting to Seattle for a visit, and a tour that went along a part of the Columbia River. The second year at the Park Jim Richards was at the South Check station and I was back at the North. As experienced Rangers, we were each in charge of our check stations the second year.

When Jim and I worked different check stations we were able to go on trips together. I recall he and I were out somewhere in Eastern Oregon on one trip, another trip on the Oregon Coast. We would generally get a ride outbound from the station with a Park visitor. Getting back via hitchhiking was always a bit dicey, but we managed. One time, and I think this must have been the second summer, we took a trip with the couple at the East check station. This is a lightly visited entrance and the years I was there a couple shared the post, with the husband being the Ranger.

Once we took a trip with the couple who managed the East check station to Lava Beds Monument in Oregon and another time did some hiking up a Mountain in Oregon. Anyway, the travel gave me a chance to learn and see a lot of the Pacific Northwest. I was enchanted with the area.

During the summer also we used time off to visit areas in the Park. Watchtower along the east rim was the location of a manned lookout and a great place to visit. We would also hike down to the lake - about a thousand feet drop in elevation. In the southwest portion of the lake is Wizard Island. It is the remains of the most recent attempt of the volcano to rebuild itself. During the second summer Jim Richards and I obtained permission from Lou Halleck, the then Chief Ranger, to camp overnight on Wizard Island. We rented a rowboat, rowed over to the island and camped on a very rocky uneven island.

The morning after our overnight on Wizard Island we got up in good time, hiked to the top of the island and had absolutely stunning

views. A principal rock formation on the lake is Llao Rock, the remains
of a huge flow of lava. I took one of my all time favorite photographs.
I also went with Dewey Fitzgerald, the first year, and took a power
boat trip around the lake. We stopped at the "Old Man of the Lake",
a great log which has been floating and drifting in an almost upright
position for at least 75 years or so. We pulled up to the Old Man so I
could gingerly get out of the boat, perch on the top of the log while
Dewey took picture. Dewey waved goodbye to me but then came back
for me.

In the very southeast section of the Lake is an island. I don't know
of anyone ever gets off a boat to explore is, but it an interesting volcanic
formation. There are numerous lookouts on the drive all around the
lake. I have always found all of them interesting.

Just a few miles north of the Park is a jagged peak by the name of
Mt. Thielsen. At about 9,100 feet elevation, it was always a challenge
for both Jim Richards and me to climb. He and I tried to climb it
the first year, but got stopped within about 100 feet of the top - too
much lose rock to follow what we knew must be the correct approach.
During the second summer I did succeed in climbing with another
Ranger and getting to the tip top. The top is very small, with a sheer
drop off of about 4,000 feet. And a 360 view. I have always regarded
the ascent as one of my best climbing efforts ever.

There was an occasional staff party in the evening. Unfortunately
we were so far out and without transportation that we only attended
one or two of them. Although we did miss out on a few tings like that,
overall, we did what I think was a very good job in seeing the Park in
some depth.

Returning home at the end of the first summer presented me with
another interesting transportation problem. I ended up taking the bus
as far as Denver. At that point I stopped by an office which I had
learned worked out arrangements for getting drivers and/or passengers
for another part of the country. I went in and told the fellow at the
desk I would like to see if I could work out an arrangement to drive
somebody to Pittsburgh.

The fellow asked me a lot of questions about myself, and then said
that he thought he had something of interest to me. He motioned to
two women sitting a few feet away who had overheard the conversation.

One of the women was Helen Reynolds. Turned out she lived not far from Columbus Ohio. She had some physical handicaps which made it difficult for her to drive long distances. She had been out working for the summer. Well, we ended up traveling together, with me doing all the driving. We had a wonderful time driving together. The next summer when it came time to go back home, I contacted her and asked her about Jim Richards and me coming to meet her in Denver and do a repeat. She was delighted. We did and it worked out well.

Both summers at Crater Lake worked out so very well for me. I remember when I arrived home after either the first summer Mother said she was so glad I had had such a good summer. But, she added, she hoped that I would never want to live that far away from home. What could I say? I was hooked on the Pacific Northwest. I mouthed some nothings, but knew that I really belonged out west.

11

Law School - Second Year

We second year law school students headed back to Ann Arbor with a little more confidence than we enjoyed during the first year. We were survivors!! We weren't all top scholars, including me, but we had survived the first year cut.

This year, too, I had a new roommate Alexander S. Trout (Sandy). Sandy was a great guy and we got along very well. He was from Detroit, where his father was an architect. I visited his parents on at least one occasion. I don't recall the event, but I liked them very much.

Sandy was also a veteran of the Second World War, and I think had a few scars remaining from the time. He was a tall man - perhaps 6' 3"plus. I say that I think he had some scars from the war, because part way through the second year he apparently was having a great deal of difficulty sleeping and took a room somewhere near campus where he slept most nights. He never discussed with me the circumstances of the second room and I never inquired. From a scholar standpoint, I recall that he and I were probably pretty well matched. I use the past tense in referring to Sandy because perhaps fifteen or twenty years ago - i.e. some time in the late 80's he very suddenly and unexpectedly died.

Sandy married a few years after law school, a very lovely woman named Marcello ("Marcie"). I had met Marcie at some point after they were married and on one of the class reunions we (Lois and I) had spent quite a bit of time with them.

By the second year I had made and then strengthened friendships with a number of classmates - friendships that in some cases have extended for a lifetime. One of my closest friends was Tom McIntosh who was from Pittsburgh. I think I have mentioned him earlier - he and I generally rode with Jack Yates, another classmate, back and forth to Pittsburgh. Tom never expected to practice law. When he finished law school he worked for a time with an advertising firm in Pittsburgh, the firm for Heinz Company. He was with the firm for a relatively short period of time and then left to work for H. J. Heinz Company where he worked for the rest of his life. I don't know whether even when he was with the advertising firm he did any legal work. He quickly got into public relations type of work, at which he excelled.

Tom was an inveterate politician and spent most of his life working very hard for the Republican Party. The Heinz and Republican work resulted him in later years being very actively involved in the election of one of the Heinz' to the U.S. Senate. I recall very clearly during the first year in law school going over to his room to listen to the election returns on the Dewey-Truman (2nd term Truman) election. As the early votes favored Truman Tom kept saying, wait until the farmer votes come in. And so it went most of the night. (That was the election when the Chicago Tribune early addition had big headlines reading "Dewey Wins"). (Tom was an inveterate cigar smoker. and unfortunately died of lung cancer just a few years ago from the time I write this.) I nearly always got together with Tom when I was in Pittsburgh.

Bill Reed was another very close friend. He practiced law in Great Falls, Montana, and again as someone with whom I kept in touch as l0ng as he lived (until a couple of years ago.). We visited Bill and his wife Elizabeth one time in Great Falls, and they visited us a few times in Seattle.

Dick Kaplan, from San Francisco lived in the same section of the Lawyers Club as I did the first year and we developed a friendship which continues to this day. His first year roommate, Warren Kawin is someone whom I got to know pretty well in Law School but unfortunately, I think, he never showed up for reunions and so I pretty much last track of him.

Bill Snell and Don Leeper roomed together all three of the yeas in law school. Bill and I have remained friends throughout our lives. When Lois and I were married he gave us a big box of I think Anchor Hocking bowls and dishes. Bill was near Toledo and his Dad was an officer in the company which made the dishes. Bill was brilliant but very unassuming and the top man academically in our class.

There were four men in my class whose last name was Jones. So we adopted nicknames for each of them. The one I knew best was Bob "eating" Jones. He ate prodigious quantities of food but was very active and kept himself very trim. He had served as a paratrooper, climbed mountains, roomed on the top floor of the Lawyers Club intentionally so he could run up and down the stairs to and from class. His father was a top official with Illinois Bell. He fully expected that Bob would join the Chicago firm which represented Illinois Bell. But Bob wanted to move to Montana, and did, so he could be close to mountains which he loved to climb. He married Lilias "Dusty", a very sweet and refined woman from a suburb north of Chicago. Not too good a fit from a vocational standpoint - e.g. she loved the arts, etc. More about them later. Lois and Dusty became acquainted while we were in Law School on the number of occasions when Lois visited Ann Arbor while I was in Law School.

There were lots of other friends of mine, but the ones above were perhaps my closest friends in school. There were 300 to 350 students in my class. A sign of the changes which have occurred over the years is that there were only six women in my law school class. One of the women married a classmate whose last name is Thomas. She was quite nice and fit in well. I recall the other women in the class as being a bit different. (Of course, I think they had a tough time being such a minority.)

I don't recall a lot of particularly significant events in the second year I think we all had pretty well settled down to the idea of getting through school and doing the best we could.

The GI bill really helped me through law school. Not only did it provide the financing for three years at Allegheny (which I completed in about 2 ½ years, but it handled a little over 2½ years of law school expenses. I recall Mother saying to me that she was very grateful for the GI will because she just didn't think that she and Dad would have been able to pay my expenses at Michigan.

By the end of the second year in law school, or perhaps a bit earlier, Lois and I had decided that we would get married at Christmas time in my senior year at Law School. (We had decided early on that it would probably work out better for us if we were not married during most of the time I was in school. This was not our first preference but the decision we felt best from the standpoint of my academic career, children, etc.)

12

Wedding

Once we had decided on the date for our wedding, Lois set to work to plan the most beautiful wedding ever. By time I returned from Crater Lake the plans were well underway. (Fortunately, our wedding was not delayed or deferred due to the Korean War!)

When I was discharged from the Navy in 1946, the service people at the discharge center worked on me, as they did on all dischargees to try to get them to sign up for the reserve. "There would never be another War. We could just sign up for the inactive reserve, put in one or two nights a month of duty, get seniority, retire in twenty years, etc. I firmly declined, and was mighty glad I did. I read in the summer of 1950, after the beginning of the Korean War that the Navy was short on six ratings—one of them was "Radioman", my Navy rate. Wow, I thought!! . If I had signed up for the reserve I could have been, and probably would have been, yanked back in to the service. It would have disrupted my law school, probably forced a delay in our wedding, etc. etc.

I don't recall when we set the date. I think it related to when the Law School Christmas break came, etc. So we decided on December 30, 1950. (Some of my law school friends suggested that we got married before the end of the year to enjoy the tax benefits from joint filing. I always assured everyone making that suggestion that with our income in 1950 there wasn't much need for tax planning. We had already decided that we would be married in Mt. Zion Evangelical Lutheran Church, in Pittsburgh, the Church which Lois had belonged to and attended all her life. We wanted to really tie the knot and have two ministers marry us—John B. Kinseley, the minister at Mt. Zion's and my Dad. I have always felt that Dad was pleased that we asked him, but I don't think there was ever any doubt that we would ask him.

Then there was the wedding party. Lois wanted her very good friend Mary "Maisie" MacQuown to be her maid of honor. We also asked my cousin Nancy, who was then eleven or twelve to be a junior bridesmaid (She is the daughter of my late Uncle Bill and Aunt Lee.) The other bridesmaids were: Ruth Eger, Lois' cousin and the daughter of "Unk" Bill and Aunt Hazel Dindinger; Nancy R. Irwin a very good friend of hers from Pittsburgh and a fellow employee at the DPS in Pittsburgh; and Helen Merseberg Mutersburgh, Lois roommate at Allegheny for at least three years, from Cleveland. For my attendants, my brother, Richard was my best man, and the ushers were my law school classmate Tom McIntosh, my Crater Lake ranger friend Jim Richards, and my Theta Chi fraternity brother, Paul Welty, and cousin Stan.

Lois planned very carefully the dress for her attendants. Lois selected beautiful fabric, with green color. Their gowns were beautiful. She very carefully selected her wedding gown, also, which was very beautiful.

As for the groom and ushers they were dressed in morning clothes. (I think that was the first and last time I was ever so attired.

The wedding reception was at the Woman's Club of Mt. Lebanon., a very fine facility. Don't know who arranged for the facility. Don't know if Lois Uncle Jack and Aunt Phame were members there or if the facility could be rented by anyone.

The Church was well filled with family and friends from both sides of the families. I don't recall who was the organist, but I do recall that the soloist was a fellow Lois had known, and I also, from Allegheny. He had a beautiful voice.

The wedding went off without a hitch. All the papers were duly signed. As we left the Church following the wedding I think my Uncle Bill was in charge of seeing that rice was properly and abundantly thrown on Lois and me.

Lois and I wanted to keep secret the hotel where we would be spending the night. So we arranged for my cousin Stan and his wife Lorene to drive us to the Pennsylvania Railroad train Station. After they left, we got a taxi to the William Penn Hotel in downtown Pittsburgh. The next day we went back to the train station and took the train to Altoona, Pa. and then a taxi to a resort hotel a few miles from Altoona. We had a very wonderful four or five days there before heading back to Pittsburgh.

After the wedding Lois and I began our married life. It was indeed a wonderful marriage. We were always deeply in love, our interests and hopes blended perfectly. We always seemed to act as a team. I think each of us always both felt that we were meant for each other. I always felt so very fortunate to share life with my wife Lois.

At this point in time I can't remember how we got to Ann Arbor. I don't think that we rode with Jack Yates. I suspect that we may have taken the train to Ann Arbor.

Before our wedding I had scrounged around and found an apartment for us to live in Ann Arbor. It was soon enough after the war that housing was in short supply. I did find a small apartment on the second floor of a house which had been converted to apartments. I think the apartment may have been on Washtenaw Avenue. I do recall, further, that it was not far from the entrance to the University Arboretum and also was just a block or two from the U of M hospital. It was a very modest apartment, but it worked out just wonderfully. It was not too well furnished. We had purchased a ¾ size hide-a-bed. For things like chairs, tables, etc we attended local auctions. We bought beautiful wood oak chairs and tables for a song. I seem to recall that we paid about $3.00 for a wood chair which would cost us a leg and arm today. Anyway, with these few purchases and wedding gifts we were well set up. The apartment was about a fifteen minute walk from the law school - quite a bit further than walking across the Quad from the Lawyers Club to the Classrooms, library, etc.

Then there was the matter of finding a job for Lois. I don't recall who suggested that she try at Argus Camera, whose headquarters were, and maybe still are, in Ann Arbor. Don't recall exactly what kind of work Lois did. I seem to recall that some one suggested that the personnel man who hired her sort of created a job. In any event, it worked out very well for the approximately five months that remained in the school year.

One of the other workers at Argus was Hilda Streich, whose husband Harvey was a second year student in the Law School. We quickly became good friends and remained their friends for their lifetimes. They were from Phoenix and planned to return there on completion of Law School. We kept in touch with them after law school, visiting them in Phoenix a couple of times and they visited us in Seattle at least once. The firm Harvey joined was small when he joined it. But it grew to over one hundred attorneys and for a number of years he was the senior and I think managing partner. Wonderful people. We continued to keep in touch until perhaps three or four years ago from now (2007) until we suddenly stopped hearing from them. Don't have any idea what happened. Perhaps we should look into it.

Life the last semester in Ann Arbor was very busy for us - classes, work, making friends, and of course having law school friends in for dinner on occasion. And then, sometime during the spring we bought our first car - a 1947 Chevy coupe, which we named Hephzibah. Lois had saved some money during the time she worked for the DPS in Pittsburgh. I think the purchase price pretty well drained our cash, but we did purchase the car without borrowing.

The second semester of my last year in Law School came the end of May or first week in June. Law School was over. I had passed and would graduate. Mother and Dad assumed that I would be participating in the graduation ceremonies. However, such was not to be the case (I have only been through one graduation of my own, from High School.) It turned out that the graduation ceremonies would not be held until something like June 11, and we just were not able to spend 10 days or so just waiting around - especially since the ceremonies at a school the size of U of M law school would b quite impersonal. Besides we already had other plans.

Sometime during the spring we learned about a trip to Europe on the Anna Salene through the Council on Student Travel. Most of my classmates were already looking for or had jobs lines up. But here we were thinking about going to Europe. The fare would be incredibly cheap, we could and did join the Youth Hostel organization. We had very little money, but we figured that if we were very careful we could stretch our dollars. I told Lois that I thought we should do it. After all, I said, it would be a long time until I would be able to take two months off, again, and I could always apply for a next session on the bar exam and could look for a job later. And so it was decided - we would so to Europe. I have said many, many times that it was one of our wisest decisions. For indeed it was many years before I was able to get away from work for two months.

So we sold a few of our meager possessions and I think packed almost everything we owned in Hephzibah and headed to Pittsburgh. Before leaving, we had to get passports. When I applied for a passport I found that as far as Pennsylvania was concerned I had never been born. Seems that when I was born Pittsburgh and Philadelphia had their own Departments of Health where they kept track of births in those jurisdictions. The kept the rest in Harrisburg. Well, Millvale, where we lived when I was born was outside Pittsburgh but the hospital (I think Presbyterian) was located in Pittsburgh. I figure each jurisdiction felt the other would keep track of my birth.

So, since Dad had baptized me, he got out some blank forms, counted back to the date Easter came on in 1926 and completed the baptismal record of my birth. (I have often wondered if there was a copyright on the baptismal record and if perhaps it was a date much after my birth. But no worry, the record was accepted and passports have come easily ever since.

I probably should add, also, that Lois' parents were very concerned about Lois moving all the way to Ann Arbor, even for a few months. After all, it was about two hundred miles from home and Lois had never lived any place other than Pittsburgh. Her Dad said that it would be ok for her to go to Ann Arbor since it would just be for about six months until Law School would be over and then we would be back in Pittsburgh. I tried to explain to him that I did not intend to practice law in Pennsylvania. It was like talking to a wall, however. Little did they know what the future held for their daughter as far as living places!!

13

Europe - 1951

It was quite an event in the Hartung family when Lois and I went to Europe. Lois' Dad had served in France in the First World War, but except for that trip abroad nobody in the family had ever traveled abroad. I think both of our parents were a bit anxious about this adventure but I think that they vicariously were very excited about it.

It was definitely going to be done on a shoestring budget. And at that time we of course did not fly. I think that Icelandic Airlines may have been flying across the Atlantic, but I don't think any other airlines, with the possible exception of Pan Am was crossing the Atlantic. We had to get to New York to board the ship. We took an overnight Greyhound Bus to get there. Then it was a day or two before we took a taxi to the dock.

The Anna Salene was definitely not luxury travel. The ship was, we understood, built as a cargo ship during the Second World War. Then it had been converted to a passenger ship. At the time we took it its principal use we understood was hauling DP's to America from Europe. Accommodations were dormitory style and food service was on a cafeteria line. The food was good, as I recall.

The Anna Salene was not a high speed ship. I think it took us about a week eastbound. Then because we got into a hurricane on the return, that portion of the trip took about nine days. We did meet a lot of other young people, traveling in somewhat the same style as we. There were lectures on board - about the countries and travel in Europe. And I think there may have been some language instruction, also.

We finally docked at Southampton, late in the day, and then had a several hour train trip to London, arriving at night without any accommodations!! I don't recall how we got accommodations, but we did. It was in a guest house or small hotel. The first night did not turn out too well because we had an encounter with bedbugs. Next day the woman proprietress expressed surprise and assured us she had not had any guests previously experience that problem. Yeah!! So we moved.

We experienced a bit of a problem in London, first off, with the language. We kept thinking people were directing us to Maable Ach. Only after a time did we realize they were saying Marble Arch, a well known spot in London. Talk about yokels on the road!!

We had ordered Raleigh bicycles for travel in Europe. We had to take delivery at the plant, which was not in downtown London. We did find it, though, but then some more fun followed. Lois had never ridden any kind of bike except ones with coaster brakes. So she kept crashing into the rear of my bike as we worked our way back to the hotel where we were staying. When it came time to leave London Lois said she just could not ride a bike in the London traffic. So I had to wheel down to the ferry dock area, then get back to where her bike was and cycle back down to the dock area. I don't remember how Lois got to the dock area. Like I say, we were novices in this kind of travel.

But we did get ourselves to the train station to get the train to Windsor. There we boarded a steam train to Windsor. I think that may have been the last time I ever took a steam train. But once in London we headed off for Oxford, the Cotswold's and other points of interest in southeastern England. We didn't have time to travel very extensively in England. We had allotted only about nine days or so for that country. We did stay in a few youth hostels and enjoyed especially the friends we made there, the very reasonable prices, etc. I do recall, though, that for one breakfast we had fried herring, which I enjoyed very much. There was one hitch though. While in a youth hostel we had morning chores. We drew KP one morning. It was the fried herring breakfast morning. There were about six of us fellows and then Lois was the only female. She sensed that the fellows would decide she should handle the dirty dishes. Lois could just not face that. Suddenly, Lois was nowhere around. Only shortly later did I realize that she had feigned illness and lay down in a bed to recover - recovery took only until someone else had handled the dishes!!

Then it was off to Belgium. We had a wonderful stop in Bruges - including a walk up the 365 steps to the tower - one for each day of the year. Our visit to the country took us to Delft, which we found dirty and smelly, and Brussels. A fairly short stay in the country, but one we enjoyed very much.

We had purchased a train ticket which we could use throughout Europe for a given amount of time - we may have purchased a 30 or 60 day ticket. We quickly learned, also, how easy it was, and perhaps is, to take bikes with you on the trains. We learned that we should just be at the track and go to one of the coaches which handle bikes, leave them with the attendant, then board the train and pick up the bike at the destination.

From Belgium we headed to the Netherlands, which turned out to be one of our favorite countries. It was there, on the day we went to Middleburg that we had one of the most fortunate events of the trip. Lois was not feeling well and didn't want much for dinner. Lois didn't want much except for an orange. At that time, English was not widely spoken (unlike today where most people speak English). As I was struggling with the waiter to make my wishes known, one of two fellows in the restaurant whom we had noticed spoke up and told the waiter in English what Lois wanted. Shortly after that they came over to our table to talk. We learned that they were Fredericus van Gulick (Fred) and Johannes Kerramanes (John). They were both newspapermen. One had a daily in Amsterdam and another a weekly in Schoonhoven. We talked all evening, and toward the end of the evening they invited us to travel around with them the following morning, which we did. As we were wandering back to our beginning point, the two of them spoke between themselves in Dutch, and the next thing we knew they were inviting us to join them in either Fred's or John's VW and travel around the country with them. There were all kinds of problems we said - getting our bikes to Amsterdam - no problem they said. They would just have it shipped and we could pick it up there. And so it went, and before we knew it we were having a wonderful trip with them around their country.

I do recall that at one point they started driving down a private lane along side which was a sign in Dutch. They asked us if we knew what it said, and of course we said no. They told us it said no trespassing. They had wanted to go down that lane for some time. This time, they said, if they were stopped they would be mute and we in our best American English would tell them we didn't understand. No problem, but we remember the event.

We stopped near the end of the trip at John's home and then took the electric train to Amsterdam. There Fred invited us to spend the night at his house. His wife and child were out of town, but he opened up his house for us and we had a wonderful night. Then the next day we headed off for Amsterdam. I recall we took a boat trip on the Grachten (canals) and very much enjoyed seeing the canals of the City. Then we went to the Rijksmuseum. Remember my first sighting of the Night Watch.

From the Netherlands we took a train to Germany. Spent the first night in Cologne. Our hotel there was a bomb shelter from the Second World War which had been converted into a hotel. It was also shortly enough after the war that the half of the bridge over the Rhine which had been bombed remained half way across the river.

We then took a memorable trip, for us, up the Rhine River, stopping at a number of cities along the way. Then it was on to Heidelberg, a truly magical City. The U.S. Army had intentionally not bombed Heidelberg because it wanted to use the City as a headquarters area after the war.

After our trip along the Rhine and then to Heidelberg, we went on to Austria. I recall as we got off the train we saw a lot of women coming toward us. One of the women stopped us and asked if we would like to stay at their home. The price would be $4.00 U.S. for the two of us, including breakfast in the morning!! As soon as we said yes she motioned and her husband and son showed up and carried our bags and took our bikes to their place, on Gasworken Strassen!! We had a beautiful room, small but very carefully appointed, and a good breakfast. I am certain we had the best room in the place.

Time was beginning to get short and so we headed to France. We did have time to spend in Paris and also went out to Versailles, to see the Palace where so much had happened at the end of the First World War - Peace Treaty, League of Nations, etc. The Arc d' Triumph in Paris and a few other sights were memorable. We also visited the Palace of Versailles.

Our bikes had been shipped ahead from I think Amsterdam and I think we picked them up again in Paris. We splurged and traveled second class from our last stop in Austria to Paris. I remember trying at this point to speak in German to a couple of priests on the train. To my shock they were American Jesuits so their response was in fine American English!!

From Paris we had to get by train to the port of embarkation to the U.S. At this point, i.e., while we were in Paris we realized we had absolutely run out of money. So, unfazed, we used the little money we had to buy a big chocolate bar and sit on a Park bench overlooking the Seine River and wait until offices opened. Nothing ventured, nothing gained. So we went into the American Express office and I asked a very nice man there if I could arrange for a little cash. I think he must have been dumbfounded. But he leaned me $50 U.S. which I promised to pay once I got back to the States. And I did pay and sent it with a very nice note expressing my appreciation.

We boarded the Anna Salene for what we thought would be an uneventful trip back to the U.S. Little did we know that a huge hurricane was brewing in the Gulf of Mexico area. It hit our shipping lane on the way back and we had three or four days floundering around in the Atlantic, making very little headway. Most people were suffering serious seasickness. We stayed active, stayed above, and weathered the storm with not a bit of sickness.

Then, as planned, we arrived back in New York and then in Pittsburgh after a couple of the most wonderful months in our lives. We showed slides of our trip to relatives, etc. and generally just reveled in the wondrous trip we had. And as I noted earlier Lois and I always felt that our decision just to take some time off and let the world go by was one of the best decisions we ever made.

14

Chicago

When we returned from Europe, Lois and I both knew that we had to make some decisions on where we were going to live, where I would practice law, etc. It was certainly my desire to head west, and Lois was prepared to go along. My parents saw no reason to go west. I recall my Dad suggesting that I could practice law anywhere, for example in the Chicago area and then take a vacation to other places we wanted to visit. It was apparent to me that he didn't grasp the concept of our desire being a place to live, not just a place to work. I'm sure my Mother didn't think that moving west was a thing do. And of course, Lois' folks were upset enough Lois just living as far from Pittsburgh as Ann Arbor that they would have gone ballistic about a move to the west coast.

So for whatever reason, and while I don't now recall that we even thought through the whole process, we decided that we would first step in Evanston for a few days to visit Grandparents, aunts & uncles, etc. Fate dealt us an unexpected blow. The day after we arrived in Evanston, my Uncle Alva, who lived in Elgin, suffered a serious heart attack from which he died later in the day. By the time the funeral was over, etc., the pressures were building for us to day in Evanston. If we had been better organized at the time for the trip west, I think we probably would have headed out. But we weren't. Pretty soon Jean

DeJong, a first cousin once removed was working on an apartment for us. We moved in and there we were. No plan in place for the move west, then. I decided that I would, as lots of new attorneys did then, try to get a job adjusting insurance claims while I waited for the Bar exam

I quickly got a job with the Hartford Accident and Indemnity Co as an adjuster. My supervisor was Clarence Hercules, a very nice person with whom we kept in contact for a number of years until he died. I had limited training for the job, and was then assigned to handle claims in the Chicago area. Lois went to the Illinois DPA and got a job with the same responsibilities as she had had in Pittsburgh.

Soon we fit into the society of the area. We both made friends among our fellow workers. I particularly remember Paul O'Connor. And Lois made several friends. We tried out Evanston First Methodist where my grandparents belonged for many, many years, but found it too stiff and frosty. So we went to Hemenway Methodist Church, more to the south end of Evanston and found a very good Church home. And of course my Uncle Bill and Aunt Lee lived in Evanston, and we were frequently guest at their place.

We rented an apartment at 1335 Birchwood Avenue, just about a half block from Lake Michigan. It was a three story brick building, built I would guess in the 1920's - no air conditioning which made it a bit hot in the summertime. Since there was no air conditioning, the apartment got hot in the summer. Tenants kept their front doors open, so the whole building was permeated with the cooking in the various apartments.

Fairly soon after arriving I filed an application for the Illinois Bar exam, and signed up for a cram course. It was all so unreal. I really did not want to live in Illinois. I wanted to live out West and thought of the whole arrangement as a temporary thing. But for the time being, we were gong to be there in Chicago. My folks were very happy that we were living in Evanston. Lois' folks could tolerate the idea of us being there, even though it was 500 miles from Pittsburgh. As a matter of fact, Lois' parents made a visit to Chicago while we lived there.

The cram course for the Bar exam was a grind. A lot of hard work, with classes, as I recall, on Saturday, etc. Finally, the cram course was over and it was exam time. I recall that I saw Bob Jones at the exam. I recall also, that I saw him after lunch on the first day of the three day exam. At that time he said it was good to see him, but that he would be heading back home in Billings, Montana. I inquired why, with two and a half days left in the exam. To understand his answer one has to understand the reason for his response.

I think most of the persons taking the exam wee veterans. The Bar had decided that at least veterans who flunked the bar exam were required to retake only the courses which they failed. Bob said that he had flunked the exam but that in preparing for this exam he had misread the letter from the bar exam and had studied all the courses he had passed but ignored the other courses. He said there was no reason to think he could pass courses he had failed before, so he was heading out. Bob did to back to Montana, took its bar exam without any cram course, and passed and was admitted to the Bar.

Well, anyway I took the bar exam and failed. I did study the sections which I failed, and passed the bar exam on the second try. Then after we got to Washington I took the cram course and passed the Bar exam on the first try. Could it be that Bob's and my mental attitude toward practicing in Illinois played a part in how we did on the exam?

Anyway, after passing the exam, Lois and I took the trip to Springfield to be sworn in to the Bar. (There was no accommodating attorneys by the Bar Association). Although most of the young attorneys lived in the Chicago area, we all had to go to Springfield to be sworn in and admitted to the Bar.

After passing the Bar exam and being admitted to the Bar, the ordinary and customary thing would have been for me to look for a law job, assuming that I had not by then lined something up. Well, even though I had put a lot of time effort and money into being admitted to practice law in Illinois, I just couldn't get myself geared up to look for a law job. My heart just was not in it. I really wanted to go west, and that was all there was to it.

Meantime, we built up more friendships in the Chicago area. We traveled around the area, spent time visiting relatives in the area (my grandparents lived in Evanston, where they had lived since I think about 1910 or so. And we visited Mother's friends, Tom and Lillian Harwood (brother and sister and their mother; the McIntosh's who had children about my age; Mrs. Cady whose daughter married a Rev.

Rocky and lived in India as missionaries; and a couple others whom I do not now recall. We also became good friends with a few of the other young couples at Hemenway Church, etc. We spent Christmas's with Bill and Lee, and enjoyed the Christmas even Lutefisk dinners which "Uncle" a relative of Lee prepared.

We drove back to Pittsburgh a couple of times, I think, to visit my and Lois' parents; we took at least one very nice vacation, part of it with Lois' parents, to Washington D.C., Williamsburg, Va., then down the Highway to North Carolina and through the Great Smoky Mountains.

It was in the preparation for this longer trip that Lois learned to drive. She had always procrastinated in learning to drive. In my frustration I told her that I would not do all the driving on this long a trip. And either she would have to learn to drive and share the driving, or we wouldn't take the trip. Well, she really wanted to take the trip, so she took some driving lessons and got her license shortly before we left on the trip - and she did share in the driving!!

In the meantime, while all this was going on I continued to do insurance adjusting. I just could not get myself motivated to getting a law job. Rather my dislike for the Chicago area kept increasing and I disliked Chicago more and more. I don't think that Lois felt as strongly about Chicago as I did, but she could see that we were stuck in a rut.

Finally, I told Lois that we had to make a change. I told her that I was going to resign and we were going to pack up and go west. I was always very pleased that Lois was very supportive of my decision that we had to move west. Actually, I think it was our decision. Lois and I discussed the move all along. I think she was very excited. But it took real gumption, knowing the opposition from her home that she would act on making such a move, to sign on enthusiastically. She always felt it was the best possible decision we could have made. (As I have noted before, Lois and I had the best possible marriage either of us could ever have hoped for. We acted in unison on all of our big decisions. And I have always been grateful.) At that time Washington had a requirement that an applicant for the bar have been a resident for at least 90 days before making application and the application had to be filed not less than 30 days before the exam. I decided that I would take the train west to Seattle, spend the weekend there, visit the Bar offices and tell them of my plan, and then of my Seattle address. Alice and Norm Mattern, very good Allegheny friends of course and lived in Seattle, so I used that as my address.

On the trip west I stopped in Billings and overnighted and had a good visit with Bob and Dusty Jones. I also lined up a job in Seattle with Campbell Husted, a very good company doing insurance adjusting work.

I had resigned before I took the trip west. So when I got back to Chicago we gave notice to our landlord who wasn't too happy and suggested that it might want to make some claim against us for breaking our lease. (I have always thought that they figured, correctly, that a judgment against us would not be very collectible). We packed up all we owned in addition to what we could take with us, in eight rather small boxes which we shipped to Seattle, I think to Alice and Norm, bid our adieu to all of our friends. We had also let our parents know what was going on. My parents wished us well, but I think were very sorry about our decision. Lois', her mother especially, put on a real mother martyr scene "they would die without ever seeing us again unless we came back to visit", etc.

With all these matters attended to, we loaded up the car and set out on one of the really big adventures of our lives. A real leap of faith. But we were both just as happy as we could be. And I sensed that I was going to make some use of my legal training. I recall that on the October 1 date we left, the Chicago temperature hit 100 degrees Fahrenheit, again!! And I was double glad we were heading out.

I have always felt that it was too bad that we spent the two years in Chicago. We were really just in a holding pattern. But that is something long over the dam. We never looked back once we made the decision to head west.

15

Washington - 1953-1954

Lois and I were truly optimistic and lighthearted when we set out from Chicago and headed for Washington. The only time consideration for our trip west was that when I was hired by Campbell Husted I said that I would come and be on board by October 15. We were looking forward to a new life in the West. Our parents, especially Lois', were upset to say the least but we felt we were making the correct decision.

It was early fall as we headed west. The weather was generally sunny and warm. I can remember as we rolled across the country we sang over and over such songs as: "With someone like you, a pal so good and true, I'd like to leave it all behind and so find a place that's known to god along, just a place to call our own, we'll find perfect peace where joys never cease and spend the rest of our lives….", Home on the Range, Tell Me Why..", etc. We really looked forward to our life "out west".

As I have been reflecting on the trip, I cannot recall the exact route we took. I do remember we stopped to see Dinosaur National Monument. And we may have routed ourselves through Salt Lake City. As we got to Oregon I reminded Lois that we should call my second cousins or first cousins once removed, Leone, and her husband Gene Webber in Walla Walla. I recalled growing up hearing Aunt Pearl talk about the Webbers in Walla Walla and of all their summer trips. I knew nothing about them, though, and had no idea what to expect.

But when we got to Oregon, just a few miles from Walla Walla, we telephoned. They were most cordial, most enthusiastic about our visit and gave us very good directions for meeting them. We met Gene in front of a bank in downtown Walla Walla, and he led us out to their place.

We couldn't have been more fortunate than to have them meet us. They were such wonderful people and we established friendships which lasted for the balance of their lives. Gene had gone I think to Whitman and majored in Electrical Engineering. He graduated about 1930, at the height of the depression. He got a job as a letter carrier with the Post Office in Walla Walla and stayed with it until he retired. In 1952 Eisenhower appointed him as Postmaster of Walla Walla. (I recall Gene telling me a few years later that in case I wondered why with his major he stayed on as a letter carrier, that I had no idea what little demand there was for electrical engineers in 1930 and by 1945 his engineering skills were all out of date)

After an overnight with Weber's we set out for Seattle. We arrived late in the afternoon. I recall that during the time I was driving (Lois really didn't spell me too much on the driving) and as we got close to Snoqualmie Pass, I told her it was her time to take over driving for a while. At that time there was no freeway, Route 10, known as the Sunset Highway was the major east-west route into Seattle. The highway was two lane, but I think there was construction underway to convert US 10 into a four lane highway. Anyway, Lois drove through some poor detour route and felt she had been treated very badly to get that part of the driving.

We arrived into what is now Bellevue on toward dinner. We got a motel for the night and then set out for dinner. At that time, 1953, the entire business district of Bellevue extended for about three blocks on a north-south basis. After dinner, I suggested to Lois that we drive into downtown Seattle, and go to Ivar's for a bowl of clam chowder. She was game. I still remember the salt smell of the air as we got to the water. I suppose we called Alice and Norm, but other than that we called it a day.

The next day was October 14 or 15, so I told Lois that I had better call Art Campbell and let him know I was here and would be in to the office the next day. I recall him saying that they had been concerned about my arrival I thought I had made clear our arrival time, but apparently they had been looking for me a few days earlier and were thinking about offering my position to someone else if I didn't show up very soon. Whew!!

It must have been the next day that we headed out to see Mattern's. They got us lined up to meet with the manager of the Northgate Apartments, and before we knew it we had signed a lease for an apartment. Everything was falling into place!!

Lois then very promptly stopped by the offices of the Washington DPA to see if they might have a job opening. They did, and Lois very promptly began working there, and continued to do so until the following year when we moved to Tacoma.

Campbell Husted proved to be a good firm for me to work with while waiting for admission to the bar. Art Campbell, the founder, had worked initially after school for the Hartford Accident and Indemnity Co., the same company I worked for in Chicago. After a time he set up his independent adjusting firm, handling work for a wide variety of insurance companies which did not maintain their own adjusting staffs in Seattle. Don Husted had been in business with Art from early on. He handled much of the administrative work of the office. I suppose there were seven or eight of us adjusters, plus the support staff of secretaries, etc.

The work was pretty much the same as I had handled in Chicago - handling personal injury claims. One of the things which the job did do was to enable me to early learn my way around the whole City. Chicago is so big that I worked only in the North end of the City. But in Seattle I worked the whole area. I quickly learned that Seattle was what I would call a nicer city than Chicago. There wasn't the rush and hurry, it was easier to talk to claimants, and generally work out settlements. Oh yes, the offices were in the Dexter Horton building in downtown Seattle.

The Northgate Apartments were just across the street from the Northgate Shopping Mall. The Mall was, I think, the first shopping mall in the country. Or for that matter for anywhere in the country. It was still fairly new at the time, and not quite as developed as it was later. It opened about 1950. A&P and Safeway both had stores in the Mall (grocery stores have long since disappeared from the scene at Northgate Mall). In any event we shopped there for groceries, and found stores as the Bon Marche, Nordstrom and Penney's were already in the mall, so shopping for the most part was very convenient.

Very soon after arriving in Seattle we started attending the University Temple Methodist Church. At that time it was a large well attended Church which was both rather convenient and a good church in the sense it had a large congregation, a minister who was a good preacher, etc. As it turned out the Sr. minister at the Church was someone whom my Mother had known at Northwestern University. I think they were both in school at the time. Mother said she had known him fairly well, I guess in the Young Peoples activities at the Church.

Shortly after we arrived in Seattle I also went in to the Bar offices. Don't know whether I had learned at my first visit about the Bar cram course. But I certainly did discuss it on this first visit. I was very pleased to learn that such program was available. I may also have picked up the forms for applying for the Bar exam, but perhaps I could not do so. At that time the Washington Bar required that an applicant for the Bar be a resident of the state for not less than ninety days before applying. The application was due not less than thirty days before taking the exam. As I say, the scheduling of our trip west was fit very tightly into the requirements of the Bar. This ninety day requirement was ruled unconstitutional a number of years ago.

I learned that a number of younger attorneys, mostly I think, ones who had come from the east and for whom such a cram course was not then available, organized the cram course. The attorneys who organized and ran the cram course were indeed good attorneys, became leaders in the Bar. One of them later became a U.S. District Judge, a person whom I always regarded as one of the best Judges I have had the pleasure of knowing and practicing before.

I think the cram course lasted for perhaps six weeks. This meant that it started within a month or two of the time we arrived. Especially since I did not study Community Property Law at Michigan, and since there were probably other subjects which I had not studied, and since I knew nothing about the position of the Washington courts on various areas of law, a cram course was a godsend for me.

When I started the cram course, I was surprised to see my classmate and good friend, Don Leeper, in the classes. Don later joined forces with another Michigan alumnus whom I never knew, or not well at least, and opened a practice in the eastern part of the state. I never saw Don much after that.

The classes met in the evening since most of us were working day time. I was most anxious to pass the exam the first time. So I asked the people at Campbell Husted if I could work half time during the course. I recall Don Husted being a bit surprised at this request. And by hindsight I think it was a bit bold to ask for a half time job just a month or so after I started. But the firm was very gracious and said it would be ok.

I made quite a number of friends at Campbell Husted. One of them, Bill Caton was a Michigan man. Another was Bob Ratcliffe whom I liked very much and one whom I would see in the courthouse from time to time over many years.

I recall dense fogs in the evening coming home after the cram course classes. I'm not certain, but I think the courses were held in the law school at UW. I know that in this area we always get a lot of fog in the mid to late fall. I've always thought, though, that the fogs were particularly dense that fall.

In due course it came time for the bar exam. By that time Washington allowed applicants to use the typewriter for the exam. This was a relief to me, given my penmanship. The test lasted two and one half days - a half day less than the course in Illinois. I recall thinking at the time that the bar exam didn't seem too tough. I suspect the feeling was a combination of the good cram course and also of my very positive attitude in preparing for the course. I really wanted to get on with practice.

And so, in due course I received notice that I had indeed passed the exam. Admission was in late March of 1954. This was the second test for the year, and not as many took this test as the one given in July, just shortly after school let out. There were just about 30 or 31 of us admitted at that time. The ceremony was held in the court t of the presiding Judge of King County. At this time I see the lists of persons who have passed thee bar exam and there seem to be several hundred for each of the tests. I recall at the time I was admitted there were jut about four thousand attorneys in the whole state (Leon Misterek thinks the number was about half that, but I think my recollection is more correct.) About half of the attorneys practice in King County and the other half all around the State. I think that today there are about 20,000 to 25,000 attorneys in the state. I realize that the population of the state has a little more than doubled since we came out, but, there are certainly a lot more per capita now than then.

So then, the next question was, where would I look for a job. This process was not nearly as structured as it now is. Given how much I hated the size of Chicago, I decided that I did not want to practice in Seattle, but that I wanted a smaller city. I have thought over the years that I would feel differently about it now. Seattle is a big City, but nothing like Chicago. I sometimes think that it might have worked out even better for me if I had looked in Seattle. But that's water over the dam, and if I had looked in Seattle, who knows how things its might have worked out.

In any event I went around to firms in a number of cities in Western Washington to see if they would be interested in hiring me. I had nice interviews in Bellingham and Everett but nothing came of it. Don't know if there were other cities where I interviewed before Tacoma but there may have been. I do recall that the first 4th of July weekend we went on a junket to Olympic National Park and at the Antlers Hotel in Forks. Somehow it came out that I was an attorney. A few of the people in Forks talked to me about how nice it would be to practice in Forks and how much business there would be - especially from the logging and forestry industry. But it was quite a big smaller than anything I had in mind.

So I decided to look around in Tacoma. When I did go looking for a job I checked and tried to go to firms where there were Michigan grads. I do recall having a good interview at the Gordon Thompson firm. The man Thompson, whose first name I won't recall, everybody knew him just as Tommy. They didn't have an opening, but he suggested that I might want to check with Ed Eisenhower, just one or two floors below. In the Puget Sound Bank building. Ed was a Michigan man, class of 1914.

So I went to see him. The firm was Eisenhower, Hunter, Ramsdell and Duncan. Ed's whole practice had been in Tacoma, and he had developed a very good practice. I think, too, that the fact his was the brother of the then President of the United States didn't hurt. We had a real good interview and either at that time or at a later meeting, he offered me a job. Starting date would be the first of July, 1954. I accepted.

Taking a job in Tacoma meant that we had to move to Tacoma. We had been spending a lot of time visiting Alice and Norm Mattern while we lived in Seattle. They were a tremendous help in making the move. Of course, we also had to find a place to live. I remember visiting Kim Comfort, a senior real estate man in Tacoma, who, with both of his sons, became good friends, suggesting that I might check the Park Towers Apartment. And so we did, and so we took an apartment. It is located at 220 Tacoma Avenue (perhaps north Tacoma Ave.) And we promptly moved in to be ready to report for work the first of July. And so there we were, ready to start another big adventure - a job actually practicing law!!

16

Tacoma 1954-1956

It was very exciting but also sort of scary for me to head off to work for my first real law job. I had a good feel about Tacoma, we had moved into the Park Towers Apartment which was a very nice apartment building, and I had landed a job with one of Tacoma's largest and best law firms.

The Eisenhower, Hunter, Ramsdell and Duncan law firm had four partners and, with me, two associates. I've mentioned earlier some about Ed Eisenhower. Chuck Hunter was in his late forties when I started and Jim Ramsdell was in his early forties. Chuck Hunter was born in Yelm, Wash., the son of a physician. Chuck was born sort of with a silver spoon in his mouth. He and his wife belonged to and lived at the Tacoma Country and Golf Club - definitely the upper end economically in Tacoma. He was also an excellent golfer and played frequently. (Ed Eisenhower was also a very good and enthusiastic golfer.)

Wendell Duncan was in his early forties and had been an excellent trial attorney.

He and George Boldt, then recently Judge Boldt, U.S. District Court Judge in Tacoma had been two of the best trial attorneys in Tacoma. Unfortunately, Wendell Duncan was suffering with cancer of the spine, or back, by the time I joined the firm. I visited him at his home on a couple of occasions, but unfortunately I never saw him in the office. He survived for perhaps three years after I joined the firm.

The other associate was Bob Hamilton. Bob had been a Tacoma resident nearly all his life, as I think was the case with his wife Sue. I think Bob was a good attorney. Unfortunately for him it became fairly apparent to me fairly early on Ed favored me over Bob. Bob left the firm three or four years after I joined the firm. He went with the City attorney's office and ultimately was appointed the City attorney for Tacoma.

On Friday of my first week in the office I had an experience which, while I did not realize it at first, was a manifestation of Jim Ramsdell's manner of practice. Early Friday afternoon one of the secretaries, I think Ann Holmlund came in to my office and told me that Jim Ramsdell had scheduled an appointment for this very time. Jim wasn't around and no one knew where he was or when he might show up. Also, I was the only attorney who was not tied up at the time. So, the secretary, I think Ann Holmlund, asked whether I would meet with the client.

Of course I would be glad to meet with them. Turned out the clients, husband and wife, were accountants and were selling their practice. I really was a bit at sea over just how to proceed. But proceed I did. The clients were very happy with me. I handled the business for them, and ended up having them and their daughter as clients for a long time.

Over time I gained quite an insight into the partners in the firm. Ed Eisenhower had come out from Michigan after graduating from its law school and opened a law practice. I don't know whether he had anyone else with him in the early years or not. I do believe that Ed worked very hard and developed a good practice. By the time I started Ed must have been about 65 and was already taking off Wednesdays to play golf. Sometime during the course of the time I was with the firm Ed started taking off Friday's. He would speak at length, however, about how hard he was working, etc. etc. He also, I learned, felt that he was entitled to the biggest share of the firm's income no matter how hard or how little he may have been working at the time. It also became apparent, fairly readily, that in some ways he was a one partner firm.

Chuck Hunter started practice with Ed in about 1932. Chuck was personally a very nice person. Very genteel, always very courteous. He really did not want to work too hard or handle law business that involved a lot of controversy. He favored Probate and Trust and Estate work. He always deferred to Ed. Chuck was well enough connected in Tacoma that I think he generated a fair amount of business.

Jim Ramsdell was pretty good trial attorney. He also did a certain amount of labor work. Personally, Jim was a very open friendly kind of person. He was well regarded in the Bar, I think. Jim started practicing with Ed in about 1935. He always would defer to Ed on issues which might come up. One thing which I noticed about Jim was that although he had been practicing with the firm for nearly twenty years when I started, he never really did generate much law business.

I very quickly plunged into whatever work was assigned to me. I found that fairly quickly good clients were starting to call me directly on items which came up. We represented Puget Sound National Bank, which generated a lot of work. Reno Odlin was president and Al Saunders was, I think, the executive Vice President and the head of the commercial loan department of the Bank. HK (Pat) Strong was the Vice President for consumer affairs. Very soon I was handling most of the commercial loan work for the Bank, work which the Bank Cashier might have - banking issues. We also represented Washington Steel and Washington Hardware Co., which were interrelated. Soon I found myself doing much of the work for these good clients.

And so it went with the firm as far as my work and the responsibilities which were assigned to me. I think that because Ed was slowing down, Chuck didn't want to work too hard and didn't want to handle controversial work, and Jim was not always able to keep concentrated, I ended up being the attorney handling, pretty much on my own, a great deal more work than is generally turned over to a young associate. Bob Hamilton handled a fair amount of work, but for whatever reason, I found myself being called directly by more clients than would ordinarily be the case, I think. I think the partners were comfortable letting me run with the work because I seemed to get good results and keep the clients happy.

Early on in the practice, when Ed's brother was President, Ed called me in to his office and said that he had one special bit of work he would like for me to handle   He told me that as the President's brother he received mail from lots of people seeing if they could get some special help from the President through Ed. Ed asked me to look over this correspondence, review it, and generally either ignore it or if it seemed appropriate prepare some response for Ed to sign. I don't recall spending much time on this assignment. I gave it very low priority and I don't recall Ed asking me much about it after that first conversation which I had with him on the subject.

After Bob Hamilton left the firm, or thereabouts, Mert Elliot was hired. Mert was Jim Ramsdell's age and a longtime friend of Jim. Mert had practiced in Tacoma in the past but then left to return to the family farm in Kansas. For whatever reason he decided to come back out to Washington. Mert was a good attorney, very workmanlike, etc. He much preferred office type work. He seldom went to court. He and I got along well and I liked him very much. He and I had a different temperament and disposition. I know I was a lot more at ease in the courtroom and in controversial settings than he was.

I felt after a few years, and also at the time I left the firm, that if I had stayed in Tacoma I would soon have been in control of the firm.

While the law business was progressing, Lois and I soon became very involved in the community. We joined Tacoma First Methodist Church and became active in Church affairs. The minister at the time, Frank Brown was a very social person but we felt a very mediocre preacher. He was the biggest reason that after a few years we left First Methodist Church and joined Mason Methodist Church where J. Henry Ernst was the pastor. He was a tremendous preacher and had a growing Church, in significant part due to J .Henry.

At First Methodist the Young Married Couples, which selected the name YOMACO was soon organized. We enjoyed the group and made a number of very good friends. Don and Gen Fisher were early and good friends. Also Ken and Muriel Spring were good friends. Lois and Muriel were especially close, in part, I think because they had a child very close in age to ours. At Church we also met Bob and Rusty Sherwin who have now been close friends for over fifty years. They were not a part of the YOMACO group, however.

We also met Oliver and Vivian Larson at Church. They were not a part of the YOMACO group either. Oliver worked for the Tacoma

Chamber of Commerce. Fairly early on he got me involved in what as known as the Industrial Bureau. It was a group of businessmen who met each Friday for lunch. I attended the meetings and in that way made a lot of friends in the business community.

We also enjoyed the Northwest very much, and spent time seeing and participating in the events. Trips to Mt. Rainier were a favorite spot to visit. We also enjoyed such things as the Daffodil Festival in the springtime. Tacoma has a wonderful large park - Pt. Defiance. Driving the five mile loop of that park was a fairly regular event for us.

As I noted earlier, I fairly quickly was given full charge of significant litigation - a rather unusual thing, as I said for such a junior attorney. On the litigation end I found myself handling a stockholders derivative action, and a Workman's Comp appeal for St. Regis Paper Company, another good client of the firm. (St Regis was one client that Ed always kept tight control of.)

We represented the Tacoma Housing Authority. This got me to court frequently on landlord tenant matters - generally evictions. We had some walk-in business at the firm. Through this I handled a few divorce actions. With one exception, they were not contested. I decided very early on, after perhaps a half dozen or so default divorce actions that I wanted no part of that law practice.

Once we moved to Tacoma, Lois left the workforce. She felt she had about as much working time as she wanted. Besides that, we felt that we wanted to have a family. Lois was determined that when children came along she was not going to be a mother working outside the home. By spring of 1955 we were fairly sure that she was pregnant. So, we looked for an OBGYN. Our family Dr gave us two names. Lois called the first name found that she couldn't get an appointment for a week or so. So she called the other, J. Edmund Deming, and got an appointment very quickly.

We very quickly became very good friends of Jack Deming and his wife Alberta. When we both learned that we each played Bridge we started getting together very frequently at the card table. Jack and Alberta lived in the McKinley Hill section of Tacoma when we first met them, but fairly soon after we met they purchased a lovely home at Brown's Point, on the waterfront just across from Commencement Bay.

Lois' pregnancy was uneventful. Richard's delivery was something else. Part way through the delivery Jack noticed Richard's heart rate was slowing. Jack suspected that the cord might be wrapped around his neck and so he started Lois on oxygen and the heart rate went back up. Jack was absolutely correct. We were so grateful that Jack had the level of skill he did.

We spent quite a bit of time working on Richard's name. I had grown up tired of always being called Junior, even though I was the third. So I said I did not want Richard to be another George. I came up, somewhat in jest, with some names to which Lois was very opposed. So we settled on Richard Lance, which we always liked and hoped that Richard liked the name also.

During the time Lois was pregnant with Richard, we felt that it was time to look for a house. We actually settled on a place the week Richard was born. It was located at 4601 Sixth Avenue, a house that Tony Ursich, a Tacoma attorney had built some years earlier. It was a house we liked very much - two bedrooms, one bath, living room, separate dining room, and a room which on the first floor which we understood Tony had used as an office. There was also a full basement. It also had a nice good sized yard.

Sort of with the house came some wonderful neighbors Glen and Royden Doud. (Don't actually know or recall what Glen's first name was). We always just called her Mrs. Doud.) They lived on Cheyenne Street which was the cross street on the corner lot on which we were located. Royden, or Roy as most people called him was retired. Glen worked for the Thrift Shop of the Junior League.

We moved in to our house a couple months, I think, after Richard was born, so it was spring when we moved in. It was so exciting - our own home!! I used the GI bill for financing for the home - 4% interest.

When Richard was born I immediately called both my and Lois' parents. Lois parents wanted her to call as soon as she got home (at that time there were no phones in the hospital rooms.) When Lois spoke to her parents they said that they would be coming out to visit!! We had lived in Washington for two and a half years and had not seen hide nor hair of them. And so they did come out, which was a treat. Before they came out, the preceding year I believe, Lois' Aunt Alma

(Elma Eichenberg, a brother of Lois dad) had come out for a visit. When she was here I had a mortgage foreclosure to handle in Chehalis or Centralia, so the three of us took an overnight trip and went down together. The weather was gorgeous, and Aunt Elma invented the word "gorgeousity" to describe the beauty.

Coming home with a baby was a challenge for both of us - perhaps even more so for me. As far as nighttime feeding was concerned, once Lois decided that nursing just wasn't going to work out, we agreed I would take the first feeing, which generally came about 1 AM, Lois would take the later feeding.

Richard grew very rapidly and we were ever so happy to have him as our son. Our friends, Don and Gen Fisher had a daughter, Jane, borne just a week or two later. She was two months premature, which unfortunately resulted in her suffering from a significant hearing loss, but Lois and Gen and the babies spent a lot of time in one home or the other.

One other sidelight into Richard's birth was the time Lois spent in the hospital before Richard was born. I took Lois to the hospital in the middle of the night, and he was not born until late afternoon that day. You will notice as I continue that getting to the hospital lost some of its sense of urgency with each additional birth.

I completed two years with the Eisenhower firm just a few months after Richard was born. It had indeed been a very busy two and a half years.

17

Tacoma 1957-1960

As I noted earlier, we bought our first house just before Richard was born and moved in within a few months after Richard was born. With the new house came all the sorts of things that living in a house rather than an apartment building brings with it. There is a yard to maintain, including a lawn to mow. I bought a used lawn mower from Ed Watts, a vice president of the Puget Sound National Bank. I started a compost box but it never did work out very well. It takes a lot of work to make a compost box work - turning the leaves and grass, working in some fertilizer, etc. I was just plain too busy to think about that. Then there was the planting, etc. With a corner lot we had a fair size of lawn to take care of. And I quickly learned a lot about plants native to the area that would look well in our yard. We had a beautiful willow tree in our back yard. I always liked it very much. In late winter or very early spring it would be a real harbinger of spring. All of a sudden in late winter we would notice a bit of green sheen to the tree - and then the leaves. One time, though the roots of the tree did spread and clog up our sewer lines.

I built a big sandbox in the back yard. I think it was about 9 x 9 feet. I think I bought a couple of yards of sand. When Richard and Kirk were young it was a great place to play.

Olympic Enterprises

By 1956 my very good friend Oliver Larson came up with the idea of creating a consulting firm. It would be a firm with shareholders who were largely retired and who had varying skills. We organized Olympic Enterprises, Inc. Inc. John Rue, the retired manager of Hooker Chemical Co., Ed Warner, who had been active in the plumbing arena; Paul Benson, a retired mining engineer; John D. Powell (Jack) who was active in Raleigh Mann, a local insurance agency; John Judy an executive with Hooker Chemical company; William M. Merrill (Bill) a banker with a bank in Tacoma; and Morrie Johnson, who was very instrumental in the management of Washington Steel Co.; and at some point Bob Clem, although at this time I can't remember what his level of skills was. While Oliver Larson was the person who conceived the idea for the company, he felt that because of his association with the Chamber of Commerce it would not be appropriate for him to be active in the company.

We met fairly often as shareholders and tried to figure out ways in which we could generate a consulting business in which we would utilize the varying skills of the shareholders. Unfortunately, we never did generate much if any business. The problem was in finding someone who would or could make the time to generate business. Also there was the need for capital to open an office, advertise, and pay secretarial or other administrative activity. I always felt that if we had been able to raise perhaps twenty five thousand dollars as capital to get the business started we could have been a going machine. The shareholders either did not have money to invest or as older retired people did not want to put in much money.

We did have a number of social events, mostly dinners, etc. where we got to know each other. Lois and I did develop very close friendships with several of the shareholders, however, so there was a real benefit from the organization. John Judy and his wife Sarah and family were long term friends; John and Molly Rue were also very good friends and through him his cousin Phyllis Ellis. Bill Merrill and his wife also were long term friends - recall attending the marriage of one of their daughters, and Bill for many many years always gave me a phone call on my birthday. Jack Powell I knew more in professional contacts; Ed

Warner was a good friend and I recall a few years later probating his wife's estate. The rest of the shareholders were friends, but not persons with whom I developed a long term relationship.

Fairly early after becoming acquainted with John Rue I was introduced to his cousin, or second cousin Phyllis Ellis. Phyllis was from New Jersey, living within sight of the lights of New York. Her husband was a Navy flyer in the Second World War, but unfortunately was killed after the end of the War, or near the end. Her property was condemned by the State of New Jersey for freeway purposes. So when John Rue introduced me to Phyllis it was with the idea that I might be able to help Phyllis in acquiring property in Washington to replace the condemned property.

I think it was about the time I met her that she was looking at 200 plus acres out from Gig Harbor. It was mostly unimproved property, but the owner had built his residence on lake on the property. I don't recall the name of the owner, but he was a Dr. who was asking ninety thousand dollars for the property. I told Phyllis it looked like a nice piece of property but that the price was much too high. I suggested that she offer the owner $20,000.00. Phyllis was shocked at making such an offer, thinking it was so low that it just wasn't possible to buy it for anything like that. As a matter of fact, being the shy person she was, she said she couldn't convey the offer and asked me if I would do so. I assured her I would be glad to do so and in fact the owner accepted the offer.

There were a lot of second or third growth trees or timber growing on the property. Phyllis offered us the opportunity to come and get our Christmas tree from the property. So began a tradition that continued for at least twenty years of going there for our Christmas tree. John Judy and his family also got their tree from the land. The trees certainly did not have the nice tailored look of trees from a Christmas tree lot, but the trees had character. Christmas tree day was always a full day affair. We would drive over in the morning, Lois and Phyllis always planned and provided for a very generous lunch, and then the rest of us were out in the bush looking for a tree John Judy and Sarah, and perhaps one or two of the children (they were older and so we really didn't see much of their children).

Phyllis had a daughter born after the death of Phyllis' husband. We continued going over to Phyllis' until not too long before her death. I recall the last year we went over. Phyllis had become a bit strange. She had always been reclusive but that tendency was more pronounced in the last year of his life. After this last year of the Christmas tree Phyllis had a stroke from which she did not recover. Unfortunately, I always felt, her daughter fairly quickly stopped being as friendly, and for many years now there has been no contact.

Life in Tacoma

Within a year or two of moving to Tacoma we got a collie, which at my suggestion we named Yorick (Alas poor Yorick, I knew him well!). He was a wonderful dog and we kept him as long as we lived in Tacoma. He always went with us to get the Christmas tree and he thoroughly enjoyed running all over the woodlands of Phyllis. Richard and Kirk knew Yorick from the very first and always liked him very much. Yorick was hit by a car one time, which caused a broken hip. He recovered well from that accident. Mr. Doud never could manage Yorick's name. If Yorick would be barking out in the yard I would hear Mr. Doud out there calling "Yorkie, Yorkie". I tried a number of times to get Mr. Doud straightened out on the dog's name, and finally just gave up.

When we moved to Seattle the decision was that Yorick would have to find a new home - that he was just too active a dog to be cooped up. So we gave him to Phyllis Ellis, who did not have a dog. Both Yorick and Phyllis were very happy with the new arrangement. Each year Yorick remembered us and romped with us just like he did when he lived with us.

While in Tacoma I made my first efforts at the game of golf. Didn't have any formal lessons and just had a set of pick-up clubs, but had a lot of fun. The real question now is whether I am doing any better now after quite a few lessons and rounds of golf than I did with my limited instruction in Tacoma. Oliver Larson and I played together a number of times. I also played at times with Cliff Ramstad, our next door neighbor in Tacoma. The most frustrating single event I recall in golf in Tacoma was playing a course not too far from home. There was a deep water hazard, where golfers had to drive across this fairly deep ravine

- perhaps fifty feet deep. There was a stream at the bottom. Some of us simply couldn't sometimes drive the ball across. When a ball settled in at the bottom, often I guess in the stream, it was only a few minutes until a young boy would show up with my ball and offer it to me for something like fifty cents, which was about what the ball cost new. Pay I did and the boys were always cheerful about selling the ball!!

We developed a lot of good friends in Tacoma and before long we were having dinner parties. I recall Bob and Rusty Sherwin always being a part of the dinner party. Then at times, there would be Gordon and Modean Hill, good friends whom we knew from Church; John and Sarah Judy whom I've mentioned before; Bill Merrill and his wife; Bob and Marry Jacobson (he was a City planner; they and their three children were close in age to ours. Rusty was an excellent cook so the food there was always superb.

I recall especially a couple of events at Sherwin's. One time when there were a whole group of guests I got to talking to Al Hooker. Rusty had made a wonderful fondue. Al and I stood in front of the bowl, helping ourselves frequently, and always referring to the dish as poi, much to Rusty's consternation.

Then there was the particular time that we did singing after the dinner. We often did this at Sherwin's. On the occasion I remember all the guests were around with their songbooks, with numbers being selected at random. At one point we got on to Civil War songs, and one time turned to the song "There will be one vacant chair." It was the sorrowful tune about how the family and friends were missing their lost family member. I recall distinctly there were four verses. After the first verse one woman whom we had not met before suggested we go on to another number. But another one of the guests whom we had not met before and I said no we wanted to continue the number. He and I were quite insistent. At the end of each verse there was the plaintive wish for changing the number, but we pushed through all four verses. Only later did Rusty inform me that the woman who wanted the song changed had lost her husband, who was in the military only a month earlier. I recall feeling very badly but the damage was done.

Shortly after we moved to Tacoma we were invited to join the Tacoma Tennis Club. Even thought neither Lois nor I played tennis, we joined because of the social program at the Tennis Club. I recall meeting quite a number of real nice people at the Club. Don't recall any long term close friendships that originated from the Club, but we were always glad that we had joined.

Then as I mentioned earlier we belonged during the latter years in Tacoma at Mason Methodist Church. It was only three or four blocks from where we lived. While we often walked to and from I think we generally drove. I do recall walking home from Church with Richard during the summertime. Quite a number of our friends went there also, and some of them were others who had belonged to First Methodist but changed to Mason.

Not too long after Deming's moved to Browns Point, Jack bought a boat. It was not a big boat - perhaps a 12 to 14-foot open boat. Deming's had a pier, or dock, sort of, where Jack could tie up the boat. He and I fairly often went out in the boat. We wandered around the outer area of the Commencement Bay, and even across the Sound over toward Vashon Island. We did have a little fishing tackle. I think Jack and I were pretty well matched on our fishing skills, so we didn't really catch a lot of fish. I do recall that once I hooked and landed a ling cod. I think it was about a ten pound fish, probably one of the biggest fishes I ever caught. But with the waste in that specie of fish there was not a whole lot of eating. Jack and I thoroughly enjoyed our trips out in the boat.

Mentioning fish reminds of a fishing event I participated in while in Tacoma. The Grays Harbor County Bar Association had, maybe still has, an annual fishing derby. As is often the case, attorneys from all over the state are invited but those attending are primarily from Grays Harbor. I don't recall how I happened to go, but it must have been with some other attorney(s) from Tacoma. In any event, I remember outbound crossing the bar, feeling very good about the whole thing. We had full stomachs because they had had a big breakfast with pancakes, bacon and sausage, eggs, coffee and tea, toast, etc.

Once we crossed the bar the skipper cut the engine so we could just drift and fish. Before long I experienced the worst bout of seasickness I have ever had. (I generally don't experience sea sickness. As a matter of fact I can't recall any other time I have gotten sick. But anyway this time I was really sick. I was so sick that I just leaned my hook against a sort of holder on the side of the boat, with my line over the side. I recall that fishing was not too great. I watched two Superior Court judges, one of whom was Lloyd Shorett, skillfully move their lines about, only to come up empty handed for their day's efforts. On the other hand, two hapless salmon hooked themselves on my line while I was just sitting there being sick. I did have the energy to get up and land my fish and went home with a lot more fish than most others on the trip. I must say, though that I never repeated the fishing experience with the Grays Harbor Bar Association.

Richard grew rapidly and we were ever so happy he was with us. He was so large and big that, perhaps because of it, did not walk as soon as he might have. In any event he spent a lot of time crawling but didn't actually getting around to walking until he was perhaps fifteen months old. But when he did get walking he was here and there, everywhere.

Kirk's Arrival

Well before Richard was walking we knew that we wanted to add to our family. I definitely did not want a one child family. And Lois was most adamant on that point. She had been an only child and grew up wishing so much for a sister or brother. And so we set about seeing if we could make it happen. And we did.

And so it was another trip back to Jack Deming. This pregnancy went well and uneventfully. I recall very clearly the difference in the time Lois entered the hospital after labor began. With Richard we checked in at the hospital in the middle of the night the day Richard was born. Labor began in the middle of the night with Kirk, but we headed for the hospital about 6 or 7 a.m. Mrs. Doud very kindly came over and stayed with Richard.

I did goof a bit on keeping track of Lois' progress. I figured Kirk would not arrive until late afternoon. So I went in to the office. Went out to lunch and then went for a haircut. While I was waiting for the barber he said I had a call from someone who said that my wife had given birth. So - rushed out and went to the hospital. By this time I had been to the hospital enough times with Jack Deming that I just wandered back to the delivery area. Just about as I got there a nurse cam out and in a horrified voice told me I couldn't go back there because I wasn't sterile. I calmly told her I knew I wasn't sterile because I had just sired a son. My recollection is that she did not see any humor in my response.

As requested, I called Mom's parents as soon as Kirk was born. They were excited to have another grandson. They couldn't figure out where we got the name Bradford for Kirk. I explained that it came out of a book of names and Lois and I both liked it and hoped that Kirk did, too. They also said, "we'll be coming out this summer". I was very glad they would be coming out. But I told Lois that she had to make clear to her parents that we were not going to provide a new incentive every two years for them to make a trip to Tacoma!!

When Kirk got home from the hospital we were all very excited to have a new family member. There was not nearly as much stress as there had been with Richard's arrival. Kirk was a real joy and quickly fit in to our family life. Our pediatrician in Tacoma was George Tanbara. A very good pediatrician, we always felt. He was a bit conservative, however in some of his ways. Along about mid June, I think, Lois asked if it would be ok if we took Kirk with us on a camping trip for the 4th of July. (George insisted that we be very conservative in care during the first three months, and Kirk would be 3 months old on the 3rd of July. George said, "you mean like rent space in a motel somewhere. Lois said "no, camp like in a tent". George was very reluctant to approve the idea. But camping we did. It was car camping on the Olympic peninsula. Kirk did just wonderfully. As a matter of fact the out of doors made him ravenously hungry and I had to drive several miles into a small town and buy more formula - he had gone through all we had for a three day weekend after about a day and a half!!.

And that camping experience was the first of many. Kirk was an early walker. He started walking when he was about 10 ½ months old and he was a whirlwind after that. Anyway, by the time Kirk was little over a year old we had a tent and started car camping. One of our favorite places to go was Millersylvania State Park, about ten miles south of Olympia. The boys and I thoroughly enjoyed camping, although real camping with backpacking is much better. Mom never took to the camping routine with any enthusiasm. She didn't like sleeping in a sleeping bag in a tent. But more than that, she hated the laundry after a camping trip. She said that all the clothes were dirty, smelled like smoke, etc. etc. But camping we did do for a while. Her camping ended not long after Gretchen was born, at which time we substituted backpacking in place of car camping. But I am getting ahead of myself.

We did take a trip to Pittsburgh the summer after Kirk was born. Naturally it was a chance to show off the boys. And I believe it was on this trip that Kirk was baptized. He got a double blessing with both Grandpa Hartung and Dr. Kinseley officiating. (Dr. Kinseley was the pastor at Mt. Zion Evangelical Lutheran Church.) (At the time I write this I am a bit uncertain when Richard was baptized. I think he, too was baptized by Grandpa Hartung but the details as to the exact time escape me at the moment.

Politics

In about 1959 there was an election of school directors for Tacoma. I had some concerns with the way the schools were being operated. A big concern of mine was what I perceived there was too much emphasis on shop type things, dancing, crafts, etc. rather than the fundamentals of reading writing and arithmetic. Jack Deming shared my concern. I think it was he who suggested that we each file for one of the two positions on the school board. Sounded like a good idea to me, so without really having a good understanding of the work that would be involved I said fine. And Jack and I each filed for one of the positions.

The difference between my filing and Jack's filing was that I committed myself to trying to win the position and Jack did it more or less symbolically. Four persons filed for the position for which I filed. The incumbent was Fred Haley, of Brown and Haley Candy Company. (I don't recall the other two.)

Fred Haley is an autocratic person and I don't think he regarded me as more than dust under his feet. Early on in the game I was invited to speak to the teachers association. I waded into that meeting without really understanding the politics of the teachers. I spoke to the teachers and expressed my concern with the curriculum, which I felt was not strong enough on what I felt were the fundamentals. I hoped that I could receive an endorsement from the teachers association. I thought I might have some chance of obtaining that endorsement because Mom was a very active member of the AAUW (American Association of University Women). They turned me down cold.

The primary election came along fairly early on in the political season. I barely stayed alive. Fred Haley received something like 48% of the vote in the primary and the rest of the votes were split among the other three. I think I got something like 24% of the vote.

Undaunted, I proceeded full tilt into the campaign. I ran a series of ads in the Tacoma News Tribune. I had checked the minutes of the School Board and found out that Fred Haley had not attended several of the budget meetings of the Board. So one of my advertisements, which were double column and about 4 to 6 inches of type was captioned "SCHOOLS CLOSED". The thrust of the article was that if all the Board Members attendance had been as poor as my opponent the schools would be closed because there wouldn't be any operating funds. The day after that Rex Coudebush, a good older attorney in Tacoma, an attorney whom I liked and respected and whom I knew to be an active Democrat stopped me on the street to discuss the article. He said he knew Fred well and was shocked by Fred's poor attendance record. Rex said he would vote for me. A boost to me my feelings. I ran perhaps half a dozen articles. I also got a number of attorneys in Tacoma to send out postcards announcing their support for me.

During the campaign I did accept an invitation to speak to what turned out to be a small group of voters at a private residence. I learned from the event. Not just because they basically were rather hostile toward me. But rather I learned that with my limited amount of time I couldn't address or meet any group unless I had a large group.

I did have one event during the campaign which Norm and Alice Mattern kidded me about mercilessly. I appeared in a TV program sponsored by a local coffee company. I took a cup of coffee even though I never drink the stuff. If that wasn't bad enough, during the meeting I felt Fred was getting too much attention, so I stood up, and I think partially blocked the image of Fred. I said I wasn't too much of a coffee drinker but this coffee was so good that I would have to get a second cup of coffee, whereupon I went over to the coffee pot and poured myself another cup. Well - Alice and Norm never let me forget about that. I 'm not sure they would serve me tea next time we went there.

Well, the campaign rocked along. My law practice was largely on hold for the few weeks of the campaign. And then came the election. After the polls closed I went up to the courthouse where the results were being posted. As I walked along the corridors I went past the open door of one of reporters whom I knew and whose support I had sought. The reporter was on the radio but he called out "George, come in here." Then he announced over the air that I had asked for his support, that he felt in his position he couldn't take a position. He said further that that he had wished me well, but that I didn't have a chance against Fred Haley. And then the reporter said, but look, George is running the closest race on the whole ballot.

Well, I ended up getting 49.4% of the vote. One vote switch per precinct and I would have been elected!! I called Fred Haley to congratulate him. Got nothing more than a frosty thanks. It was an interesting experienced and I learned a lot from it. But it is the only public elective office for which I ever filed. I learned later, after the election, that Fred was leaving a couple weeks after the election for a trip to Russia. I wished I had known that. Given the feelings at the time about Communists, I think if I had known that and made it public I might have picked up enough additional votes to win.

There is an addendum many years later to the Fred Haley storey. Fred served on the School Board for many years. When he retired, perhaps ten or fifteen years ago, he criticized the then curriculum of the Tacoma schools. His criticisms sounded much like my position in the election many years ago.

Backpacking

In the summer of 1960 some of us began the backpacking tradition of our family. Richard and I, Bob Sherwin and son Bob, Bob Jacobson and daughter Mia backpacked into Klapatchie Park on the slopes of Mount Rainer. It was a magnificent trip. The weather was clear, sunny and warm. It was abut three miles each way, and had about an 1,800 foot elevation gain. By today's standards the area was very uncrowded.

I think there was not more than other party. I can still remember it was a moonlit night. I can remember being kept awake from the sound of hoofs of deer racing back and fort across the meadow.

There is a small pond at the Park. Bob, Mia and Richard found a log in the pond and treated it as a boat. A seasonal ranger, I think somebody from like Chicago, told us that we really violated park rules by treating the log as a boat and thereby boating at the park, which was against the rules. We ignored him and just enjoyed the time

This backpacking trip was the first of many, of course over the years. But it was wonderful and I think made a very favorable long term impression on the young ones on our trip.

We did have one tragedy in the summer of 1960 - my Mother died. She had not enjoyed robust health at any time. She had sinus infections, a couple of surgeries and generally was not well. And she did not eat well. Even at that time I didn't think much of her favorite lunch - bacon and Velveeta cheese sandwiches.

Sometime in the late 1950's she went under the care of a cardiologist. I remember Mother telling me that her doctor said she had the heart of a high school girl - something I just couldn't buy off on. In any event she suffered a major heart attack and did not survive. Unfortunately, at that very time Dad was in the hospital for some prostate surgery.

The four of us took a red eye special to Pittsburgh. We arrived to find out that Dad was not aware of Mother's death, my brother was very, very upset and the doctor was asking who was going to let Dad know of Mother's passing. So I was elected. The doctor was in the room at the time and told me later that he thought I had done a marvelous job in letting Dad know. But it was a loss to all of us.

I don't think at the time that I appreciated fully the impact on Dad of Mother's passing. He did manage to cope surprisingly well, however. Dad never did remarry and as far as I know never developed any romantic relationship with any other woman. Dad lived until 1974 and I thought then and have always been sorry that Dad didn't make an effort to find some woman with whom he could share his life.

Consideration of a change in area of practice

After three or four years in Tacoma I began to wonder whether I really wanted to spend the rest of my days practicing law in Tacoma. The residential areas of the city were and are delightful. The downtown was another story. The downtown was getting pretty dowdy, she smell from St. Regis Paper Company permeated the town regularly and I didn't think the City was as vibrant as Seattle. I began to wonder whether we should make the move to Seattle. But that thought just sort of perked with me for quite some time. I was so busy that I had little time to think about it. Also, we had made a lot of good friends during the time. The practice was going well, I was generating some clients and was more and more, I felt, ingratiating myself with the clients to the point they were thinking of me as their attorney. At one point I spoke to Warren Peterson, another attorney in Tacoma, about breaking away and starting our own firm. Warren's income was so much more than mine (I really became impressed with how underpaid I was in Tacoma and how much the more senior partners were taking advantage of me.) There was also the question of how we would survive during the first year or so. We didn't have that much financial reserve etc. etc. So nothing came of that. Warren was a wonderful attorney and good friend and I'm confidant we would have made a success of it. Unfortunately, Warren died within about a ten years from cancer and so we couldn't have had that much time to practice together.

My thinking of where to practice was spurred by an event that occurred somewhere in the 1958 to 1959 area.

In the course of representing the Puget Sound National Bank I handled the Easterday Trust case. This was a case in which the beneficiary of a trust created by Mr. Easterday, a deceased former attorney who practiced law in Tacoma, ceased to exist. The heirs of Mr. Easterday felt that the trust should be terminated and they should receive the assets in the trust—a trust set up to provide benefits to unmarried mothers. The Bank felt, based on my advice was that the trust should be continued for the benefit of an organization(s) provided similar benefits. This would require the application of the doctrine of Cy Pres, which provides for such a treatment where the charitable organization beneficiary has ceased to exist. At the time there was no authority in Washington for the application of the doctrine. I brought the case, tried it successfully for the Bank before Frank Hale, in the Superior Court for Pierce County. The heirs appealed. The Supreme Court affirmed the lower court, applied the doctrine of Cy Pres and held that the trust would be administered for the benefit of three organizations doing business in Tacoma.

The heirs were represented by Bob Comfort, a Tacoma attorney I knew well, and by Cameron (Cam) Sherwood of Walla Walla.

While the case was still on appeal Cam called me, complimented me on the quality of the work I had done on the case, and said that he would very much like it if I would join him in the practice at his offices in Walla Walla. The offer was attractive enough that I felt Lois and I should go to Walla Walla and check it out. Gene and Leone Weber, my cousins in Walla Walla were very excited about the prospect of our moving to Walla Walla.

We had a very nice weekend visiting in Walla Walla and discussing with Cam the nature of his proposal for practice. At the time he had one associate practicing with him, so it was a small firm. Lois and I thought seriously about it. I finally called Cam and said that I would accept his offer.

I had some nagging concern about the idea of moving to Walla Walla. It is a lovely town. Whitman College is located there which was a real plus. But as I thought more about it I reflected upon the fact that I had been drawn to the Northwest by the Mountains, Puget Sound, and similar things. The more I thought about it, Walla Walla is more like a typical Midwestern town. So within a couple of weeks I called Cam and told him that I appreciated very much his offer but that because of what had drawn us to the Northwest, I just could not accept his offer. Cam was very gracious about it and we remained friends for the rest of his life.

Train Travel

After Richard was born we began to give some thought to getting back to Pittsburgh for a visit. We hadn't been back since we left in the fall of 1957. We gave thought to train travel. This was before the time of jets and travel by train seemed like a feasible plan.

In the summer of 1957 we took our first trip back to Pittsburgh. We rode the Milwaukee Road which at the time had service originating in Tacoma. Richard was about a year and a half old and was walking. I think that we rented a sleeper. I recall going up with Richard in to the dome car. He managed to stay awake for a while, but then the motion of the train put him fast asleep. We had a good visit with my parents. My mother's health was getting worse and she especially was so glad to see us. And of course, we took the opportunity to visit all the relatives. I think it was on this trip that my Dad baptized Richard. Actually, he had two ministers baptizing him. He was baptized at the Lutheran Church with Dr. Kinseley and my Dad officiating. (Or as Richard said, "rapitized".)

We made another train trip to Pittsburgh after Kirk was born and before my Mother died. I'm not positive, but I think it must have been in 1959. It would have been on the Milwaukee Road, again. I recall that on this trip we went out to the Wohlgemuth's. I'm not sure if either Uncle Louis or Aunt Lydia Wohlgemuth were still living, but at least cousin Alma was still going strong. I recall that on this trip my cousin Everett and his family were there. I recall also that Everett's first wife Virginia was just starting to come down with MS. It turned out to be a long illness for her. In the course of the illness their children really managed the house.

It was on this trip that Richard made a prescient comment and my Mother made an unforgettable response. We were having lunch in the dining room at the duplex on Martsolf Avenue. My brother was there at the time. All of a sudden son Richard asked if Uncle Dick had any boys and girls. There wasn't time for anybody take a breath before Mom said "not that we know of." My Mother was totally flustered, my Dad stuttered thinking of something to stay, and Mom and I laughed and had a story to tell for the rest of our lives!!

By the summer of 1960 I decided that train travel was going downhill and that we should rally take a trip to savor the trains of the period and also to travel while Richard and Kirk would not be charged a fare. So we decided to take the Shasta Daylight to San Francisco, then the Coast Daylight from San Francisco to Los Angeles. (Our good friends, Don and Gen Fisher drove us to Portland to get the train for San Francisco. Then we took an overnight train from Los Angeles to Phoenix (we had a day of sightseeing in San Francisco and then part of a day on Los Angeles to see some of the old Spanish section.

In Phoenix we had a very nice visit for a few days with our good friends Hilda and Harvey Streich. I recall we were there on at least part of a weekend because Harvey was able to drive and show the area. Then we rented a car for a trip up to the Hopi Indian reservation. I recall we rented the car at Sky Harbor, the Phoenix airport which at the time was a very modest size airport. I had been checking on the prices of cares and had decided on a compact car. At the car rental agency desk the woman asked me where we intended to go. We told her up through the Hopi Indian country and then on up to Utah to get the train back. I guess she had some concerns about the reliability of the car, concern about a family with young children getting stuck. But in any event she offered a larger car at the same price and took it.

The trip through the Hopi country was truly memorable. Then we wound our way up north and picked up the train in Idaho where the transcontinental rail line had been completed many years earlier. It was truly a memorable trip. We all saw a part of the country which we had not really had a tri to visit before, except for my slight contact with a part of it when I drove a car across the country.

Partnership

By 1959 Ed Eisenhower was taking off two days per week, still taking the lion's share of the partnership net income, and still saying continually that a he was working so very hard. By this time there generally were just the five of us in the firm - Ed, Chuck, Jim, Mert and me. By this time Wendell Duncan had passed away. We had two younger associates during the late 1950's and 1960. None of them stayed very long. Larry Ghilarducci, who was a great guy and from a long time Tacoma family, Ed Lowry, and perhaps another one whose name I do not recall. Neither or none of them, including Bob Hamilton, ever really discussed with me their reasons for leaving. I learned also that not too long before I came with the firm Ed's nephew had been with the firm. Seems he did not get along with his uncle. Seems that one night the nephew came in to the office, wrote a letter to Ed telling him his feeling for his uncle (not good), packed up his office things and left town without ever saying good bye to his uncle.

During 1959 I continued to be extremely busy. My relationship with most of the good commercial clients continued to get closer. As we got toward the end of 1959 there was a partnership meeting at which Mert and I were offered partnerships in the firm. Mert and I were each offered a ten per cent interest in the firm. That seemed like a fairly stingy amount, especially considering the contribution Mert and I were making toward the business. Ed told us though that it was his intention at the end of 1960 to take ten percent of the partnership income going to him and share it between Mert and me. No statement as to how that ten per cent would be split. Mert and I reviewed the financials for the firm and decided to accept the offer. I was not aware at that time of how the remaining eighty percent was split among Ed, Chuck and Jim. By hindsight I should perhaps have asked. I learned later that Ed received 40% and Chuck and Jim each received 20%. I learned later, also, that Chuck and Jim had each been receiving 30% but that when Mert and I became partners they were each reduced to 20% and Ed continued to receive 40%.

Little changed in the way the firm operated after Mert and I became partners. Ed still regarded the place as his personal fiefdom. I didn't realize that as much as I did later. I did become aware, though, that I was not being very well compensated given my years in practice, the nature of the work I was handling, and the relationship I was enjoying with the clients. My feelings intensified, though, as the year progressed, that I would like to consider a move to Seattle.

It became fairly easy for me to keep to myself my efforts to relocate. By 1960, for example, I was handling an appeal to the Tax Court of a determination by the appellate staff of the internal revenue service adverse to a good furniture company we represented. I was also handling a major tax case involving issues of the status of several companies in the co-op business - I think the issue revolved on the issue of whether the members were employees or had a similar status. I handled the major work on this case until it came time to meet with the IRS and the client group, when Ed took over the negotiation even though he was not that well informed on the facts.

I experienced a similar Ed takeover of another matter which involved the acquisition by an Illinois company of Washington Steel, Inc. I handled all the work on the local level, then went back to Chicago to negotiate the final terms at the corporate headquarters of the acquiring company. But when it came to the shareholders meeting Ed attended the meeting as attorney and did not include me in the meeting. My good friend Gordon Hill, who was a shareholder in Washington Steel, told me that at the shareholders meeting Ed stumbled around, couldn't answer questions of shareholders about matters with which I was very familiar. I can't now recall my express feelings about these matters, but I think I probably was a bit frustrated.

By 1960 I could go to Seattle to do work on client matters, but then simply take time to interview with Seattle law firms. I had become acquainted with senior partners in several of Seattle's fine firms so I had fairly easy access to the firms. I spent a fair amount of time talking to firms during the years. The whole hiring process was much different than it is today. Today firms of any size have hiring partners, the desire of the firms to consider hiring is better known, the contact is maintained at the firm level rather than with an individual partner, etc. I recall receiving a firm offer from what was then about a five attorney firm, but which today is abut a 100 attorney firm - now goes under the name of Lane Powell. The offer was to serve as a litigation attorney on insurance defense claims. I was not interested and so turned down the offer. Then through a Michigan alumnus, a practicing attorney in Seattle, I learned that LeSourd and Patten might be in a hiring mode.

I called for an interview, spoke to Fran LeSourd and had a very good meeting. Either at that first meeting or the second meeting I met Woolvin Patten. I was very favorably impressed with them and it appears that their regard for me was also good. The attorneys in LeSourd & Patten had been part of Little LeSourd Palmer Scott & Slemmons. They broke away in the early part of 1960. Brock Adams was also a partner of L&P. Max Crittenden and Stan Allper were associates. I learned later that one of Tacoma's fine firms had inquired of me from a partner in that firm and received a very favorable recommendation. I knew that things probably were proceeding well for me with L&P when there was an event at the Eisenhower firm which made my decision easier.

In early December 1960we had a partnership meeting. At the meeting Mert Elliott asked Ed how the 10% which Ed had discussed a year earlier—the ten percent which would be divided between Mert Elliott and me would be divided between Mert and me. Ed responded that business had not been too good during the year and there would not be anything more coming to either Mert or me. That response told me a great deal about the dark side of Ed. I was so angry that I nearly stood up and walked out of the meeting. By hindsight perhaps I should have done that, but I didn't. But in any event, doubt as to which way to go was resolved. I would accept the offer of LeSourd & Patten.

Subsequent to my departure I engaged Vern Pearson, a very good attorney in Tacoma and a very good friend of mine to represent me in a claim against either Ed or the firm. Vern interviewed both Chuck and Jim to tie down Ed's statements. They both denied that there had been any firm offer of any specific amount. Vern told me that with no support from Chuck or Jim, he didn't think there was enough chance of prevailing to bring the suit. He also said, "you know, George, that as far as Ed is concerned the wrong guy had left the firm." I was told later that a few months after I left that the Puget Sound Bank was so dissatisfied with the quality of the work it was receiving that it told Ed either he would have to work out a merger or get someone else to take my place or the Bank would have to leave. I don't know whether that really occurred, but I do know that within six months the firm did work out a merger with Carlson, Newlands Reha and Sinnitt. Whatever the situation, there was a change made at the Eisenhower firm.

Our friends were rather shocked that we were leaving the law firm and even more that we were moving to Seattle. And of course, it was a hard decision to make. In the six and a half ears we had lived in Tacoma we had made a great many friends, had become involved in a number of organizations, and made our life in Tacoma our life. But I thought that I was making a correct decision and that it was time to move along.

The law firm was rather docked about my departure. From comments made to me by Cluck Hunter and Jim Ramsdell, I think that they felt Ed had pushed things too far. And I think that Ed was sorry for my departure.

18

Seattle - 1961-1963

Locating in Seattle

Since my decision to leave Tacoma and the Eisenhower firm was made late in December, 1960, and since I had announced that I would be leaving at the end of January, 1961, we had to move promptly with the many things which we needed to do before we moved to Seattle. Perhaps the number one priority item was to find a place to live in Seattle. Certainly I did not want to engage in a daily commute - or at least do so for any extended period of time.

We knew that we would want to live in the north end of Seattle, but beyond that we really did not have a clue. Somehow, however, and I don't now recall any of the details, we went to Loyal Realty on 24th Ave NW near 85th street. We spoke to a woman whose name I do not now recall. I think she may have made a couple of suggestions about places to rent. I do recall that one place she mentioned as being for rental was located on a street which ended at the south end of Evergreen Washelli. It seemed to us that it would be a quiet neighborhood, but perhaps a bit quieter than we had in mind. There may have been one or two other ideas she came up with, but in a short period of time she mentioned that there would be a place for rent on Bayard Street in Blue Ridge. Blue Ridge meant nothing to us, but we decided to take a look.

The Blue Ridge house she mentioned was owned by the Santelman's. Mr. Santelman worked and lived much of the time in California. The Santelman's had one daughter as I recall. Anyway, the real estate woman did not go with us for the house inspection. So Lois, Richard and Kirk and I showed up at the door. The woman looked at us and said "oh, you have two boys", in a tone that made clear she was not happy about Richard and Kirk. Mrs. Santelman's comment immediately alienated Mom from the woman. We looked at the house and decided it would work out well, and signed a one year lease. So, step one was taken care of, but then came the questions of what to do about our home at 4601 N 26th Street.

As I think I have noted earlier, we purchased our house in Tacoma with GI bill financing - 20 year financing with a 4% interest rate on the mortgage. We decided that we did not want to take a loss on the sale, but on the other hand we did not want to be saddled on a house in Tacoma while we lived in Seattle.

So we listed the house at a figure close to our purchase price. Either the first or second weekend after we put the house on the market we sold it. It was possible to sell with an assumption by purchaser of the mortgage indebtedness which gave an attractive deal to any purchaser. The purchasers accepted our proposal and the paperwork was put together, which provided for a closing on the transaction in the early part of February. So, the second high priority item was taken care of.

Then, of course was the question of how much "stuff" we would move with us and how we would get that to Seattle. There wasn't much doubt that we would take with us virtually everything we owned at that point in time. I think the Santelman house was vacant at that time, or would be by the end of January, so it was possible to move in by stages. I think the Mattern's helped us move a number of things. I think Norm and I made a few round trips moving smaller things. Then we engaged a moving company to move the rest of our things to Seattle. It all really worked rather smoothly.

Very shortly after I accepted the offer of employment, Fran LeSourd and Woolvin Patten and their wives scheduled a party at Patten's house so that we could all meet. At that time, the law firm consisted of Fran LeSourd, Woolvin Patten, Brock Adams, Max Crittenden, and Stan Alper. I don't think that Max or Stan were invited to the party, but we did meet Burgess LeSourd, Katherine Patten, and Betty Adams and a couple of the secretaries. It was Lois' first meeting with any of the firm and/or spouses. She was most favorably impressed - and so was I. Patten's at that time owned a grand old mansion on Capital hill - three stories built in the early part of the century. Complete with hitching post on the curb line at the front of the house.

As it turned out, I did have a couple of weeks of daily commuting, before closing on the house sale. The commuting was a bit of a drag and I was glad it did not last for too long. The commuting trip home was interesting. A client, I think, of the LeSourd firm commuted and he offered me a ride home - on his boat. The boat trip was a bit scary because of the high speed in the dark at which he drove the boat.

A Couple of Memorable Cases

It felt very strange going in to the office. It was a whole different environment. And at least at the beginning I was concerned because I wasn't that busy. But that soon changed. Fran put me to work on matters for an insurance company of which Duke Frisbie was president and Carl Meitzen was either Vice President or Treasurer. Then, very quickly, Brock Adams got me involved in the case for Miles Construction. It was an appeal from a default termination by the AEC and alleged default by contractor on a contract for a nuclear reactor exhaust decontamination facility. I had handled one case before a federal contract appeals board on a tax case for a furniture company we represented in Tacoma. But this was a whole different case. Jurisdiction of the case was before the Atomic Entergy Commission Board of Contract Appeals.

Dick Miles was president and owner of the firm. When the government defaulted him on the contract, Dick was basically out of work and close to broke. The suit had destroyed his bonding capacity.

The Miles Construction case proved to be quite interesting. Dick told me that there just wasn't any way he could provide the government the airtight facility called for in the specs. We took the position that the specs were impossible of achievement, which under government contract law constitutes a change. The problem of course was to prove the impossibility. I contacted my fairly longtime friend, the older of the two Anderson brothers who had developed Concrete Technology in Tacoma (Concrete Technology was a pioneer in the reinforced concrete field and had been delivering large amounts of concretes bars used in the construction of the I5. The Anderson brother I contacted (I don't remember his first name at this time) was a very bright fellow, PhD from I think M.I.T, etc.

He studied the specs and in a fairly shot time came up with his answer. The specs provided for a seamless air tight bonding of steel or aluminum and concrete. He very soon gave me a learning period and explained to me that the coefficient and rate of expansion varied between concrete and steel or aluminum. Especially since the construction was in eastern Washington, with great and rapid daily changes in ambient temperatures, there was no way the two products, steel and concrete would provide an airtight joint unless there was a flexible bonding agent between the two members.

The case was large enough and complex enough that it took a lot of exhibits and documents to put the case together. But put it together we did. Brock had been the one leading the case for some time, but I quickly became very much up to speed. The case was set for hearing in Richland in about June or July of 1961 I had intended to be working the case with Brock, with him being the lead attorney. The case was intended to take several days, and indeed did take a week and a half to try. After the noon recess the first day of the trial Brock explained to me that he had a schedule change. At the time, Kennedy had just been inaugurated. Brock was very active in politics. Bobby Kennedy told Brock over the noon hour the first day of the trial that he, Brock, had to come back to Washington D.C. right away in connection with his intended appointment as U.S. attorney for Western Washington. So, Brock said "George you are going to have to try this case." Bingo, surprise. And so I did.

After the trial we had to submit briefs and then want back to Washington D.C. for closing argument. By the spring of 1962 the hearing examiner of the AEC Contract Appeals Board rendered his decision. He found that indeed the specs were impossible of achievement, there was a change in the specs, and he ruled in favor of Miles.

Then there was the mater of calculating damages. I think that perhaps we didn't go back to Washington D.C. until the damages issue was before the court. In any event by 1962 Miles was awarded about $800,000 in damages. Dick Miles was suddenly solvent, we had a big fee (the case had been taken on I think a 10% contingent fee and we had about an $80,000 fee which was one of the largest fees we had seen for a long time.

While the case was still working its way through the court system on the damages issue, I had a call from the bonding attorney for Safeco telling me he wanted to refer a case to me which he thought I knew something about.

All during the Miles case the government had been talking about the witness they were going to produce - a witness who had put together successfully an airtight nuclear reactor exhaust decontamination facility with specs identical to those for Miles. The Government never put on this witness. Well, the witness the bonding company provided me was another contractor, who also had a problem. Here was the no show witness the government had been talking about!! I handled that case also, although we didn't have to go to trial.

I ended up doing a fair amount of construction law work which I enjoyed very much. A problem I had, though, in really developing this specialty was that I didn't have any backup attorney etc. So the specialty never really went too far.

(The Meeks Crystal Mt. case follows later. I had initially intended it to be one of two cases to describe.)

But, back now to life in Seattle. Richard was now in first grade at Crown Hill School. Kirk was at some point that year, I think, in preschool. Seattle did not at the time have a kindergarten program. Richard's teacher was Mary Peterson. She and her husband belonged to Trinity Methodist Church and also lived in Blue Ridge.

Buying our house

Shortly after we moved to Seattle we decided to start looking for a place to buy. We didn't want to be pushed at the end of the one year lease. So, we started out looking at different areas of the city. We considered Blue Ridge, looked in Laurelhurst, etc. In all, I think we must have looked at places in perhaps half a dozen sections of the city. We met more squirrelly real estate women and learned a lot about different areas of Seattle. We did find one real estate woman with whom we could relate and who made sense to us. He name was Kay Sainden.

After several months, and probably in mid or late summer of 1962 she stopped by our place and said she thought there might be a place we would like. Turns out the house was not then on the market, but had been. The people who owned it had changed their mind. Ms. Sainden said she thought they might change their minds again. Lois was surprised and shocked when Kay. Sainden saw no problem in contacting the people to see if they would like to reconsider. Well they did, and lo and behold it was the house we bought.

We knew immediately when we looked at the house that this would be our dream house if we could put it together. I said that I didn't want to put down more than 20%, wanted interest at not more than 6% and wanted to have 20 year financing. Well the negotiation went on for a bit of time. There was a big of haggling over the price. But ultimately, we bought the house for about $32,000.00!! By today's standards, that is substantially less than the down payment for the house.

We arranged the closing so that we would move in to our new house in January of 1962. It was and is our dream house. Neither of us have ever had any thought of selling or moving. We have always felt fortunate to have been able to acquire the house.

The people who were going to rent the house on Bayard called us shortly before we moved and asked if they could get together to take a look at the house and see what they were leasing. We of course were delighted to do so. It turned out to Thorpe and Lucinda Kelly. Before the end of the first evening we knew we each enjoyed playing bridge. And this was a game we enjoyed for many years.

The move from Bayard to Valmay was yet another move. This was a much easier move from a distance standpoint.

We did engage a moving company to handle most of the moving. I can still remember sitting in the living room of our new house, on perhaps the day we moved in, looking at just how big the living room was, and thinking that I had never lived in any place like this and felt so fortunate to have the house.

Even though we were delighted with the house, there was work to be done. We were the third owner of the house. The first owners had owned the property from 1935 when the house was built, until 1955. They took very good care of the yard, I am sure.

Then there were two owners who held the property for just three years each. Why they ever bought the house I have never really understood. I don't know much about the first of the two although we did meet them a couple of times.

But the people from whom we bought - the whole thing is a mystery to me. She was an interior decorator, or sort of was one, and she lived to fix up the house on the inside and she did make a number of changes. Earl liked to work with tools, but I don't think he ever did much with the yard.

By the time we moved in the whole back hillside was filled with morning glory and blackberries. I spent almost all of the first summer clearing and weeding the hillside. It was a matter of going about a square yard an evening. I made certain that the two plants never again got place in our yard.

Very shortly after we moved into our house we met the Wacker's. They live on Mary Avenue., and attended Trinity Methodist Church. They were both Michigan State grads ant the two schools had a joint party the first year we were in Seattle. Anyway, Jerry provided us a lot of good advice on the yard. So I had a plan for re-landscaping much of the back yard and spent a whole lot of time doing that

Nineteen sixty two also brought a change at the law office. Dwayne Copple was hired. He and his wife Claire were both people we enjoyed very much and with whom we became good friends. Nineteen sixty two also brought another change in our lives - skiing. Fran had been a skier for many, many years. Also, he was one of the founders so Crystal Mt. which opened for skiing in 1961 or 1962.

I had a pair of skis when I was growing up - for a short time. Never had any lessons and never really learned how to ski. But I always dreamed about doing more with it. So Fran encouraged us to get on with our skiing. We bought a pair of skis, bindings, boots etc. We also signed up for beginner's lessons. I enjoyed learning how to ski. Lois was not as enthusiastic as I but she was a good sport and tried. Unfortunately, she did not enjoy it that much. One problem which she had, and which I had to a lesser extent was a great difficulty in letting her skis run. She just could not let her skis run. And was still doing snow plows, for example long after she should have moved beyond that.

A couple of years after we had been skiing, we took a week at Crystal Mountain with the Kelly's. Unfortunately, about the second day out, Mom turned her ankle and wasn't able to ski the rest of the week. This really dampened her enthusiasm for the sport and she never really did do too much after that on the ski front.

Early on in skiing, with Fran's help, I was able to buy a unit of Crystal stock. A unit was 20 shares. With the ownership of a unit, I got the discount ticket benefit. – one adult daytime ticket for 10% of regular ticket price for each share of stock owned. Ticket prices initially were between $5.00 and $7.00, depending on day of the week, etc. After a year or two I succeeded I purchasing another unit of stock. I paid more per share for the first unit than the second year. My average price, though, was I believe $1,500.00 per unit. With ticket priced now over $50, my return on the investment has been very good.

As soon as we moved in to Blue Ridge we checked in to see about getting some lessee Blue Ridge Club membership. We succeeded in joining within a month or two of moving in to Blue Ridge. At that time, and for many years thereafter, Blue Ridge had an active Social program. Part of the program included four dinner dance events each year - spring dinner dance, the summer barbeque, the fall dance and the New Year's evening party. We seldom missed any of the events. It was most enjoyable and a very good way to get to know a lot of the families in Blue Ridge.

Life in Seattle - The First Years

Promptly on moving to Seattle, we began attending and then very shortly thereafter joining Trinity Methodist Church. At the time it was a very active Church and Olin Parrot the minister was a great person. His wife Lou was also a live wire person, and organized a bell choir. I think Lois may have been in the bell choir, but am not sure.

On the legal front, 1962, or perhaps 1963, but I think 1962, brought the Ward Meeks Crystal Mountain litigation. Ward Meeks was an opportunist who tried to take advantage wherever he could by fair means or foul. In any event, the triggering event was a patented mining claim in the Crystal Mt. area. The whole area had been, and perhaps still is part of a federal mining area.

At one time, there was a lot of mining in the Crystal Mountain ski area. Nothing of much value was found as far as I know, but lots of people tried. Most of the claims were unpatented, but there was one patented mining claim. When Crystal Mt. was organized it went to the Attorney General of the State to have a long delinquent corporation dissolved. In the process, only one shareholder was found. As the only shareholder, he received all the assets of the corporation. The assets consisted on the one patented mining claim. While the dissolution process was in mind, Meeks courted the old miner, who was very elderly. Exactly what happened will never be known. What is known is that in some way there was ten thousand dollars in the dissolved corporation. I think most of it put in by Ward Meeks. In any event, when the smoke cleared, the miner got almost nothing but Ward Meeks was in control.

Ward took the position that with the patented inning claim he had a right of access. He proceeded to take vehicles across the Crystal Mt. ski area, when skiers were present, and when the snow pack was light, and generally cause a lot of problem to the corporation. So LeSourd & Patten was engaged to solve the problem and I was the one who brought the suit. I was new enough in the firm that I think Fran wanted to see how I performed in Court.

The case came on for trial before Bertel Johnson, a Superior Court judge of Pierce County before whom I had appeared many times. After the first morning Fran left, which I took to mean Fran felt I knew y way a round and knew enough about the case to handle it. I prevailed in the trial and an injunction was entered against Meeks. Meeks paid little attention to the court order and continued to violate the order. I was in court repeatedly or the matter. Ultimately the last time I was in court was on I think the third citation for contempt. Judge Johnson told Meeks that he didn't seem to understand the English language. But just to make sure, he told Meeks that if he ever violated the order in any way, he would be sent to jail. Meek heard this and the case came to an end. The case was the subject of discussion at home many many times over the two or three years that the case dragged on. It wasn't a very important case from a legal standing, but it was really a talking point

Several of the heirs of the old miner, who died shortly after Crystal got underway, called about suing Meeks. I had to tell all of them that dead men carry no tales. There simply was no evidence of what Meeks said to the miner.

Nineteen sixty two brought yet another change to the law office. Leon Misterek joined the firm. When they first moved to Seattle they lived fairly close - out about 10th street. So we saw a fair amount of them. Leon also helped with a few things around the house. We had a very large maple tree in the back yard when we first moved in. Within a year or so Jerry Wacker, a landscape architect who helped us with some planning told us that the tree was rotting. So we had to take it down. We had maple wood from it for several years. We also gave a lot of wood to Misterek's. Leon had a wedge and sledge and split a fair amount of the wood.

Sometime during the first year that Leon was with the firm we added another attorney, Joe McKinnon. Joe was then in his mid 40's and had done a lot of litigating. By this time both Max and Stan had left the firm.

The summer after Joe joined us would have been, I think, 1963. We had been doing some camping, etc and maybe a little backpacking. But I was anxious to do more. And so we did. Joe McKinnon was interested also. So we, and I think Joe Matsen and is son Jay, went on a pack trip into the Enchanted Valley, in the east fork of the Nisqually Valley, in Olympic National Park. It was about a twenty mile round rip. By that time, a young man by the name of Dempsey who lived over in the Olympic Peninsula had a burro rental agency. So we rented a burro for the trip. I bought a set of saddlebags, etc. I discovered that burros are very good animals to travel with. They walk at a human pace, are gentle kind animals and a joy to have with you. They can be a bit stubborn. And they will eat anything in sight. I think it was on the way out when we were having lunch that I learned more than I then knew about watching out for burros and food. While we were eating lunch I heard a crackling noise, looked around, and saw that the burro was devouring a two pound sack of prunes!! We were glad that we didn't have to clean out the trailer at the end of the trip! Anyway, I rented burros two or three times and enjoyed each of the trips with them.

Fire Engine

Mid 1962 was an eventful year. The City decided to auction off a number of overage fire engines. By that time we at the office had hired Ginger DeLeeow as bookkeeper. Her husband was Fell DeLeeow, whom I soon became acquainted with. Well, somehow I spoke to Fell DeLeeow and Carl Meitzen and we decided to try to buy a fire engine. The sale was being conducted at a firehouse near by. Imagine our surprise when for I think a few hundred dollars we were the successful bidders on a 1926 Seagrave Pumper. (Vintage year!!)

The fire engine was sold as is where is. It was also sold with all emergency equipment working - siren, flashing lights, etc. It was a big triple sparked engine. No enclosed cab. The brake and gear were all big things operated manually. Well, we had to move our purchase and it ended up at our house.

The plan was, among the three of us, that we would each have the fire engine at our house a part of the time. Didn't work out quite that way. First, Carl never kept it at his house. Somehow he got us involved in driving the fire engine at a 4th of July Parade in Bothell. I drove, wearing my Uncle Nick's old street car conductor's (was he a driver?) white shirt with black arm bands. It was a kick.

The fire engine tank held twenty five gallons. The engine got one mile per gallon. Fortunately for us, gasoline prices at that tie were very cheap.

Fell DeLeeow tried keeping the fire engine at his house in Madison Park. Unfortunately, after about a month a none-too-pleasant neighbor of his called and said it was unlawful to park that large vehicle in his driveway for a long period of time. So - the engine came back to my place which turned out to be its happy home.

The fire engine proved to be a boon to kids living in the neighborhood. When I turned the engine over, kids came out of houses like termites out of the wood work. They would all clamber in to the empty hoses bin and wait for the ride. The kids rang the bell, shouted, etc. etc. I immediately decided that I would have to have a dad on the back of the truck to be sure no kid tried to jump on or off while the vehicle was moving.

Kirk felt his place on the fire engine was in the seat beside me -

and that's where he always rode. Either he or others constantly rang the bell so I almost lost my hearing. In any event the fire engine was a real neighborhood attraction. Soon kids would call me Friday evening to find out if I would be going out the next day. When I said yes, he told me he would be there. And sure enough he would be there with a dozen friends. I drove all over Blue Ridge. Sometimes I used the emergency equipment, even though it was against the law. I figured that if anybody turned me in the kids would find out and trash that owners house the next night. In any event, I never had a problem that way.

Keeping the engine in the driveway proved to be a problem. In bad weather I put a plastic sheet over the cab part—but the wind would tend to blow it loose, etc. Lois said the engine was good for providing directions. If anybody wanted directions for someplace in the neighborhood, Lois would say she told them to first find the house where there was a nut who kept a fire engine in the driveway. From there on the directions were simple. It wasn't long until I realized that the red pigments in the paint of the engine did not like sun - fading set in. Then there was the problem of trying to keep antifreeze in the rig.

I think we kept the engine for about two years. Then it was time to move on. I donated the engine to a big PONCHO auction. I understood that the successful bidder was a rancher in eastern Washington who could use the rig out around the fields. Never did verify this.

For a few years after the rig ownership, I would receive mailings from the City about other auctions. I recall one evening coming home from work to find Richard and Kirk very excited. They had seen a mailing from the City and told me that we could bid on a hook and ladder truck. Well, that just wouldn't fly.

The memory of that rig was remembered for years. For perhaps twenty years I would be accosted by a young man asking if I wasn't the man who had the fire engine, etc. Even today some people remember the rig. And I did keep the big brass bell. It's in the basement now. And given the price of brass these days, the metal alone makes it worth something.

We always took vacations. In the early 60's I came up with the idea of driving one way and flying back the other. Since it was our car, I always opted to drive out. We did this two times. Once, and perhaps the first time, we did this with the DeLeeow's. They were from Niagara Falls. We drove east, stopped in Pittsburgh and then delivered the car in perhaps Buffalo. They parked their VW at the airport in Seattle and we used it while they were traveling.

The second time we did this was with Kay Church and a friend of hers. Kay was the office manager, secretary, etc. She was in her early 60's I think when she did this. They wanted to go to the Southwest, so we flew somewhere in the Southwest, and delivered the car there to them. Actually, I think this may have been the year when we went to the Grand Canyon and when I rode a mule down on to the Canyon. If this is the trip, it was the time when we went to Bryce and Zion parks. This far away in time I have trouble remember just which year we went where. I do know, though, that the day after Kay and her friend got back home, the car died and the battery was dead. I always would have had the car checked before going on a trip but just was never aware of the problem. Fortunately, they didn't get suck out in the boonies.

We have had lots of friends and acquaintances who would say that they didn't know how we could take these long trips. They said "the kids just can't travel that way." Their problem, we found out, was that they planned to lock the kids up in a car and drive all day long except for lunch breaks. We, on the other hand stopped everywhere every hour or so for county and city parks, had picnic lunches, etc. and travel that way was a pleasure for everyone.

At the end of 1962 I was very pleased when Fran and Pat extended an offer to become a partner in the firm. I decided that I must have been doing things to their satisfaction. And I was very happy with Pat and Fran. So, 1963 started out with a new setup.

Nineteen sixty two was the World's fair in Seattle. It was also one of the times when Lois' parents came out or a visit. This time they didn't tell us how long they planned to stay, but after two or three weeks her Dad said he's better get seat reservations for the train back to Seattle. Well, as might be expected, but couldn't get seats for another two or three weeks. Well, at this point I decided something would have to be done. For a long time I had harbored the idea of renting a trailer. And, I said this was the year to do it, and so we went forward with the idea.

We had about a fifteen foot trailer. It slept three or four. So, Lois and Kirk and her parents slept in the trailer and Richard and I camped outside each night. Well, it was a good idea except that the 1954 Plymouth Station wagon was woefully underpowered. It was so underpowered that we heated up going slightly down hill. But we did travel. We went up to BC, then cut across to Kelowna, then back to eastern Washington and up over Stevens pass. The car heated up continually. On each big slope, we would have to stop one or two times to let the engine cool off, add water, etc. I would stop the car, keep the engine running, I would get the hood open, then her Dad would pump water from our supply in the trailer, her Mom would walk to the front of the car and give me the water and I would pour it into the steaming engine. Mom always said we met the nicest number of State patrolmen on the trip. The police cars would stop when they saw us on the edge of the road, ask if they could help, etc. Anyway, it was a very nice trip, although there were problems. I told Mom that I was going to take our $25 deposit back when I turned in the trailer, open a savings account at a bank, and then if I ever again had an idea to rent a trailer I would use the deposit to go and spend half an hour with a psychiatrist!!.

By 1963 Lois and I began to discuss the possibly of having a third child. Mom said she loved Richard and Kirk very much, but she just didn't know if she could manage three boys. I assured her the third one would be a girl. She expressed some doubt as to my ability to predict sex, but we decided it would be a good idea. This time, instead of Jack Deming, Thorpe Kelly was her obgyn.

I recall that we took a big vacation in the fall of 1963. We went through a big chunk of the southwest. We went to Mesa Verde where Mom had a real fright having to climb the ladder out of one of the cliff dwellings. Then we drove to a high peak near Albuquerque and being pregnant the 9,000 feet altitude got to her but it was a good trip.

The fall of 1963 was the usual busy time, with office work being very busy, with Blue Ridge activities, etc. But pretty soon we were into December, 1963. About the evening of the 12th Mom told me she thought we were about to have our third child. We were relaxed about getting to the hospital. With Richard we were there twenty four hours before he appeared. With Kirk we were there six or seen hours before the firth. With Gretchen, Thorpe Kelly was so worried he was calling us to see where we were. We got to the hospital about 45 minutes before Gretchen was born. I saw her born, saw it was a girl and was doubly elated.

Sometime after we moved to Seattle and were living in our Valmay Avenue home, we invited the Doud's over for the weekend. An impetus for inviting them was so that I could graft some new apple species to one of our apple trees, both of which are transparent. Well, Doud's arrived and Mr. Doud had grafts for King, Winter Banana, and one other specie. Mr. Doud and I did the grafts, and in the process I learned a new skill. Fortunately, all the grafts took. There isn't enough sun in the back yard to enable us to grow large apples, but we have received apples each year since. And often the apples were so plentiful that we would have apple picking parties with other people from the office. Then we would make apple sauce—our family, that is, and froze a large supply for the coming year. One thing about the grafting process, however, was that Mom insisted on referring to me as a grafting attorney.

One thing I neglected to mention earlier. I had been anxious to get a dog. Earlier in 1963, I think, we got a beautiful shepherd we called Duke. I trained him and he became a very obedient dog. He was so well trained, and so intelligent that he would come on hand signals. The only drawback was that he was definitely a one man dog. I encouraged Lois to work with him but she didn't. So Duke would respond to me instantly, but Lois was just another person he didn't need to pay attention to. When Duke was a pup he decided he liked to chew on shoes. Lois thought it was funny. I encouraged her to keep shoes away from Duke. Well, she didn't, and his appetite for shoes increased. It got so that he would wander the neighborhood, find shoes, bring them home and chew them up in the front hard. Most embarrassing. There was no leash law at the time so Duke was out at night, daytime, or whenever. He never hurt anyone. Just a friendly dog but responded to only one person - me.

The December Gretchen was born, I got a TV. We had been talking about it. We hesitated, but when Richard and Kirk started going to other houses and we didn't have control over what they saw, we decided it was time. So Mom spent many of her first days after Gretchen was born, in the hideabed in the living room, watching TV, caring for Gretchen, etc. There was one problem, however. Then someone would come to the door, Duke woofed and would not pay attention to Lois, so she had to get up, get Duke put in the basement and then go to the door. This got to be a very old routine very soon. She said that Duke just would have to go. So it was. Fortunately, DeLeeouw's were delighted to get Duke. He was lonely, I think DeLeeow's lived several miles from us, across Lake Union, etc., but one day he showed up at our front door!! Duke faced a sad ending, though. When he was only five or six years old he developed testicular cancer and had to be put down.

And do we wound up with 1963 being another very eventful year.

19

Seattle - 1964-1968

Gretchen brought a whole new sense of vitality to the family. It also made our lives even busier and in the first few months resulted in a bit less sleep. Everyone was very excited about her arrival. Richard and Kirk were very enthusiastic about having a sister. And it wasn't too long before she worked into our style of living.

We took Gretchen on our first camping trip in June, 1964 when she was about six months old. It was car camping at Camano Island State Park. As had been the case with Kirk, she thrived. We had a good trip, but it was the last car camping we did. From there on when we went camping we had packs on our back and headed into the high country.

With the purchase of a TV at the time of Gretchen's birth we embarked on a new way of spending Sunday evenings. Oh yes, this change was also made possible because we had a plentiful supply of wood from the maple tree.

Quickly, it became a family tradition to build a fire in the fireplace Sunday evening and to have Sunday evening dinner on the living room floor, with the table cloth on the floor, etc Then, we would be sure to have dinner in time to watch the TV on Sunday living - Lassie, Walt Disney, etc. We all enjoyed and looked forward to those Sunday evenings together. Once we watched a movie which to our surprise scared Richard.

It was the Wizard of Oz. I don't recall what scene spooked Richard, but he was frightened, cried and fell asleep.

Mom was so pleased to have a girl. It had been a long time dream of hers to have a little girl whom she could dress up in all kind of frilly clothes, etc. Gretchen turned into a big disappoint to Mom in this regard. As soon as Gretchen got out of baby clothes, she wanted to wear the same kind of clothes as her brothers - jeans, sport shirts, etc. None of the frilly stuff for her. Mom came to accept that her dream about dressing Gretchen would just not come to pass.

The Family Car

I've mentioned our cars, but haven't said as much as I intended about car philosophy, public transportation, etc. Mom and I got our first car in 1951, just a couple of months before I finished law school. It was a 1947 Chevy club coupe, black in color. Bought it in Ann Arbor from a mechanic I met somewhere. We named the car Hephzibah. It turned out to be a good car for us and was with us for a number of years. It brought us out west, served us all our time we in Tacoma before 1956 and a couple of years after that.

Part of my philosophy about cars was that they basically are a box with four wheels and a motor up front. Styling and special features meant little to me. Not a good philosophy as far as the car manufacturers are concerned. We also bought used cars. I never owned a new car until about 1985.

By the time Kirk came along, the car, number 1, was getting a bit old and also it had suffered a little body damage when Mom had a little problem. But even more importantly, with two boys, a club coupe was just not big enough. So, from a local Chrysler Plymouth dealer whom we represented, we bought a 1954 light blue Plymouth station wagon. This car we named Esmeralda. As with the Chevy, it was stick shift. Automatic transmissions had just started to come in in the 1950's I think. This car served us very well, but by about 1962, and when the car had about 120,000 miles on and when it was showing wear and when the engine was getting toward the end of its life, we moved on.

The next car was also used. Bought it from a fellow we represented.

It was a BIG Mercury station wagon. It was also stick shift as I recall, but it did have overdrive. It was white in or other light color. I don't recall that we ever did really give it a name. Fortunately gasoline prices were low. We drove the car on cross country trips, long vacations around the country, etc as well as around time. This car lasted us until I think about 1966 or 1967, or perhaps a bit longer, until we moved into the Pontiac station wagon phase - again with a stick shift as I recall.

We did not have a second car until about 1985. I rode the bus to work in Tacoma and then in Seattle until 1985. It worked out well. I read my legal periodicals on the way to work in the morning and then the evening paper on the way home. Sometimes I thought that I perhaps should have a car so I had more flexibility during the day, in case I wanted to get out to meet with a client, or some other event. But I never did it.

Mom learned to drive in 1952. I think I recalled earlier that she had just stalled about leaning to drive until I told her in 1952 that we would not be able to take the big trip we had planned to Williamsburg Va., on the Skyline trail through North Carolina and on to Kentucky, unless she learned to drive. Well, Mom was really intent on taking that trip, so she took a few lessons and got her license just a couple of weeks before we took off. And she did share the driving on that trip, which we took in part with her parents.

Mom would have had to learn sooner or later in any event. She just would not have stood still for being house bound during the day. She never was really enthusiastic about driving, but she did it well and took in all the events she wanted to participate in, e.g. the AOUW in Tacoma, Blue Ridge affairs in Seattle, shopping, etc.

Continuing with Life in Seattle as Richard, Kirk and Gretchen were growing

The boys were beginning to grow and develop all kinds of interest by the time we moved to Seattle in 1962. Richard was nearly six years old and Kirk almost four. Mom and I were so pleased to watch them grow.

I think that by about the time Kirk turned six, just about the time Gretchen was born, he started taking piano lessons. Ida Belle

Hanna lived in Bayard Avenue, close to where we lived, so it was very convenient for Kirk. Kirk immediately took to the piano. Over the next very few years he turned in to Ida Belle's star student. I recall a recital for her students at a time when Kirk was perhaps ten or so when he was the star and played, well, the most difficult number of any of Ida Belle's students.

By about the time that Richard was in second grade or perhaps early in third grade, we became concerned about Richard's attitude toward school and studying. An event I particularly remember occurred on a vacation trip in 1964 or 1965, when Richard was in second or third grade. Mom went to the teacher and got assignments for Richard to do in our car as we traveled on a big vacation. Mom and I became concerned when Richard would complete the assignment for a whole day in less than a half hour. He insisted hat he had completed all the work, and indeed when we checked it, it was complete and accurate. Richard was becoming less interested in studying, and a bit bored. Mom went up to talk to the teacher about it. She was a nice person, and heard Mom out. She then said that Richard was very bright but there was no way she could provide him with additional work. She said she had so many students who were just barely getting through that she really had to put her attention on them. But, she added, Richard will always do well because he is so bright.

At about this time, a new organization was created in Seattle. It was the Northwest Gifted Child Association. We joined and found ourselves meeting and dealing with parents who were facing similar situations with their students. As a part of our effort to deal with the issue three or four of us members of the NWGCA, made an appointment with Forbes Bottommly, who was then the superintendent of the Seattle Schools to see of there was some way to introduce some gifted child programs into the Seattle Schools. The meeting was a bust. When Bottomly started looking around and musing as to just what a gifted chilled was, wondering whether his child or children were gifted, and when he then postulated that he thought the best system would be to bring all students of an age into one big room and let each learn according to his or her own ability, we knew we had really lost it with him. We continued our membership with the NWGCA for a number of years but dropped out as our children became older.

But we knew we had to do something if Richard was going to progress in line with his ability. Bottom line was that we had Richard tested and after he showed his learning ability and level applied for and got Richard admitted in to the coed primary school section of the Helen Bush school. And that's were he went for grades four through six. We were pleased with the program. I think that at that time the school provided its own bus for transportation. So as I recall Richard was picked up right from home.

The Blue Ridge Club offered swimming lessons, and so fairly early on we got Richard and Kirk signed up for lessons, and then later Gretchen later also took lessons. We have always been happy with Blue Ridge and participated in the social program and other events of the district.

The Mattern's moved around in the northwest, and I think also spent some time in California. But wherever they were we managed to get together with them fairly often. We always played bridge on evenings we were together. Alice and Lois developed the expression "hotsy totsy" when they got a good hand. The expression would drive Norm especially wild. We were always glad to maintain our contact with these long time friends from Allegheny.

Then we also played bridge frequently with Thorpe and Lucinda Kelly. When the children were young we would take them along, either or place or theirs, and put the children down to sleep while we played bridge.

Yard and lawn care took a chunk of my time. After I got the back hillside under control I worked on other parts of the yard. I did the mowing and watering of the lawn during all this period of time. I sometimes wonder how I managed to do all of this with all of the other things going on, but I did. Fairly soon after we moved in at Valmay, I developed a veggie garden. I guess was just my farmer self. I had had small pea patch in Chicago, a few blocks from our apartment. It worked out well. In Tacoma we just did not have space for a garden. But then when we came to Seattle I developed a small but productive garden.

Law work continued to expand during this period of time. I found myself doing more litigating that I had originally. I found myself developing clients, doing work for other clients, and found before long that other attorneys in the firm were turning to me to handle some of the litigation. We added a number of new attorneys - Dean Little in I think 1967, and then within a year or so we added Rod Waldbaum and Larry Hard. Pete LeSourd also joined the firm sometime in the 1960's

Skiing

As I mentioned before, we all - except Gretchen at that time - started skiing in 1962. As time went along, skiing became a way of life for us. We would sometimes, depending in part on snow conditions, initiate the ski season the Friday or Saturday after Thanksgiving. We always said that the rocks tended to be pretty fast that early in the season, but most of us were anxious to get out on the slopes.

Again, as I mentioned earlier, we started taking ski lessons in 1962. After that Richard, Kirk and I took at least one set of lessons. Then when Kirk became eight or nine he went on to Mighty Mites. This is a program for skiers up to 9 or 10 years old. It's designed to give young skiers a sense of confidence in skiing all the slopes on the mountain. A skier must be able to ski any of the slopes on their own before being eligible to we in the mighty mites. I think ten years of age is the maximum.

The Mighty Mite program began a half hour earlier than the rest of the lessons - 9:30 or 12:00 or 10:00 or 10:30. So the year Kirk was in the program we really had to be out of town early. We would have to leave not later than 7:30 a.m. and then make tracks. I figured that at that time of day I could have us at Crystal Mt. in about 2 hours. This would provide just enough time to get equipment out and up to the beginning part of the slope. With Kirk's natural coordination, he was a natural on the slopes. He really enjoyed the program except for the one Saturday when his class went all the way over to Northway - the then farthest way out and one of the most difficult runs on the slopes. That weekend we were staying with the LeSourd's at their unit at Crystal Mt. We had planned lunch for about 12:30, but Kirk never showed up for the longest time. Finally, he came in a bit after 1:00, cold and wet as could be. He threw his gloves down, shouted that they had gone to Northway and he had had it.

Anyway, for several years we went skiing the majority or more of the weekends from January until April. We generally skied with the opening of the season and kept going until the very end. Lois went along the majority of the time, although it was a bit of a drag for her at times because she had effectively pretty much given up on skiing after her early experience the week we went there with Kelly's.

Gretchen started skiing when she was five or six. She enjoyed it, but I don't think as much as her brothers. I recall that one spring vacation we made a ski week out of it. We had a day or two at the ski area near Wenatchee, a couple of days at Crystal, and another day at perhaps Snoqualmie. It was a fun time except for Gretchen the time we went to the area near Wenatchee. It was the only time ever skied that slope. Gretchen was maybe seven and she and I went together on a slope which I thought had a better exit than it did. We ended up near the top of a fairly long steep slope and she was petrified. I ended up side stepping with her down the slope.

Then after all the effort on downhill skiing, Gretchen announced when she was about 12 or 13 that she really preferred cross country skiing!! It actually worked out fairly well for her because she took her skis with her to Carleton and in the wintertime skid from one building to the other.

Anyway, skiing was a big part of our lives for several years. I have really treasured those years. Today, Richard keeps up his skiing skills with about one trip per year. I don't think Kirk has skied for several years.

Hiking and Backpacking

This sport also became a way of life for us. I've mentioned earlier a couple of beginning pack trips. But soon, we were out on the trails many times each summer. Each of our young folks was out on the trail by about age five. They started carrying packs, small ones, by about the time they were eight or nine or less. I remember one trip we went on with Ted, Greg and Gordy Teufel over in the Olympic National Park. Kirk may have been only about seven or eight, but he wanted his own pack. So we made a small pack for him to carry.

The farther we could get in to the back country the better it was as far as we were concerned. At that time there were no requirement for permits, no limit on number of parties who could camp at a particular sight. There just weren't enough people out in the woods to make it crowded the way it is now.

A number of years Richard and Kirk and I would go packing with Dwayne Copple. We always had a good time and enjoyed his company very much. On one pack trip on which we went out from an area near Salmon la Sac, we were on our way out when Richard came out with a kitten which he found on the trail. It was a pretty cat but not ours. I told Richard we would have to check with the ranger to see who belonged to the cat. We left our names, etc., but nobody claimed the cat. So Surchat, which Richard named the kitten, went home with us. He was a very good kitty. Unfortunately, he must have been hit by a car because we found it dead in our driveway a couple of years later.

We had two or three cats in addition to Surchat. I think there may have been two of them at one time, but generally it was just one cat at a time. Kirk also got into keeping fish, so for a time we had that to deal with also. The fish weren't too much of a problem if we were going to be away for just a couple of days, but longer it grew harder - but we managed.

I tried time and again to get Lois to go on a pack trip with us. Her reply was to corrupt the scriptures. She said "I shall lift up mine eyes, but I see no reason to drag my body up there." I was always sorry that she didn't join us. I thought it would have been nice for the whole family to be on the slopes together. But Lois just never did enjoy sleeping in a tent, sleeping on the ground, being without running water and inside toilets, etc. so it didn't work out.

Some of the best memories I have of those time was sitting around the campfires in the evening, just watching the fire, enjoying the out of doors and occasionally a bit of conversation. Those experiences are unforgettable for me.

A few times over these years I told Mom that I really thought it would be nice to have a sailboat and sail. Her response was," What do you think you would do it." With the first now flakes in the fall you have your skis our, and as soon as skiing ends you want to be in the mountains on pack trips." I tried to explain that there really was about a two month period in late spring and again in late fall when we could sail. Well, I know she was really right. And I wouldn't have wanted to give up either the skiing or hiking and backpacking.

Fourth & Pike

In the late fall, I think, of 1967, Fran turned over for me to handle a claim by disgruntled partners in I think the Colman building partnership of the management practices of Morton Beale and Mortenson. Seems they felt that the management of several buildings by common management was handled in such a way that the Colman partnership was bearing more than its fair share of the operating costs. I think there was some unfairness involved. Anyway, after I resolved the issues to the satisfaction of my clients, I was contacted by Bob Colwell and Bob Dunn to see if I had people who would be interested in buying the 4th & Pike Building..

After some negotiation, I did find an interested buyer - and I was one of them. Thorpe Kelly, Frank Crealock, Don Hesch, Fran LeSourd and I were the partners in Fourth and Pike Associates which bought the building effective June 1, 1968. Our purchase price was about $1.8 million dollars. The purchase price actually ended up a bit lower. A second mortgage was held on the building by an elderly attorney whom Fran knew well. Fran negotiated a cash settlement of $200,000 for the $400,000 balance on the note. So we ended up with the building. For a number of reasons the seller was in a tough way. There were past due payables, delinquent taxes, etc. But we got the building, and with it we got the services of Bob Kuehnoel to be the on site manager of the property

But more of the history of the building and other things in the next segment.

Other Activities

As I mentioned earlier, we joined Trinity Methodist Church in Ballard as soon as we came to Seattle from Tacoma. At the time Trinity had an active congregation. It had two services on Sunday morning. There was an active Sunday school with enough students to have a class for each grade. I don't recall if there were enough students for classes for each of the two services, but it was a large Sunday School. Fairly early on Mom began teaching Sunday school. She did this for several years.

I think she probably continued all the time Richard and Kirk were in the elementary grades. I soon found myself involved in Church affairs, also.

First I was on the Official Board of the Church, and quickly progressed (?) to Chairman of the Finance Committee. Then it was on to Chairman of the Official Board. I do tend to run a pretty tight meeting, observing Roberts Rules of Order, etc. The meetings did not drag. We succeeded in covering the agenda at the meeting. There were a handful of members who were a bit miffed when they were not afforded an open forum to talk on and on, but my style seemed to be appreciated. I think I continued at least two years in that position.

Later, after the period I cover in this section, Richard became very active in the Youth Group. He enjoyed the social interaction with all the group and made a number of good friends.

Since Mom was not employed she had the opportunity to become involved in activities of interest to her. She became very involved with MOHAI, the Museum of History and Industry. For a few years she was involved in taking Tillicum boxes to various elementary schools around the city. The Tillicum box was filled with all kinds of old artifacts that portray the history of Seattle - old items of clothing, items that were used in cooking, etc. She would go from home to the Museum, pick up the box, go to the school, and two boys from the class before whom she was speaking would come out and haul the box in and out. Mom enjoyed this activity very much.

It was also during this period that Kirk became involved in scouting. During the time covered by this chapter, Kirk was in the Cub Scouts. As I recall, at that age boys could join Cub Scouts at age eight, be in it for three years and then advance to the Boy Scouts. The Pack met at Crown Hill School, which at that time was still an active school in the Seattle School System. The Pack met once a month and then the individual Dens met weekly, generally at the home of the Den Mothers. Lois embraced the Cub Scout program fully and served as a Den Mother for the Den in which Kirk was, for much of the time Kirk was in Cubs. Kirk was very involved in all the events, all the steps for advancement. He also was in Webelos, which was the section of Cubs for the boys to enter their last year in Cubs - when they became ten years old. The events for boys ten years of age were designed for boys a bit older than the younger groups, and were designed to serve as a bridge to Scouts

I also became involved in the Cub Pack and served one year as the Cub Master. I got the full uniform, etc. In addition to the monthly meetings, there were some Pack activities aside from the monthly meeting. The activity I remember the best was the annual Hobo Hike. The idea was to dress like a Hobo, then hike around the district and then have a lunch somewhere. I can't now remember where we had the meal and I can't recall if we built a fire, etc. When I was a Counselor at Epworth Woods we had Hobo hikes. At that Camp everybody would scavenge all kind of items, come back to camp, and then build a fire and make Mulligan Stew. I remember the Epworth Woods Hobo Hikes very clearly, but unfortunately, I can't now recall whether we made the Mulligan Stew, etc. I know however, that David Wolter (Bob and Betty Wolter's son (they lived on Blue Ridge Drive.) took a number of pictures of us dressed for the hike. David a few years ago dug out and provided me with copies of a number of the photos which he took at the hikes.

20

Seattle - 1969-1974

Lakeside

This period of time saw us again revisiting the issue of schooling. As Richard began sixth grade at Helen Bush School, Mom and I knew that we had to make arrangements for Richard outside the public school system. We had continued our involvement with the Northwest Gifted Child Association, but we realized that the School District would not concentrate any special efforts on the 5% of students at the bottom end of the bell curve and that it would ignore the needs of the 5% of students at the other end of the bell curve of learning abilities. We were aware of the Lakeside School and decided to look into that school as a possibility for Richard.

Based either on testing already done, or on additional testing at this time it was apparent that Richard looked like a good candidate for The Lakeside School. We visited the school, make application for Richard's admission, and were pleased when he was accepted.

So, the seventh grade started for Richard at yet another school. As I recall, we worked out a carpooling arrangement with a family in Olympic Manor who had both a boy and girl in the school. (I think the car pooling arrangement I describe was instigated when Richard started Lakeside. It is possible that it was in place for a part of the

177

Helen Bush school experience, but I think I am correct as described above.

We were always extremely well pleased with The Lakeside School. We felt that Richard obtained an excellent education. I think he enjoyed the experience more than did Gretchen, but that is an account for later.

Lakeside had a number of dinner meetings each year with the parents to improve relations between the school and parents. We always took in those affairs if at all possible. We frequently shared a table with Bill and Mary Gates, parents of the now famous Bill Gates. I had known the father since we first came to Seattle. At the time I met him, he was doing insurance defense litigation at a firm that handled a number of cases from Campbell Husted which went in to litigation. Bill was one or two years ahead of Richard. We knew who Bill was, knew he was a bit of a geek about computers which were just being invented and developed, and knew that Bill's parents late were very upset when their son left Harvard at about the end of the second year because he didn't feel Harvard could teach him anything more about the all consuming interest he had in computers.

When Kirk turned eleven, in about a 1968, he joined Scout troop 123, which met at the Crown Hill School. With his three years in Cub Scouts, it was a natural transition for Kirk into Scouts. He quickly took to Scouts, and in fairly short time had become a Tenderfoot, then Second Class and then First Class Scout. Kirk went to Camp Brinkley one or two years. He enjoyed it very much ant then after his years of working there, he had a summer on the camp staff. As I recall, he worked in the kitchen the year he worked for the Camp.

I became very much involved with troop 123 also. It was not long before I was certified as a merit badge counselor for the various civics related Merit Badges. In about the second or third year of Kirk's membership in troop 123 I offered to teach interested scouts the Morse code and other requirements to get a Radio Merit Badge. I know that Kirk, Bob Kern, Gary Hansen and I think that one or two other scouts were in the class I offered. My skills with the Morse code were not nearly as good as when I was in the Navy, I could still use a key and tap out messages at speeds far in excess of that required to pass the Merit badge requirements. I know that Kirk did, and I think the other boys in the class, went on and got their basic government radio license Kirk had a transmitter as well as the radio, so he had the capacity to get on the air, but I don't recall that he ever did very much in that arena.

Troop 123 had, and perhaps still has had a very active hiking program. At the time Kirk was in troop 123 the Troop had hikes twelve months of the year. One of the winter hikes would be to Camp Sheppard, located near Crystal Mt., and so on that trip camping was not done outdoors but the Scouts did get to ski. But with the exception of one of two months, the troop camped outside. I went on a number of the hikes and so I remember some very cold camping experiences.

When Richard turned eleven, he joined Scouts. I had hoped he would enjoy the experience as much as Kirk did, but unfortunately it was not to be. At the time when Richard went in Bernie Hamry was Scoutmaster. Bernie and his family lived in Blue Ridge. He was a very dedicated person, and did his best to lead the troop. Unfortunately, he started each meeting with a long, long list of announcements. During this time the scouts stood bored, listening to the interminable list of announcements. The Dad of one of the scouts, (I can't at this time remember the name of this Dad) and Bernie Hamry decided that it would be good graining for the scouts to learn drill marching. So each meeting there was perhaps a ten or fifteen minute section of close order drill marching. The boys were bored. Richard was especially bored. I couldn't seem to get Bernie off the idea of this drill marching. In any event, Richard was thoroughly turned off. He made tenderfoot scout, but was so turned off that he said goodbye to the scouting program at the end of the first year. I really couldn't blame him for his feelings.

Kirk was committed to progressing to Eagle Scout and fortunately both Gary Hansen and Bob Kern were also interested. All three of them proceeded, almost in lock step, to advance on through the Star and then the Life Scout ranks. And then the three of them became Eagle Scouts at the same ceremony. Mom and I were so pleased that Kirk achieved the Eagle Rank. I guess I vicariously enjoyed it also, thought that if I had lived in a town where I could get the training, or if I had gone to a camp like Camp Wesco I, too, might have become Eagle Scout.

During the summers when Kirk was going to scout camps, Richard was attending the Y Camp Orkila in the San Juan Islands. Richard seemed to thoroughly enjoy the program. Then after a perhaps three years, or was it four, as a camper, he joined the staff as a counselor. Richard's first year on the staff he was archery instructor. (At Lakeside he had had instruction in archery, had purchased a very fine bow and arrow, and very much enjoyed the sport.) After this first year on the staff, Richard became a counselor. Richard was involved in the Orkila summer program all through both junior and senior high school.

I participated actively in the hiking program of troop 123. Richard went along on a number of the hikes. I figured that if I was going that Richard should be able to go. If he couldn't go, I just wouldn't lead the hikes. And there was always a shortage of Dad's to lead the hikes. Russ Kurtz and I served as co-hike leaders for the troop for quite some time.

The Troop also had, and I think still has, a tradition of taking one fifty mile hike each summer. I went on once on a hike which I can only described as a somewhat organized mob. There were about twenty five scouts and Dads - far too many for a good hike. We went to interesting places, etc. but I decided that I would not repeat the process.

So the next year I offered to lead a hike into the Olympics, but on the condition that there could not be more than eight or ten scouts and two adults. There was enthusiasm for the hike, although some dads complained about the limitation on the number of scouts. I told them that some other Dads could lead a hike - have two 50 mile hikes in a summer. But I held fast to my view that the groups on the trip would be smaller, and that the size group I proposed was the maximum number there should be on a hike.

I suggested that a couple of other Dads could organize and lead another hike. Three or four Dads gave excuses why they couldn't do it, and so there was no second hike.

Jim Stevens volunteered to be the other leader. Jim and Elaine had come out from the east. I don't know if Jim had ever been on the trail before he went on this hike. But he was a great person, he and Elaine were good friends of ours for many years and Jim had the time of this life. We had a fantastic hike on the route I planned. We had only one big problem. One boy had been sick the week before, he never let us know, and he was still not well enough to do the hike. His inability to do the trip was not discovered until we were on the trail the first day. (Neither he nor his parents disclosed the health problems of the previous week.) So, Kirk "volunteered" with me to bring the boy out the morning of the second day. This turned the trip into about a 65 mile week of hiking for Kirk and me. But we saw some of the most beautiful area of the Olympics.

When Gretchen turned seven, she wanted to and did get in to Campfire Girls. Lois stepped up and agreed to be one of the leaders for the group. Mom and Jane Boitano were the joint leaders of the group. Gretchen advanced through the ranks to the very top. Unfortunately, I can't remember the name of the various ranks. But Gretchen thoroughly enjoyed the experience. And she went camping two or three years at the Campfire Girls camp on Hood Canal. Mom and I went over to the camp a number of times for different events.

During the time all of the events involving Richard, Kirk and Gretchen were going on, there were big changes occurring in LeSourd & Patten. In 1968 or 1969, but I think 1969, there was a merger which much changed the size of the firm and the nature of the practice. Fran LeSourd, Woolvin Patten and Brock Adams had practiced with the Little firm. They left the Little firm in I think 1960, just a few months before I joined the firm. When I joined the firm, we practiced in the Washington Building, a very new building on Fourth Avenue and, I think, Union Street. Little, Palmer, Scott & Slemmons (the Little firm) had continued to practice in the Hoge Building.

In the summer of 1968 or 1969 discussions were held regarding the merger of the two firms. The decision was made to merge, but then came the question of where to locate. At that time, almost none of the new post World War II building spree had occurred. Except for the Washington building and the Norton on Second Avenue, the downtown looked much as it had since the 1930's. We couldn't find space in the new buildings. So we went in to the Seattle Tower, formerly the Northern Life Tower building. We built out a whole floor. That merger doubled the size of L&P.

Then not too long after the merger Don Fleming joined the firm, and the name was changed to Little, LeSourd, Fleming and Hartung. We also began to hire young associates, so that by the 1980's we were a firm with twenty five or so attorneys. With these changes, i.e. with the addition of all the new attorneys we made a couple of additional moves. We left the Seattle Tower and moved, I think, into the Seafirst Building, aka the "Black Box", which was then the home of Seattle First National Bank Building. (The locals kidded that the building was the black box that the Space Needle came in.) And a few years after that we moved into the Seattle Tower, the Martin Selig creation which I think is still the largest building, on a square foot basis in downtown Seattle.

I found some changes in the practice also. At the time five of us purchased the Fourth & Pike Building, or very shortly thereafter, I was designated the Managing partner for Fourth & Pike Associates, a position I held for forty years. Also I had begun to represent Owens Corning Fiberglas in about 1962. And also in the 1970's I became involved with Joe McKinnon representing plaintiffs in security fraud actions, brought primarily under rule 10b5 of the Securities Act.

The work for Owens Corning Fiberglas, which I soon referred to as OCF expanded greatly. OCF won the contract to provide all the insulation for the Alaska Pipeline. It built quite a factory in Seattle to produce the insulation. I found myself involving environmental issues related to the pipeline, in a class action discrimination case by I think blacks who wanted work in connection with I think the pipeline materials, in an age discrimination case brought against OCF by a local manager with whom I had worked while he was an employee of OCF, etc. So there was a whole new range of types of work, and with some client changes also. I also handled a fair number of construction lien foreclosure actions. And especially when some of the interstate and utility infrastructure work was going on I handled eminent domain cases. I was very pleased one year to receive a letter from Superior Court judge Horton Smith who wrote me a letter telling me that in his opinion my handling that year of an eminent domain case, which I tried before him to a jury, was the handled the best of any case he had heard that year.

Mom and I also became more involved in Blue Ridge affairs, also. I think it was between 1968 and 1970 that I ran for a position on the Blue Ridge Board. By the late 1960's we had become well acquainted in the community and so I guess it was no surprise that I was elected. The community was not as complex in its structure then as it has become. Nevertheless being on the Board did take time. And I was elected

Secretary, a position which I held for two years, and then on the third year of my term I was elected President of the Club. This involvement obviously involved some significant amounts of my time.

Then, as I went off the Board, at the end of my three year term, Mom was elected to the Women's Board, for a three year term. Mom really thrived on all the action of the Blue Ridge Women's Board. She chaired at least one of the Women's Spring Luncheons. She and I chaired one year the annul Blue Ridge Barbeque. All of these activities took time but we managed to thrive with all the activity.

By the late 1960's the Playfield behind our home, off Woodbine, had fallen into very serious disrepair. There had been talk about "doing something". So Mom and I called a number of our neighbors to a meeting at our home to plan an improvement of the playfield. The decision was made that we would clear out the blackberry bushes and other weeds, we would replant grass, we would install a basketball court area, and we would install a lawn sprinkler system.

There was wonderful cooperation among the neighbors. Jim Stevens, who had been in the house fixer up business, would be in charge of clearing the weeds, etc. There were so many weeds that with the help of equipment he loaded four ten yard bins with weeds, etc. Then we had to spade the field, level and cultivate a great grass field, put in a sprinkler system, etc. Much of the work was done on Saturday mornings and done on a volunteer basis by neighbors. For about three or four months I spent almost every Saturday morning down there with other members working the problem.

Near the end of the project, the question came as to whether to operate the sprinkler controls manually of with automatic electric power. There was talk about manual, with "wives" volunteering one day very couple of weeks. I told everybody that system would work the first year, and then we wouldn't be able to find volunteers. So the decision was made to go automatic. We needed to get power to the field. So Jim Stevens and I "bootlegged" an electric line up the hill and ran the power, with controls into our basement, where they have been ever since. It's my observation that there was a lot more voluntary support for these kinds of activities then there is today.

Gretchen started school at Crown Hill in I believe 1969. Before beginning school, she had spent a year in a preschool program sponsored by an organization which operated at an Episcopal Church at about 155th street, between Aurora and Greenwood. Gretchen and Karen Stevens, the closest of friends, started at Crown Hill at the same time. But at some point, Karen started going to the North Beach School. (By that time the Stevens had purchased a new home in a different section of Blue Ridge.

Gretchen and Karen were both very bright, and again, were not much challenged by the public schools. But the Seattle School District, when Gretchen and Karen were both in fifth grade, created the Decatur Program. I was held at the Decatur school. Thus the name. The district decided that the best student from each school would in the sixth grade participate in an enriched program at the Decatur school. Gretchen and Karen both thrived in the program.

In the spring of the sixth grade, Lois went to see the principal of Whitman school to inquire what special schooling Gretchen would receive after the wonderful Decatur year. The principal, who I understand was a man about to retire, a man who did not want to rattle any cages, answered each of Mom's questions, by saying the Gretchen would have the "regular program". So Mom and I found ourselves in the same fix as we had been with Richard. What to do? Well, we had Gretchen tested and then see about Lakeside. Gretchen tested very well, we applied for her admission to Lakeside and she was accepted. So much for the public school system helping the five percent at the upper end of the bell curve. Gretchen went to Lakeside, said she had a wonderful education, but she did not enjoy the social atmosphere. She just didn't care for the personalities of most of the girls in her class. But more of this later on when we get into to the next section.

In the mid 60's on through the 70's we continued and expanded our backpacking trips. By the mid-sixties Richard and Kirk were getting big enough and strong enough that they could manage multi-day trips and even better could carry ever bigger and heavier packs. I recall that during this period

Richard, Kirk, and occasionally Dwayne Copple went on trips along sections of the Wonderland Trail around Mt. Rainier. We packed the south side of the park, the north side of the park, both on multi-day trips. We also had wonderful trips into the Olympics. I recall one trip in the Olympics where we started at either nine or seven lakes basin, up over the High Divide, down into and out the Hoh River valley. I remember on the Olympics trip, during the time of the Republican presidential campaign, hearing for the first time about Spiro Agnew. We generally had pretty good weather on our trips, gut we were equipped to handle wet and old weather as well.

On our trip through the Olympics I mentioned above we had arranged for horses to bring our food to the High Divide. Kirk was nine years old at the time. The packer failed to bring the food to the agreed point. We went back to the lower level where I found a radio in a ranger backcountry tent. I radioed Park HQ to explain the problem. They checked and said the packer would be back in the next day.

The next day, as we were about to set out, a young and, I am sure, seasonal ranger came by and charged us with unlawful use of government property. We were not supposed to have used the radio. I explained the problem, told him we had packed several miles and were out of food. The ranger said it wasn't an emergency. I told him Kirk was nine years old and asked him how many times he had packed eight or nine miles with pack at his age. The fellow said it was irrelevant and proceeded to issue a ticket for the violation. I told the fellow he could do as he wanted but be could be assured that I would see that his act got media notice in the Seattle media.

As it turned out, I wrote to the Superintendent, explaining what had happened and what I thought of the ranger. I got a nice letter response. The Superintendent or maybe the Chief Ranger) said he was sorry we had had the problem, the government would not pursue the matter, and he hoped that we would come back and spend more time in the park!!

Gretchen was anxious to get out on the trail with us and did go on her first pack trip when she was four or five. We went on a fairly easy trail in the northwest section of Mt. Rainer Park. She did just fine and enjoyed every minute of the trip. Gretchen rapidly advanced her skills and also the size of packs she could handle. And as Richard got older and had other demands on his time Gretchen, Kirk and I would be out together. The three of us had one very memorable trip into the North Cascades which I will never forget. I recorded the high point in a photo of Kirk which hangs on the wall at home today (and Kirk has his own copy, also). On this particular trip we also had a problem with a ranger who said we couldn't camp where we intended. He was insensitive to the fact that Gretchen, who then was perhaps nine or ten years old, had packed many miles, was exhausted, etc. We struck some middle ground on where we would camp.

As I have mentioned before, the backpacking experiences were the best of the best for me, and I think for Gretchen, Kirk, and Richard also. I could easily have spent a lot more time out in the back country, but the need to earn a living pulled us pack home.

In later years, and this probably mould have even in the 70's, the number of people out in the woods was increasing and the Park Service and the Forest Service responded by requiring permits, limiting the number of people who could go in go and where, etc. Hard, but I think necessary limitations to preserve the beauty of the back country. At that time, though, and perhaps today, the restrictions were much less if you were back in the wilderness areas. One time Kirk and I were I Mt. Rainier, out from the Carbon River entrance, into a fairly remote area. I still remember that after dinner we had a fire doing to do the dishes, etc., it was very quiet, and all of a sudden we saw a doe Mt. Goat with two fawns less than fifty feet from us. She must not have heard us because when there was just a slight noise she must have heard it and all three left immediately.

Then in later years, and I think at times beyond the period I talk about in this chapter, Gretchen and I would head out on pack trip. She and I had the same great trips that I had with the boys. Just wish there would be a repeat now of the pack trips.

There was a special benefit as the children got older. By the time they were eleven or twelve years old they were able to take care of the lawn mowing, edging and trimming. I have often refereed to these as my halcyon days with the hard. Richard started the mowing when he was about 12. At that time, or by the time Kirk turned about 11 he would do the edging and trimming. By the time Kirk became about 12 year old he and Richard would both manage the lawn mower and also the edging and rimming.

I excused Gretchen from the mowing, but by the time she was eleven or twelve I told her she was old enough to do the edging and trimming. Gretchen always did a terrible edging and trimming and job. She always sort of burned the edge of the grass. I showed her and showed her, but to no avail. However, having a bit of brown was preferable to my doing the edging and trimming, so I suffered with the poor duality of the work.

During much or all the time Gretchen was doing the edging and trimming I had a little power device with a string that spun very fast and did he cutting. Gretchen hated the work. Richard and Kirk weren't enthusiastic about it, but at least there was no sign of rebellion. Gretchen admitted to me later - much later - that she intentionally butchered the yard in hopes that I would give up on her!!

I continued over the years to do a great part of the yard work. After everyone had left for school, and by sometimes in the 80's I did have a lawn mowing service, which I have continued to use to this day. Much later, and I am now talking about on into the 90's I think, I did continued to prune the yew hedges each year., except for the section that goes down over the steep hill. Kirk was able to prune that part of the hedge very nicely, but after he finished, I just always had that part of the work done.

By the time we got into the early 70's I could see that the halcyon days with so much lawn work done by my local unpaid help was going to be coming to an end. Richard would be graduating from High School and heading off to college. In his junior year in High school Richard took the PSAT and a year later took the SAT. He was a national merit scholar semi-finalist and was thinking about and getting busy planning for college. As the college catalogs came in I found myself pouring through them within as great an interest as Richard was showing.

During I think Richard's junior year in High School he became involved in what I think is call the Junior businessman program, which I think is supported the Chamber of Commerce. In any event it involves a lot of planning the development and operation of a business. There was class one night per week. I drove Richard to the class, which was not too far north of the downtown. Richard enjoyed the program very much and I'm sure he gained a lot of very useful information.

Richard had some very good choices among colleges. His interest was turning to the international arena. He thought about the Thunderbird School in Arizona. For whatever reason, he did not follow-up on that. He did think he would like to go to Georgetown. I was concerned abut the costs associated with going there. I've always regretted not being more responsive to that interest of Richard. He did decide though to apply to and was accepted to Pomona College. He opted for Pomona - an excellent choice.

I recall that shortly before school started Richard told me he would have to take a foreign language and he didn't know what to do. He had had nine years of French, didn't care for German, and so what to do. I told him I thought Pomona offered Japanese in case he was interested. The only response was, "oh." He did sign up for it. I think he may have forgotten my suggestion. And it was less than a month or so later that when he went to Pomona that he signed up for Japanese. And it was less than two months after that he wondered if it would be ok if he applied for a study abroad. I asked about it and found out it would be at Waseda University, he said "the Harvard of Japan.". He didn't think he could get in as a sophomore, but I told him to try and see. And so, not long after that he found out that he would be able to participate in that study program.

By the time he was sixteen, Richard was interested in learning how to drive. I was not in much of a position to question it, given how I had worked on my Dad. So he had some lessons, passed the driving and written test, and got his drivers license by, I think, when he was seventeen, or perhaps late sixteen's. Richard did not do a lot of driving, but it worked out well for him to have a license. He did have an accident where he totaled the car. It was when he was at a dance at Lakeside. Fortunately, nobody was hurt. So we would place the car— and did so with another Pontiac Station wagon - I think the same year as the one in the accident.

And so in June 1974 Richard graduated from High School. He had an excellent record, and we felt he had received a very good education. On the flip side, however, Richard's graduation from High School marked a change for our whole family. As each of our young ones have graduated from high school, we have noticed that it represents the end of the time when they are living at home on a full time basis. They are all spreading out their wings and getting ready for the world. And so it should be.

By the time Kirk was about twelve or thirteen, he was most interested in studying the organ. I was very fortunate that Ludwig Esksildson, the then minister at Trinity, was agreeable to the idea of allowing Kirk to practice organ on the Church organ. So quite a few days after school, before Kirk was old enough to drive, he would take his bicycle and head in to Church to practice. Little did we know at the time that it would become Kirk's vocation.

In about 1969 or 70, I think, when Kirk was in sixth grade, I asked if he would like to go to Lakeside. He had taken tests, down quite well, and I felt that he would be accepted. Ingraham High School had just opened. Kirk decided that he would rather to school with Gary Hansen and other friends with whom he had been going to school for seven or eight years. I had hoped that Kirk would decide to go to Ingraham. As it turned out, however, Kirk went to Ingraham during the first years. He got an excellent education at Ingraham. At that time Mr. Maxey was principal. He fell into disfavor with the administration of the school district, allegedly because he was a tough disciplinarian and academic. Would they had that kind of principal now!! Anyway, for his efforts Mr. Maxey was given a choice of retiring or become principal at an elementary school. He retired. Somehow, I wish the school administration would change.

In the late 1960's we remodeled what we now call our rec room. When we moved in to the house the lower level, or basement, was unfinished. The remodel was great and ever since has been a much used room. I just don't know why it took so long for us to get around to it, because we would have used it a lot in earlier years also.

The early 1970's we did have downsides. By the 1970's Dad was in failing health. He had had two heart attacks, one in 1955 and the other in 1962. He came back from there well, and we were really blessed that he was able to join us on perhaps three vacations. And he did not have a fear of flying as Mother had had. So he flew out to visit us on each of his several trips after Mother died.

Then in I think about 1971 Dad had a fall and broke a hip. He got around afterward with what I will call a walking stick, but he was not able to continue his customary walks. He just couldn't get over the congestive heart failure that dogged him in the last years, and so, in January of 1974, just after he had turned 84, he passed away.

Mom's parents lived until the late 1960's or very early 1970's. They never did fly, and so any visits to our home were by train travel. We did enjoy their visits to us. There was the long visit in 1962, and then

I think they visited us again in the mid 60's. But in these later years we did get back to Pittsburgh a number of times. But it did get hack to Pittsburgh a few times in the 1960's and 1970's, but it became difficult for the whole family to make the trip given the schedules everyone faced to get back as often in the 1960's and early 1970's as we had earlier

With the passing of Dad and Mom's parents, Mom and I found ourselves the older and then the oldest generation of the family.

21

Seattle 1975-1980

September 1975 - Richard was off for Japan, for a year of study at Waseda University. It was an exciting time for all of us, but things did not work our initially quite as planned. The idea for housing was that the student would live with a Japanese family. Fine!! But in Richard's case he learned after the fact that the wife was interested in having a student stay with them and the husband was opposed. So I think probably the husband made life intolerable for Richard.

Richard was told that he was to be by home 9 p.m., no exceptions, and they would not give him a key so that he could get in. Very shortly thereafter, Richard arrived home a little after 9 p.m. and could not get in He had no key and nobody would answer the door. So Richard spent the night on a park bench.

The next day, with the help of Stanleigh Jones, the faculty coordinator, Richard got a new family and moved with a family anxious to have him. The Tajimas turned out to be the family and they were indeed a great family. The Tajimas had a son and daughter. Hisao, the son and Richard became very close friends, and the friendship continues. He is just about the same age as Richard. Then there is the daughter Nobuko. She's a nice person, but a bit different. Mr. and Mrs. Tajima were just great. He served in the Japanese Navy during the Second World War and so he and I, with Richard as interpreter, talked about our service in two different navies. Mrs. Tajima is a very gracious lady. At the time Richard lived there Grandma lived with the family, as I recall. She has since died and I don't recall much more about her.

At home, in the meantime, Kirk was working his way through his junior year at Ingraham. He continued participation in Scouts, but once he had achieved Eagle rank, I think the big push was over. By the time Kirk was a junior he was sixteen and then seventeen later in the year. He had other fish to fry.

Kirk's interest in organ study increased. He was doing well enough that in his junior and senior years he was at the organ at Trinity Church a couple of times. About 1974 or 1975, and after Kirk became sixteen years of age, he too decided that he would really like to learn how to drive. And so it was. He didn't have the car to drive to organ practice after school because we still had only one car. But the bicycle proved adequate for his transportation.

Gretchen, though, was still going full tilt with Campfire. Mom and Mrs. Boitano were continuing to serve as the adult leaders for the Campfire group. The meetings of the group were held after school. Since Mom was a bit late getting home dinner preparation was fairly quick. We fell into the routine of having what we all knew as the Camp Fire dinner - hot dogs in a tomato sauce over rice. The dinner was one aspect of the Camp Fire experience that we could all forget.

In February, 1976, Mom and I took off for Japan. We had a marvelous time. Richard met us on arrival, of course. At that time Tokyo was still using the airport at Haneda for all flights. We spent the first couple of days sightseeing in Tokyo, meeting the Tajima's, etc. We had dinner with them during these first few days. Then we took off on sightseeing. Richard went along with us for the first three or four days. After that time he took off for Korea on some school vacation and Mom and I were on our own. We found travel in Japan remarkably easy. We used JTC (I think those are the initials) for train travel and hotel accommodations. I recall that the first time we stayed at a Ryokan (Japanese hotel) we went in, and everybody was rather stiff. Then Richard opened up in Japanese and everybody was much more relaxed

We traveled a large part of the southern half of Honshu Island and a major part of Kyushu. I recall particularly one incident in Tokyo when we were in line to visit the palace. There was along line of visitors waiting in line. One boy, perhaps seven or eight years old put his one foot up against Richard's foot and I am sure was talking with the other boys about the size of Richard's foot. Richard watched patiently and then very calmly started talking to the boy in Japanese. The boy was surprised, shocked, etc. All others in line laughed at the event. We had a second dinner with Tajima's just before we left Japan. Mrs. Tajima told Mom that she was using chopsticks much better than on our first dinner with them.

Our trip to Japan was our first international trip since our trip to Europe in 1951. It marked the beginning of a great deal of international travel over the next twenty years. While we were overseas, we engaged Jean Herman to stay with Richard and Kirk, cook, do laundry, etc. It worked out very well. She and her parents and brothers were long time residents of Blue Ridge. This trip to Japan was another of our landmark trips. It piqued our interest in the Orient even more, it resulted in our making changes in our diet, and Mom later took Japanese cooking lessons.

By the time we returned from Japan, it was getting on to spring of 1975 and Kirk was thinking about college. As I recall, in the spring of his junior year he took the PSAT and then the following year, early in his senior year he took the SAT. Kirk did very well on the tests and that combined with his good academic record at Ingraham meant that he had a choices of colleges he could attend.

We continued with our skiing program during what were Kirk's junior and senior years. I don't recall that we were on the slopes with quite the regularity as in some earlier years. Lois was not that enthusiastic about skiing - period, and Gretchen had decided that she enjoyed cross country skiing more than downhill. More crimps in the skiing program!!

Then our backpacking took a bit of a hit because Kirk was a counselor at Orkila and also worked a summer at Camp Brinkley, so he was away all summer. Kirk, Gretchen and I did squeeze in some backpacking and camping, and sometimes just Gretchen and I went backpacking. Gretchen was a very enthusiastic backpacker and I thoroughly enjoyed getting out with her.

By the spring of 1976 Kirk was ready for graduation. He had made a good academic record at Ingraham, he had decided that he was going to attend Whitman College, and he was ready for graduation. Gene and Leone Weber were very glad that he decided to go there, too. I recall that as a part of the whole end of senior year Kirk attended the senior prom. I recall he went with a very nice girl by the name of Leann, or was it Luann. She and her family lived on Capital Hill. (She has since gone to medical school and practices in Seattle. Kirk has maintained contact and I think has seen her a couple of times.) I particularly recall the prom because we only had one car and Mom and I ended up chauffeuring Kirk to the prom. I don't recall why Kirk didn't have the car for the event. And I don't recall why we chauffeured.

We drove both over and back to Whitman while Kirk was in school there. We always thought the college had a beautiful campus. I don't recall Kirk's roommate the first year, but the remaining three years he roomed with Phil, whose last name now escapes me. Especially on our trips home in the spring we would pick up asparagus, which was widely grown then in the eastern part of the state.

By the late 1970's I was very involved in handling securities fraud cases. One case I particularly remember was the case against Computer Sciences Corporation. Since Computer Sciences headquarters were in the Los Angeles area I had a lot of travel back and forth on depositions, etc. I recall that the travel made it possible to visit Richard a couple of times when I was in L.A. for depositions.

The Computer Sciences case had a tortured history. First of all I lost the case on a motion for summary judgment. Then I appealed that decision and the U.S. 9th Circuit Court reversed and sent the case back for trial. Then I tried the case with an associate from L.A. and proceeded to lose the case a second time. I appealed the case to the 9th Circuit, which affirmed the trial court, and then the Supreme Court declined to take the case. Our client was Bill Marx, an accountant and a long time friend of Woolvin Patten. I always felt that we had put together a very good case. My associate attorney from the L.A. area knew the district court judge very well and he felt that the judge just made a mistake. But that's the way it goes.

I spent a fair amount of time for a number of years handling security fraud cases. It was a frustrating experience however. It seemed either

I lost a case, or I won and the defendants didn't have money to satisfy the judgment.

It was along in the late 1970's that we made a Church decision which did not work out, in one way at least, as well as it might. After Olin Parrott left Trinity, Ludwig Eskilsdsen was appointed. He was a rather dour and somber kind of minister. I enjoyed his sermons find, but Lois did not. Ludwig stayed longer, I recall, than he should have. So, Lois said we needed to make a change. We looked around, and ultimately decided to join First Methodist Church, in downtown Seattle.

I think we may have handled the Church change badly. We did not involve Gretchen very much, if at all, in the decision. She was very unhappy about the change and refused to attend First Methodist except on a few occasions. I simply did not realize what Gretchen's feelings were or would be on the subject. In any event, David Aasen was then the minister at First Methodist and we found ourselves, or at least I did, with a long term arrangement at the Church.

In the spring of 1980 I decided to take a sabbatical leave. The firm policy then was for three months for such leave. I didn't take the three months, but took two months to visit Australia and New Zealand. It was an absolutely fantastic trip. In New Zealand I did the Milford trek. Sorry that Lois wasn't inclined to join me but she did some traveling on her own in the south island while I was packing through a beautiful section of New Zealand.

We covered a wide swath of Australia, even including three or four days in Tasmania. We flew in to Sydney. There we were met by a young man who had spent about three weeks with us in Seattle, and his parents. They showed us the city very well. The father tried to teach me, unsuccessfully, how to play cricket. We went to the outback - one of the highlights of the trip there was climbing Ayers Rock (climbing was then permitted). Just as we were leaving Australia I found an advertisement in the Sidney newspaper by a man who wanted to find some one to invest in deer. I pursued the matter. Never did go forward, but have always been a bit sad that I didn't go into to it. We did enjoy, and each time we have been there enjoyed the venison which is served at most all restaurants in New Zealand.

Before we hardly knew it, we were getting in to the spring of 1980 and Kirk was getting ready for graduation. Mom and I naturally went to the graduation. We did have a big event that year which had an impact on all sorts of things. It was in the spring of 1980 that Mt. St. Helens erupted. The eruption occurred just a few days before commencement. Our route to Walla Walla took us almost to Portland as I recall because of highway damage in the Chehalis area. Then there was a small follow-on eruption the morning of commencement. I recall the President of the college coming on the stage before the services to tell us that there had been a slight eruption a few hours earlier. He told us that at that very time all roads to both Portland and Seattle were closed because of the eruption. He expressed the hope that things would clear before long and urged us to go toward and enjoy the commencement. Which we did. As I recall, getting Kirk with all of his gear back to Seattle was a bit of a challenge. We returned with a very full car.

During all of these years I was extremely busy with the law practice. Then I also had many responsibilities as Managing Partner for Fourth Pike Associates. By about this time, the securities work was coming to an end. Work for OCF was going full tilt, however, and this with the other work kept me very much involved.

I also found myself very involved in Lions activities. I had joined Lions when we lived in Tacoma. Then when we moved to Seattle, I transferred my membership to Seattle Downtown Central Lions Club. When we first came to Seattle, or shortly thereafter, the Club reached its maximum size of about 115 members. I became more active as time went by. Ultimately, but this was in the 80's, I served on the Board and then served a year as President of the Club. Unfortunately, it was during the 80's that service Clubs began their gradual decline in membership. Our Club suffered the same problems as such organizations generally. But more of that later.

Kirk gradated from Whitman College in 1980. So then two of our three had finished College school, and now the second one was about to take wings.

In the fall of 1976, or 1977, Gretchen followed her older brother and started Lakeside. We didn't plan this originally, but after Mom visited the principal of Whitman to discuss Gretchen's program after the year at Decatur, and after he advised that Gretchen would just have the regular program, we decided we needed to do something for Gretchen to keep her interest in school.

Don't know now just what prompted us to do so, but we decided that in the summer of 1980, we, all four of us, would take a trip to Britain. This may have been our first trip overseas since our trip to Japan in 1976. But anyway, we headed to Britain at the very end of May or the first of June. I recall that Gretchen had to make arrangements to take one or two final exams before the end of school.

I remember flying to Britain. The days were so long that it was hardly dark on the overnight flight. We spent about a week seeing the London area. Then we rented a Ford Escort and set out to see the country. We stayed at a lot of B&B's, etc. We covered England well, lots of Wales and went way up in to the northern part of Scotland. We drove 3000 miles in the month we had the car. Kirk and I shared the driving and navigating. Mom and Gretchen rode in the back seat. It truly was one of the best trips we ever had.

I think Gretchen probably was a counselor at the Campfire Girl camp that summer. Kirk was very much involved with his organ music work.

22

Seattle - 1981-1990

This decade was a full one for the whole Hartung family. Everybody had events of significance to him or her and to our whole family.

By the time he completed Pomona, Richard knew that he would like to work for the U. S. Foreign service. The process for hiring for such work is time consuming, and so the immediate thing is to get at least interim employment. Richard arrived home from Pomona just as Lois and I were taking off for a trip somewhere. Richard told us he had had an interview or two for a job, but nothing more. Mom and I left on our trip believing that he and his new car (new for him) would be at home when we returned.

Surprise - while we were away, Richard got a job offer from Security Pacific Bank in the L.A. area, accepted the job, and was long gone by the time we returned. I think Richard felt he had a pretty good job and one that would provide income for him while he worked on getting into the Foreign Service.

Getting employed by the Foreign Service was indeed a long term event. Richard had to go through the application process and then the interviews. Apparently, something unfavorable happened in the first interview, and so Richard had to go through the process all over again. Finally, though, by, I think, late 1980 or early 1981, he was hired as an

FSO (Foreign Service officer). We were very pleased and proud of his accomplishment

The Foreign Service had at the time, a bidding process for job assignments. Richard bid for a post in Japan. He was informed, however, that the only open post in Japan was one which required only English language skills. The Foreign Service determined that it wanted to send Richard to South Korea. Beyond that, it decided it would send him to the Services' Korean language school - a six month assignment before the actual appointment to a place in South Korea. So, Richard was off to Washington DC, where he would have the language schooling.

Gretchen, in the meantime, was continuing in Lakeside. She had an outstanding academic record at Lakeside. Also, significantly, she took the PSAT and then the SAT. She did so superbly that she was an SAT finalist. In addition to the honor of being an SAT finalist, she was awarded a $1,000 scholarship. Gretchen always said that she received a very good education from Lakeside, but she did not enjoy the school because the girls with whom she was associating with as classmates had different values than she did.

I think that Gretchen graduated from Lakeside in 1981. What I do know is that by 1980 she was beginning to think seriously about the college she might attend. She applied to a number of schools, and with her academic record and with the results of the SAT test she was accepted to just about every school, perhaps every school, to which she applied.

Then came the winnowing process. I recall that there were at least three colleges to which she gave serious consideration, but she finally settled in on two. One of course was Carleton. The other was Grinnell, in Iowa. It was a tough process for Gretchen to decide between these two schools. She struggled about which school to attend right down to the very deadline. I recall that the night before the deadline she suggested to Mom that we cut her in two and send one half to Carleton and the other half to Grinnell. When all the smoke had cleared, she decided on Carleton. We always felt she had made a good choice.

When Gretchen left for school, she headed out by herself. Richard had done the same when he left for Pomona. Kirk was the only one we took to school. My thinking now, is that we perhaps should have gone along with Richard and Gretchen. But we didn't, and they did fine. I think that all three of our young folks were very mature and were well equipped to handle themselves at the college of their choice.

I don't recall with whom Gretchen roomed her first year at Carleton. I do know that the first year she met Monica Stevens, that the two of them got along very well, and that the two of them roomed together the last three years at Carleton.

As it turned out, Gretchen's switch in skiing preference from downhill to cross country worked out well at Carleton. I recall that she said that in the winter she and her classmates would ski from one building to another.

We got back to Carleton only once during the time Gretchen was in school. I believe it was in the fall. I know that we were very impressed with the beauty of the campus. We were also impressed with the whole program at Carleton. Indeed we felt that all three of our young folks made excellent choices for college.

Beginning in the early '80's David Aasen at First Methodist talked me into becoming involved in a plan to remodel and restore First Methodist. The Church was built in 1909, and was un-reinforced masonry. By the 1980's the building was showing its age. It was not designed very well to withstand seismic stress, and had suffered some damage in earthquakes over the years. The plumbing, heating, and electrical systems were all in serious disrepair.

The initial idea for the Church was to do a major restoration and remodel of the facility - the "new" section, which was used for administration and some education, was built in, I think, about 1950 and was still in pretty good shape.

First Methodist dated back to, I believe, 1851. It was the first Church in Seattle. The building constructed in 1909 was the third home for the Church. It had always enjoyed a good strong membership. Many Seattle leaders were members of the Church. It had a good organ, a very good music program, so it seemed like it would be a good plan to rehabilitate, although there was the recognition that replacement might be necessary. David was glad that I agreed to help out.

Before we really got started on the program, the Church was nominated for Landmark status which set the stage for a multiyear involvement on my part. On behalf of the Church I appealed to the City the proposal to designate the Church as a landmark. After a lengthy series of hearings, and after what seemed like an interminable time while the administrative body considered the issue, the City rejected the appeal

So the next step was to appeal to the Superior Court. I don't recall all the bases for the appeal, but I do know that we took the position that designation would violate both the federal and the state constitutions of Washington. The Superior court ruled in favor of the Church, which set the state for the next review.

The City appealed to the Court of Appeals. After another year or so working our way up through the appellate process, the Court of Appeals heard the case. It proceeded to affirm in part and reverse in part. A partial victory for the Church was not at all what it wanted or felt it needed. So it was up to the Washington Supreme Court. The Supreme Court reversed the Court of Appeals and basically reinstated the determination of the Superior Court. It determined that designation would violate both the federal and state constitutions, although it put the greatest emphasis on the State Constitution. It was not a slam dunk process however. The court was split either six to three or five to four.

The frustration over the matter did not end with the court decision. David Aasen worked diligently to find an institution willing to rehabilitate the original building. We finally found a company that was interested in providing the necessary money to rehabilitate the 1909 building, to the tune of two to four million dollars. The proposal was that the new educational section of the Church would be demolished and a thirty three story skyscraper would be built on that portion of the Church property. It looked like an excellent solution. I suggested that the Church not convey title to the company doing the financing, but rather that it grant a long term lease.

The design for the rework was submitted to the congregation. A segment of the congregation felt that the sanctuary portion of the building would be moved into the basement. Without going in to the details there was a lot of opposition expressed. I have always felt that a big part of the opposing was that there were a group of parishioners who didn't like David. I have always felt that they sublimated the best interest of the Church for getting even with David. Anyway, the whole plan went up in smoke. I think the whole process lasted for about six years - a lot of my time and effort, especially.

While all this Church turmoil was going on, lots of things were happening at home. Gretchen was working her way through Carleton. As Gretchen was proceeding through Carleton, I asked Gretchen if she would like to study a year abroad. She said "Oh Dad, it probably would be to France or England or some place like that and it would be boring". I suggested to Gretchen that there were other countries to which she might go, and urged her to take a broad brush approach. Which she did, and to our surprise she came up with the idea of studying a year in China. This was not too long after the Mao period and shortly after the country had opened up. Anyway, she was accepted and headed to China. The program was for one semester at Nanjing University and one semester at Peking University.

Gretchen seemed to thrive at her life in China. And of course, with her there, what better time for us to consider travel in China. In January or February Gretchen wrote and said "Mom and Dad if you will come to China I will be your guide and interpreter!!" What an opportunity!! So in the middle of May we arrived in Shanghai with no reservations of any kind. We had a fantastic month seeing a large part of the country. We saw several cities close to the coast, got to Xian, west to Chengdu, in Sechuan, down the Three Gorges, etc. We simply could not have made the trip the way we did without Gretchen's help.

Traveling with Gretchen in China was a lot of fun. We rode trains, local buses, etc. Never flew. I recall that many days we had picnic lunches. For a beverage we would buy a quart bottle of beer. This was to have something to drink since tap water was and probably still is a no no. Then our arrival in Xian was memorable. We arrived very early in the morning after an all night train ride. No taxis were operation. So I asked Gretchen to line up two like rickshaws - one for Gretchen and luggage and one for Mom and me. I paid the two 20 Yuan to take us to up to three hotels for accommodations. When we went by one hotel, the rickshaw men said they understood space would be available there. I told Gretchen that the hotel had been the Russian building and was not a very good place. I told Gretchen to ask the drivers to take us to the Bell Tower hotel. They did, and Gretchen did get us space. When she came out of the hotel she said she had also lined up a tour of Xian, leaving momentarily. So we got in a bus and took off. I don't know if Gretchen knew the tour would be in Chinese. No problem, because Gretchen told us what was being said. Our visit to the tombs came not too long after they had first been discovered.

Traveling in China at the time we visited was especially interesting because the Chinese were very curious about maps, cameras, etc. Any time I opened up my map I would immediately be surrounded by a lot of Chinese. Same thing when I went to use my camera. I recall one time letting a young Chinese fellow look through the lens of my camera to see what I was photographing - he was so excited. Then amidst a lot of austerity in China, I recall our hotel stay in Nanjing. On the top floor there was an orchestra, obviously with older Chinese because they were playing tunes from the 50's.

I also learned on the trip how little the sales people knew about marketing. When I stopped at a hotel in Chengdu, or a nearby town, to try to get reservations for a boat down the Three Gorges, the woman to whom we spoke suggested that we just go down to the river in the morning. Then, if there was no space available for that day, we could return the next day and check, on availability of space, etc. I said no, we needed some certainty as to when we traveled and that we wanted to go down the river on the boat pictured in a catalog which I had with me. I showed her the catalog with a picture of the boat in it. She looked at the picture and said "Oh that's very expensive." I finally convinced her that in this case certainty was more important than cost. She said she would try. I gave her two Yuan to try. She said it would take about two hours to find out. I figured she would get the info in about a half hour. I was correct, and she did have the reservations.

At the time we were in China it had two currencies - renminbi, for the locals, and FC's (foreign certificates) for foreigners. Gretchen always encouraged me not to spend my FC's when I made a purchase, but rather to use her renminbi and repay her.

We had the same kind of experience when we got to Chongching when I tried to get train reservations for the route from Wuhan to Beijing. First of all the agent said he couldn't sell me tickets at that time, then when I insisted, he finally said that for 2 Yuan and about two hours time he would try to get us reservations. But he said I was wasting my money since he was not allowed to sell me tickets. We came back about an hour later, from lunch, and found he had gotten the reservations for us. So, anyway, these illustrations are typical of some of the things we experienced on the trip - things which made the travel even more interesting.

During this general period, we also turned into camp followers and went to South Korea while Richard was posted there. Excellent timing!! Richard was very gracious, made many helpful suggestions on sightseeing and also on places to make purchases like celadon vases and figures. We had a special opportunity, thanks to Richard, to make the acquaintance of and have dinner with a very wealthy family of Koreans. While Richard was working at his consular post in Seoul, a Korean classmate of his from Lakeside came through the office, seeking a visa for the U.S. Through this event, we ended up making the acquaintance of the people to whom I refer.

After graduating from Whitman, Kirk took a job as the music director and organist for St. John's Catholic Church in Seattle. He had played there a number of times, as I recall, while he was in school.

It worked out well for Kirk in at least two ways. First of all, he had a chance to see how he enjoyed life as an organist and choir director. Second, it afforded him the chance to meet Diane and court her. Fairly quickly, it became apparent to us that Kirk and Diane were quite serious about their relationship. We liked Diane and were glad to see their relationship blossoming.

It was about this time that so many things were happening that it is hard now to sort out exact dates of the various events. I think, though, that it was in about a 1985 that Kirk decided that he wanted continue his music education. He decided that he would like to gain an M.S.M. (Masters in Sacred Music) from Boston University. And so in about 1983 or 1984 he applied for and was admitted into the program. We had enjoyed having Kirk at home for a spell after Whitman, but it was good to see him advance his interest at one of the finest universities I the country for the program he enrolled in. And so it was that Lois and I really found ourselves living with just the two of us for the first time in a long while. We were glad for all three of ours, but it did make a change in our lives. Kirk's studies were in the school of theology at B.U.

I think I should have noted earlier that after Kirk graduated from Whitman he took off a couple of months and went to Europe. I think that would have been in 1981 or 1982. But as I say, there were so many things going on at that time it's hard to get the dates all sorted out without a road map. Anyway, Kirk headed off to Europe and spent a couple months traveling around on his own. So while Kirk did not have study abroad, he did have the opportunity to travel abroad.

We did get to Carleton for Gretchen's graduation. I believe we did meet Monica's parents at that time. My uncertainty is that it was not long thereafter, or at about that time that they were divorced. Anyway, we had a delightful time at the commencement. We also had an opportunity to meet the "kleptet" - the group of girls who had roomed together in a small dorm under the football stands - girls who had become very close friends during school. At least one of the girls was heading out on a short trip that I could have enjoyed - a canoe trip to the Boundary Waters Wilderness. That's a trip I would very much have enjoyed, I think. So all in all, we felt Gretchen had a great experience at Carleton.

I think it was just after Gretchen graduated, or perhaps it was the next spring, that Gretchen announced that she planned to hike the whole length of the AT (Appalachian Trail.). Lois was very concerned that Gretchen planned to do this on her own. Gretchen assured Mom that it was safe, and who were we to tell her what she could or can't do. So she took off from Springer Mt., Georgia the middle of April. And she did cover the whole 2,100 miles .She and friends she had met on the trail found themselves on the top of Mt. Katahdin, Maine, on the 12th or 13th of October. The day after they finished the trip a snow came in and the trail, or at least the high end part, was closed to travel until the following year.

Gretchen did have one interlude of on the trip. Sometime earlier, Kirk and Diane had become engaged. They scheduled the wedding for the summer of I think 1987. The wedding would be in the summer of 1987 at St. John's. That did pose a bit of a problem. Diane had been divorced and so a Catholic Church wedding was closed to them. However, a very resourceful priest at St. John's said, let us check the records. It turned out that the priest who had marred Diane and her first husband wasn't very good at record keeping. The priest had failed to enter the marriage in the Church records. So the priest at St. John's told Kirk and Diane, that since in the eyes of the Church she, Diane, had not been married, her's and Kirk's wedding could take place in the Church. And so it was. It was a beautiful wedding. Diane's parents and some of her family were there. Gretchen interrupted her AT hike for a week to come go to Seattle for the wedding (at that time she was somewhere in Virginia or perhaps near New England).

As I have noted, an awful lot of things were going on in our family during the 80's. In about 1984 Richard was transferred from Seoul to Singapore. Naturally, when that occurred, Mom and I turned into camp followers again. We planned a trip to Singapore. Then we decided also, that we would drive through Malaysia and would also take a trip to Burma. The trip to Singapore was quite interesting. It was the first time for us to visit that area. And the driving trip up along the west side and then down the east side of Malaysia was most it interesting. Our trip then included a junket to Burma. At that time visa length was limited to five or seven days. We saw a fair portion of Burma on that trip - including Mandalay, which I find a very interesting city.

We had a very attractive young lady as our guide in Burma. I noticed that Richard didn't seem to spend all of the time in Mandalay with us, but seemed to be spending some time with our guide. Little did we realize that our guide was Sherral and that it wouldn't be too long before she would be our daughter-in-law!! Oh yes, one other aspect of our day in Mandalay. The U.S. at the time still owned property in Mandalay which had served as the residence of the U.S. consul to Burma. There was no longer a consul there at the time. Richard as an FSO could reserve the residence for accommodations. There was a woman still there who served as cook, caretaker, etc. She prepared some excellent meals for us.

Richard had been debating, I think, whether to leave the Service soon or make a career with the Foreign Service (I may be assuming things not really correct. This was just a perception.) In any event he decided to leave the Foreign Service after two years in Singapore. He decided that he would like to attend the Stanford University business school. It was also at this same time that Richard and Sherral became engaged. I don't have the chronology exactly correct, perhaps, but I think that they became engaged in about 1985. I recall having some discussions with Richard about their engagement. In any event Richard and Sherral were married during I believe Richard's first year in Business School.

Somewhere in this time frame, and I think this may have occurred before we took our first trip to Singapore, and not too long after she completed the AT hike, Gretchen decided that she would like to go to Louisiana. This would have been not too long after she hiked the AT. She met a few people from Louisiana and decided to spend time in the old French section of Louisiana. I think that she was there less than one year. I don't think it worked out all that well, although Gretchen never said too much about it. I do know that she had difficulty getting work. At a time she was examining abstracts, or some such thing, for a title company. I know that I was concerned about how she was managing. While she was there, or shortly thereafter, and I think the later Mom and I made a trip to that part of the country. We saw some of the bayous, visited the factory where Tabasco sauce is made, etc.

Sometime after Gretchen returned from Louisiana she decided that she would like to go to Taiwan to work. I think that a fellow she had met on the AT told her that getting a job would be easy. In any event she went and was there for a year or two. As I recall she got work as an interpreter. She did some interpreting or working for a couple of businessmen in Taiwan who gave or sold her very cheaply a motorbike or motorcycle. I recall that Gretchen was very glad that helmets were required. As a blond, blue eyed American she stood out too much for her liking. The helmet made her much less conspicuous.

Once again, Mom and I took the opportunity to be camp followers and took a trip to Taiwan. It was an interesting trip and it was made much better because we had a guide who could also speak Chinese. I recall while we were there we visited a great art gallery where much of the art work which Chiang Kai Shek took from China is stored. I recall also that there were thousands of weddings going on at the time. Seems that the next year would be most favorable to have a child and all the couples wanted to get married so they could have their child the next year.

Richard completed his studies at Stanford in I believe spring of 1986, although it might have been 1987. Mom and I drove down to Palo Alto for the Commencement. We had a great time. We met a number of Richard's classmates, and the parents of at least one of his classmates. We also loaded up on apricots on the way down. (We found California produce very seductive. In the past we had loaded up on avocados. One time I overdid it with avocados, but not enough to spoil my taste.)

About this time, i.e. 1984, I began to experience some angina pains on exertion. By 1985 I knew that I had to have a health check. Kas Skubi, my primary care physician, referred me to John Petersen. It was discovered that I had some narrowing of three coronary arteries. The question was just what to do. I felt that I did not want to go for the balloon and metal stent. In those fairly early days of the technology, there were fairly frequent and often sudden collapses of the balloon. So I opted for bypass surgery. The surgery went well and in a month or so I was back at the office.

By the later part of the 1980's grandchildren began appearing. Kimberly was the first to arrive, in October of 1988. By that time Richard had completed his studies at Stanford and was working in Tokyo for Citibank. Understandably, Mom was very excited and decided to go to Tokyo for a couple of weeks to help out with Kimberly. I think that especially with grandchildren, we began the practice of taking annual trips to the Orient or wherever our family was.

It was some time in the late 80's that Gretchen decided that what she really wanted to do was to go in to nursing. Because of where she went to school, I think she made the decision about the time she returned from Taiwan. In any event, she made application go Stamford University in Birmingham Alabama, was accepted and headed off for her career learning. We visited a couple of times while she was in school. I recall that one trip was scheduled to that we would visit Kirk and Diane in Framingham and also visit Gretchen and go to Florida. The weather got all mixed up on that trip. Winter was warmer in the east and colder in Florida, but we had a good trip, nevertheless.

Especially as the 80's went along, I noticed that it was becoming more difficult to generate new clients. I guess I was getting to the age where people looked at me and decided that if they were going to engage a new attorney they wanted to hire a younger person. Anyway, this was not exactly an ego builder but it was a reality. In the late 1980's I found myself serving as the Managing Partner for LeSourd & Patten. This was definitely a mixed bag. If I had followed past experience, I would have served only for two years as managing partner. The next one probably in line to be managing partner was John Colgrove. John was a very nice person, very bright, etc., but not a manager type. I recall at least one of my partners urging me to continue longer in that role. I did so, and later regretted that I had stayed so long in that role.

The demands of the job limited the time I would have had available to try to generate new business. But, that's water over the dam.

By the time 1990 came along, the firm had perhaps twenty five attorneys. We had not developed a strong business reputation in anything other than taxation so we were at a bit of a disadvantage. Woolvin Patten was disabled with strokes by that time. Fran was setting on into his 80's and so was not thinking about expanding the practice the way he probably would have done when younger. In any event in 1990 a few of the younger attorneys decided to break away from the firm. The break involved enough of the attorneys that it effectively adversely affected the firm itself.

I found myself on the outside, as was the case also with Leon Misterek and Dan Woo. Leon and Dan had been working together closely and it was natural that they would stick together. They invited me to join them, which I did. The firm breakup was extremely unfortunate from my perspective. I was 65 years old, my practice had been somewhat limited in size, especially because of the time and effort I put in to being managing partner of the law firm. And so I found the whole experience to be a bit shattering.

At the time I was involved in a very interesting and rather complex condemnation proceeding begun by the Port of Seattle. Also the Church landmark case was still chugging along at the appellate level. And of course, there was a fair amount of 4th & Pike work. But with the break up of the firm it appeared to me, and the perception was correct, that the likelihood of my being able to hold onto an office in a retired status, doing to a reduced workload (a practice very common at the time in larger firms) was rather diminished. Overall, my future looked a lot different than I had hoped and imagined over the years what it would be when I got to retirement age.

In 1990 I still enjoyed good health, Mom and I were still very much on the travel trail, taking at least one long international trip each year, the house mortgage had been paid off for some time and we were debt free. So things could have been worse. It's just that my hopes for the future had become quite a bit different than I had imagined and hoped would be the case.

23

Seattle - 1991-2000

Nineteen ninety one was a big year for grandchildren. Both Benjamin and Colin appeared on the scene. I don't recall any specific items or events tied to Benjamin's birth. Colin, though, was a bit different. He and Diane were in a hospital located along the route of the Boston Marathon. Diane and Colin had intended to leave sometime in the morning of Marathon day. The route of the Boston Marathon being what it was, the entrance area to the hospital was closed because of the runners. So, Diane and Colin left the hospital a couple hours later than planned. Both grandsons' births were uneventful and we were delighted to welcome them into the family.

Nineteen ninety one was the first full year that I practiced law with Leon and Dan. I recall also that I was still working on the condemnation action brought by the Port of Seattle and also the appeal of the landmark case of First Methodist. And of course there was the ongoing work for Fourth & Pike.

Gretchen was continuing her nursing studies at Stamford University during 1991 and 1992. I think that she graduated in 1992. We found our way back to that part of the country a few times while she was in school. And we did some traveling in the area when we went to visit Gretchen. I recall that one trip took us to the store in I think northern Alabama where Northwest Airlines has a store selling all of the merchandise from lost luggage. Quite a store. I looked at a suit or jacket but, as might be expected, the sizing was not quite right. But the price was certainly appealing. I think it was during this period that we took the trip to Louisiana that I have mentioned earlier.

Gretchen enjoyed the pediatric hospital work the most, I think. She seemed to really concentrate on that area of care. Then when she graduated she went to work for Alabama Children's hospital in Birmingham. Overall her favorite hospital, as I recall, was in Bellingham, but she very much enjoyed the work at the children's hospital.

Mom and I did not attend Gretchen's graduation from Stamford University. I can't now recall just why we did not. But I do have a recollection that for some reason Gretchen did not encourage or want us to make the trip back there.

Richard had left Citibank in about 1990. He lined up a job with MasterCard which turned out to be much more satisfactory for him. The change in employer did mean a move. Either at the time he joined MasterCard or very shortly thereafter, they moved went to Singapore. The move to Singapore meant, of course, that we ended up with a new destination to which to travel on our annual junkets to see Richard and family.

It was during the late 80's or early 90's that Seattle Downtown Central Lions Club effectively came to an end. The demise was part of the decline of service clubs generally during this period. By the time that the club had dwindled to perhaps ten members, and the weekly meetings had changed basically to Friday lunches with five or six Lions, I, too, joined the exit. The Club simply wasn't large enough to engage in the service projects which should be such a large part a of a service club organization.

I think that it was in 1993 that the Supreme Court heard and decided the Landmark case for First Methodist. I was very pleased that the court ruled in favor of the Church, and basically reinstated the judgment of the Superior Court a few years earlier. I decided after winding up that case that it was time for me to discontinue my litigation work. It was a matter of recognizing that as I was getting older and the stress and long hours of a longer case were getting too tough for me. Also, my volume of work had declined with the changes in the practice arena. I felt that I did not have the volume of trial work necessary to really keep abreast of all of the court rules, and also that I was not keeping abreast of the changes in the law. I felt that it would be prudent for me to avoid failing a client by continuing to work in an arena where I knew that I wasn't as competent as I had been for forty years.

Gretchen, in the meantime turned in to a bit of a nomad as far as the medical work was concerned. After a year or two at Birmingham Children's hospital, she signed up for the traveling nurse program and was hired by a hospital in Pocatello Idaho. This was not a very successful tour. First of all, she faced twelve hour shifts which she found too exhausting. Then she found Pocatello as basically a blue collar town was not as interesting a place for her to live as other places in the country. Pocatello also lacked a good book store. There was another town in that general part of Idaho which did have a good book store, but it was not convenient for her.

We did visit Gretchen at least once when she was in Idaho. We did have a very nice trip. And our trip did include a visit to Craters of the Moon National Monument, which we enjoyed very much. And of course, a real plus on the trip was that Gretchen did have a couple of days to spend traveling around with us. Feeling as she did about Pocatello it wasn't that long until Gretchen decided to move on to a different location. This time it was to Moses Lake. It was a smaller city than she had lived in before. They have, I think she felt, a good hospital, but Moses Lake is not large enough to have the facilities of hospitals in larger locations. We did get over to Moses Lake to visit Gretchen at least once during her fairly short stay in that city. I enjoy eastern Washington, even though I would not want to live in that section of the State.

As the early 90's moved along, Leon apparently was becoming restless. In any event, it was, I believe, sometime during 1993 that Leon announced that he was going to retire. The news came as quite a surprise. Leon was then only in his early 60's and as far as I knew retirement at that time was not in his plans. Anyway, the announcement was a surprise to everyone. With his retirement, we would be heavy on staff. We responded by terminating a very good secretary, simply because with Leon's retirement we would not have enough need for secretarial services to keep all the employees on staff. Then I think we may also have given up a part of our space. Anyway, about the time everything was in place, all things done, Leon changed his mind and decided that he would indeed keep practicing. I was glad he did, but we all could have done just as well without everything that came with his announcement of retirement.

After another couple of years of practice, at the end of 1995 or 1996, Leon again changed his mind and decided to retire. I learned about it from Dan in a phone conversation since I was on the travel trail when Leon made the announcement. But this time, Dan said no way. He'd been through this retirement gig before with Leon and wasn't going to do it again. Dan simply said that the firm would fold up. By this point in time, my practice, which had continued to decline, was not big enough for me to do anything about it if the firm wound up.

So the question for me was, what to I do now. I was not prepared to retire, even though it was at the seventy year mark. I decided that the best thing would be for me to try to sublease space in another law firm's offices. After giving some thought to it, I spoke to Dwayne Copple and worked out an arrangement to sublease an office in their space. Theresa Lawrence, a very good secretary at Misterek and Woo, and at LeSourd & Patten before that would be my secretary, etc. I was very happy in the arrangement and hoped that it would continue for an extended period of time.

But lo and behold, after about eight months or so, Dwayne told me that the firm was very happy to have me there but they no longer had space for me. And of course I knew a number of the attorneys there, so it hadn't been as if I had gone in to a firm where everybody was new. Williams, Kastener and Gibbs, the law firm, had given up space a few years earlier and now found that they needed portions, at least, of the space they had given up. So there I was, once again trying to figure out how to deal with this situation.

This time it wasn't so easy to find a new home. I quickly started looking around. I spoke to a number of firms I in hopes that I might find space there. But no such luck. I didn't, at that point, have a large book of business. The economics of the law practice had changed. Since I did not have a good book of business which might result in economic benefit to the firm where I might office, the firms just weren't interested. The economics of the practice of law had indeed changed significantly since I began practice.

So I looked around and found space in Two Union Square on its Executive Suite floor. I was able to rent space, the manager of the floor would provide secretarial help as needed, etc. So at the end of 1996 I moved again and began my era of solo practice. As part of that move, I had to face the reality that my practice was not large enough to hire a secretary. To deal with that, I bought a computer. I recall one or two secretaries from the L&P side said they never thought they would see me using a computer. But, necessity is the mother of invention. So I bought a computer and proceeded to learn enough about it to have it as a valuable tool for secretarial, legal work and other miscellaneous items.

While the changes were occurring in the office there were some changes in another aspect of my life. I decided in I think 1995 that I would volunteer for service to Blue Ridge Board and would run for the position. I was elected and began my second three years of service to the Blue Ridge community.

During the 1990's, I later realized, changes were occurring of which I was not then aware. I knew that Mom seemed to be making some changes in her interests - e.g. over the years we had had dinner parties every so often. Both of us enjoyed the dinners. By the early 90's Lois was not interested in having people in for dinner. I guess that also Lois was becoming more irritable with me, and was not willing any longer to do a number of things we had done routinely in the past. I realize now that these changes were a precursor to much darker things.

By late 1996 or early 1997, Mom was becoming very forgetful. She just would not remember things. These changes continued to magnify as 1997 progressed. During 1997 I realized the tragic reality that Mom was manifesting definite signs of Alzheimer's disease. Gretchen and I had lots of discussions of the matter. During all of this period, all of the 90's, Mom manifested the ability to conceal her problem from most people.

By the end of 1997 or very early 1998 I contacted the Alzheimer's section of University Hospital. The facility is, or was, located on Beacon Hill, or near to it. I scheduled an appointment for her evaluation. Gretchen and I at this point met with Mom to discuss the nature of the problem and the need for an evaluation. Mom listened to us and then expressed shock. She said "I never thought you would say to me the kinds of things you have." She was totally unable to cope or deal with the reality.

After the first visit and some further examination and testing, I was told by the staff that Mom was suffering from mental deterioration. It was not then diagnosed as Alzheimer's. But life at home became ever more difficult. Unfortunately, for all of us, Mom manifested the aggressive and combative form of the disease. The problem was made even more difficult because Mom's hearing was declining and I had to arrange for her to get hearing aids.

Mom never did adjust to hearing aids. Worse than that, she simply would not wear them much of the time. Further, she couldn't remember to take care of them and she lost one of the aides at least once.

We took a trip to Singapore in early 1997. It was a very difficult trip. Mom was just so restless and agitated that she could not rest on the plane. We traveled on an overnight flight, e.g., with all lights on at our apace, and with Mom thrashing the whole night. It was the last long trip that Mom and I ever took together.

The next year, in early 1998, Mom was tested again. This time there was no equivocation. She was diagnosed with Alzheimer's. I was told that positive diagnosis could be made only by biopsy but the Hospital's record on diagnosis was better than 90% correct. Further, the Dr. told me in no uncertain that Mom MUST not drive a car any longer.

The need to give up driving was especially hard on Mom. She had wanted a red car for many ears. In I think 1996 or 1997 I found a 1990 red Cadillac in very good condition. I bought it for her. Only to find out fairly soon that she could never again be at the wheel.

Difficulties at home increased. Mom simply lost her ability to cook, etc. But worse, she would not recognize the limitation. Thus a piece of the sink is now missing-- a piece of tile popped out because Mom put a very hot pot in the sink. I arranged for a time to have women come and stay with Mom in the afternoons. Mom so opposed and resisted this that she literally drove away at least one of the workers. She once slammed the front door so hard in the face of a new worker that it almost broke the door. The worker turned and left and never came near again. Later I succeeded in getting Mom in a daycare program at a facility near Northgate. The bus picked her up right in front of our place, returned her about 3:30 and then I tried to have a person there at about the time she got back from the care facility.

As time went by Mom became More and more combative and aggressive - both verbally and physically combative. I began to consider the need to place Mom in some kind of care facility. Gretchen was very familiar with what was going on.

It was at about this time, probably about a 1998, that Gretchen left Moses Lake and took a position at the hospital in Bellingham. She enjoyed it there very much and often said it was the nursing position she liked best. When she and Darin were married his job was not portable, but Gretchen's was very portable so she left the hospital in Bellingham. It was wonderful to have Gretchen so close. I started to go up to Bellingham fairly frequently, in part just to get away from home.

While she was in Bellingham Gretchen started looking for a house to buy. She met a very nice real estate woman who showed her a number of places. Gretchen thought about buying five acres with a blueberry farm on it. I suggested it might be difficult to both nurse and care for a five blue blueberry farm. She did find a very nice house a few miles south of Bellingham. She considered it seriously. Fortunately, in light of what happened it was fortunate she did not go through with any house purchase

In I believe 2000 I learned about what sounded like a great air safari to the southern part of Africa - South Africa, Namibia, Mozambique and Botswana. I very much wanted to do it. I was sure that Gretchen would enjoy it, and indeed she was interested. But what would be do about Mom who obviously would not be able to make the trip and was not really able to be by her self for three weeks. The trip Gretchen and I took to Africa was one of the best trips I think either of us ever took. And it was such a great plus to be able to take the trip with Gretchen.

It turned out that Mom's very good and long time friend Marion Karn was in much the same situation as Mom. At about that time I read about a cruise of the New England area. I came up with the idea of Mom and Marion making that trip together, while Gretchen and I would be on the air safari. And so we did work that out. And they both enjoyed the trip so much. I think it was the last trip that either of them took

At the time that Gretchen and I took the air safari Gretchen had mentioned that she had had a date or two with somebody in the Bellingham area - or at least that's where I thought he was from. When we got back from the trip, she had a beautiful bouquet of roses from this "date" I had heard about. I said to myself, this is more than just a casual date.

And so it was in this way that I learned about Darin Anderson. When I met him I liked him immediately. His courtship proceeded with vigor and they became engaged just before the end of the year. I think it was at about this time they decided that they wanted an early wedding. Perhaps even at this date they decided on February 29, 2001, Leap year's extra day.

Gretchen and Darin had a very beautiful wedding at home. Kirk made the trip to Seattle to play for the wedding. A good friend of Kirk's from B.U. performed the ceremony. There were just a handful of us in attendance for the wedding. After the wedding we had a very nice lunch at the Palisades. Darin was, I think, so excited that when he went to the restroom to change his trousers for the wedding trip, he accidentally found himself changing in the women's room - from which he exited as quickly as he could. But they got off for a lovely honeymoon.

By 2000 I was at the point were I needed some respite. Gretchen at least, and to some extent Richard also thought I should consider putting mom in a care facility at that time. (It took Kirk longer to realize the scope of the problem. He was not here much and so didn't have a chance to see Mom in action. I recall) that it was after Kirk made a visit to Seattle that his thinking changed. I think it was about this time, when Kirk came on board with the idea that we might have to put Mom in a facility that Richard sent me an email where he said of Kirk's change, "Hallelujah, brother, we've got a convert."

By mid 2000 I contacted I arranged for Marlyce Bowers to come over midday Thursday and spend Thursday and Friday nights with Mom. Then I would come home about noon Saturday. . Marlyce had been our receptionist at L&P for a number of years. Gretchen said to me, "Dad you are exhausted every Thursday when you come to our place. It takes you until Saturday morning to recover, and then start over for another week." Gretchen and Darin very graciously insisted that I stay with them the two nights each week when I was away on respite time.

The arrangement with Marlyce worked well for about six or seven months. Marlyce and Mom took a few trips together, etc. and got along well. But by late 2000 Mom had declined to the point that Marlyce wasn't sure she could continue for long. It was one time when I returned from my two day respite that Mom looked at me and said, "Now are you my husband or father?" Shock for me!! I knew we were fast approaching the state where Mom just could no longer be at home. Actually Gretchen and Richard felt earlier that I should make the change. But I was determined to keep Mom home until I satisfied myself that it just was no longer possible for me to do it.

Only later did Gretchen tell me that her westward march for nursing jobs was because she had recognized by the very early 90's that something unfortunate was happening to Mom. She certainly recognized the signs before I did. And I was eternally grateful for the effort and sacrifice Gretchen made to help

At the end of 2000, December 30, 2000, Mom and I celebrated our 50th wedding anniversary. Richard did most of the work in planning a dinner for a few friends. We held it at the Columbia Tower Club at the Columbia Tower. The invitees included son Richard and Sherral, Gretchen and Darin, the Copples, the Mistereks, the Matterns -long time friends and perhaps one or two others.

We had a lovely dinner. Mom succeeded well in keeping her disability under control. She had a new dress, a new hair treatment, etc., all with help from Marlyce. I'm not sure Mom even recognized the event or the significance. She was quiet, subdued, smiled at everyone but said little, etc.

I was so glad that we had had such a big party to celebrate our 40th wedding anniversary. I recall Mom saying at the time, that she thought it was well to have a big fortieth party because a lot of people never get to celebrate a 50th. And I think that is so true. And while we had a wonderful 50th party, I don't think Mom really understood what was going on.

And so we celebrated our fifty years. It had been a remarkable journey. I was just sad that Mom wasn't able to enjoy it that much, or even comprehend the event.

24

Seattle 2001-2005

The years 2001 and onward were some of the best and some of the worst of my life. Those among the worst were Lois' declining years. Among the best and worst were Gretchen's high points and low points.

By early 2001 it was apparent that Lois would not be able to continue living at home. Even though Lois' health had deteriorated very seriously I was determined to keep her at home until I was satisfied that it was just impossible to do so. By this time Richard, Kirk and Gretchen were telling me that they felt that I should proceed to place Lois in a care facility.

The inability to keep Lois at home was also affected by the fact that Lois had deteriorated to the point that Marlyce would no longer be able to care for Lois for my weekly respite. Mom had reached the "sundowner" state where she was all mixed up between night and day. She started bringing coffee to Marlyce at four a.m. and asking what Marlyce would like for breakfast. Somewhere in this stage Mom reached the point where I could no longer leave her medicines out. One evening I discovered that she had put out on the kitchen counter from a bottle of her medicine many of the Arricept tablets in a medicine bottle. I had no idea, and neither did she, whether she had taken any of the medicine, and if so, how many. I found myself at 10 or 10:30

that evening calling the Poison Control Center for help. I was told there was a wide range of safety on Arricept, but that I should just watch her during the night in case she tried to get up and was too wobbly to negotiate her way.

Faced with these problems I looked around and found Faerland Terrace. It was a new facility, located at 1421 Minor, fairly close to my office and not too far from home, etc. I checked it out and it seemed to be just the sort of place that I was looking for. So I got Lois registered. I wasn't certain how she would react. To get her to go in peacefully I told her that I had a little business trip and that I wanted to be sure she was taken care of while I was away and so she would go there. Once she went in, she never left. And just as I was told would be the case, she adjusted fairly quickly and that was home for her.

Faerland Terrace was close enough to my office that I could walk up there and have lunch with Lois. During the firsts couple of months, when I was about to leave, from lunch I explained that had to get back to the office. She was concerned about how she would get home. "Oh" I would say, "I will stop by for you on the way home." That calmed her down, of course and she promptly forgot about my coming back for her.

Unfortunately, Lois' combative and aggressive practices increased fairly quickly. She began engaging in practices which we all found unbelievable. She would bite and scratch, and kick at the nursing care staff, etc. It got so bad that I had to put her in to Northwest Hospital for a week where they started her on mind altering drugs, just to calm her down. The aggressive combative practices did calm down but of course it slowed her down, also, in other ways.

By the time I put Lois into Faerland Terrace I was experiencing some angina. I went to John Petersen, was tested and found that I had significant arterial blockage and that it looked like I would have another time in the hospital for repair. John Petersen told me the risks on a second bypass surgery. I told him that I wasn't going to be a cardiac cripple and we should go forward. The surgery worked out well. And over the years since then, John has said a number of times, that having that surgery was really the right decision.

And then, this time period brought some of the best of times. Gretchen and Darin were so very happy and so obviously very much in love. It just gave me a good feeling all over. And they found a house to buy in Sammamish, a house that very quickly became a home. I became a frequent visitor and they were always so gracious to me.

But all too soon Gretchen's health took a terrible turn. She suffered kidney failure and was seriously ill. Then followed a course of dialysis. The three times a week visit for the cleansing with dialysis fairly quickly became a real burden.

The question was, should Gretchen have a kidney transplant. Richard and Kirk both were checked out to see if either could be a good prospect for a donation of a kidney. Kirk turned out to have a very good match and made the lifesaving decision for Gretchen to donate one of his kidneys. And so, after about a year on dialysis she and Kirk had surgery in May of 2001 and Gretchen received one of Kirk's kidneys. (The surgery almost coincided with my second bypass surgery.)

As I believe I mentioned earlier, the law firm with Leon Misterek and Dan Woo came to an end in about 1996. It was then that I started practicing law on a solo basis. I rented an office on the executive suite floor of Two Union Square. The space worked out well for me although practicing alone resulted in a whole new way of practicing. I had decided in 1993, after the wind up of the First Methodist Church case, that I would hang up litigation work. The stress and time demands when in trial were becoming just too much for me to handle. Also I found that as I was getting older that it was becoming increasingly difficult to generate new clients. And, many of my business clients were getting older, retiring, selling their business, or dying. None of those scenarios were conducive to an increase in the law practice

In about 2003 two fellows who engaged in the bond business leased space next to mine in two Union Square. I quickly became acquainted with them - Ed Riley and Brian Bertsch. Fairly soon I learned that Ed had a plan to open a stock and bond brokerage. Not too long after that Ed came in to my office to chat. He told me of his plans for a brokerage firm and further, he wanted me to be the attorney for the business - not house counsel, but an attorney who would office with the firm.

I told Ed I was flattered that he would ask me, but told him that there were three things which might affect his plan. First, I said, I don't get in the office until 9:30 or 10. Fine, Ed said. Then I said that I only worked three days a week. Fine, Ed said. Then, third, I said, I take a fair amount of time off to travel. Fine, Ed said. So then I said that I was sure we could work out an arrangement satisfactory to both of us, which we did. In exchange for serving as attorney I would get rent, phone, office space etc.

Fairly soon thereafter, Ed leased suite 5300 in the Washington Mutual Tower. When we all moved in to the building there were 10 to 12 of us - total staff. To help out with the organization costs, start up costs, etc. I helped them find and secure a bank loan, which I guaranteed. I also bought a block of preferred stock with a kicker of a block of common stock for $.01per share. And there I still am today. The firm has grown from this one office to a multi-office firm, with several offices in Washington and also offices in California, Idaho, Arizona, Colorado, Oregon, etc. with a total count today of one hundred plus. With the vast expansion in the scope and size of the business it now needs legal support in several different disciplines - a need which I can't myself fulfill. So in 2007 the firm has engaged the Davis Wright firm, with its 200-300 attorneys with a broad range of skills to handle the legal work. I continue to occupy the space in the same way as always, except that I don't have an obligation to provide legal services.

Serving as attorney with my schedule worked out well, I enjoyed the work and appreciated the opportunity to serve as attorney for E.K. Riley Investments. Even though I was out of town frequently, it was not difficult to provide legal services. I recall, for example, a few years ago, when in Romania, and found an email outlining a need for my services. With email and phone I took care of he firm needs while on the trip.

Living by myself, for five years, kept me very busy. Three days a week in the office, housekeeping, cleaning, shopping, meal preparation, yard work, etc. etc. kept me going on a very fast pace.

I did take time during these years to make my annual trip to Singapore. And I also kept going in other international travel. Son Richard got me tied in to the Stanford travel program. Even though Mom and I had almost always traveled independently, I found that the good tours operated by Stanford worked out well. My travels included a great trip to India, and a trip to Cambodia, Laos and Vietnam.

Within the year of when Lois went in to Faerland Terrace I located help with house cleaning. I found young women working independently, to come in each week, to clean, etc. Then pretty much at the insistence of Richard, Kirk and Gretchen, the house cleaning was institutionalized. Merry Maids was engaged to clean every other week. That took a pretty good load off my back - just had meal preparation, yard care, shopping, plus of course the office work. It was still a very busy time for me.

As the years went by, Mom's health continued to decline. I always got in to see her two, three or four times each week at Faerland Terrace. Within the year of when she went into Faerland Terrace it was not possible to have lunch with her. She just couldn't manage to handle her meal. Then her walking skills declined. The first couple of years we would have good walks all around Faerland Terrace. But then her walking skills became more difficult. I did continue walking with her until probably about 2004 but as time progressed she became unable to walk without quite a bit of assistance. As time passed, her verbal skills declined. After mid or late 2003 there was no real conversation. Her recognition of me became an uncertain sort of thing by 2004. She always seemed to have a slight smile of recognition, almost to the end. The staff were certain that she recognized me. But it was all very tenuous.

Gretchen's health went through changes, also, after the transplant. In the early years after the transplant she was able to do all the things she had always done, although she did not have the stamina she did before surgery. It seemed that she had so many side effects from the transplant. She developed some intestinal problems that I am sure caused her a great deal of pain. Gretchen never complained, however. She maintained her confidence in Dr. Tung, her doctor, and seemed to accept all the various side effects and limitations on her activities. During this period she also became involved in driving people who needed a ride for medical care, shopping, etc. etc. She continued to do this faithfully every week until mid 2007. Toward the end it must have been very difficult for her, but she never seemed to complain

By the summer of 2004 Lois was pretty much bedridden. It became apparent to me that her nursing needs were such that Faerland Terrace could no longer provide the intensive care which Lois required. So by late summer I arranged for her to be admitted to the nursing home section of Providence. Much more intensive care - feeding, bed care, etc. Lois was bedridden for the rest of her life. She was unable to talk, for all practical purposes could not walk, although I did for a short time walk with her, holding her, knowing that if I let go she would fall.

It was during the Faerland Terrace and Providence periods that we were very glad that we had many hears earlier purchased Long Term Care insurance. I had a fight with the insurance carrier, which insisted that the policy provided only nursing home care. It said that Faerland Terrace was not a nursing home and that the policy did not cover her care. I engaged a woman attorney at Williams Kastener and Gibbs to represent me and together we got GE, the insurance carrier to agree that "on a one time basis" it would reimburse me for Lois' care. We showed that Faerland Terrace provided each service which the policy said must be required by the patient before coverage applied. Lois and I had purchased the policies when we were about 65. Our monthly premiums were about $200 per month for each policy. Lois care at Faerland Terrace and Providence ended up costing well over $200,000 so I have always felt that we were very fortunate to have the policy for her, and peace of mind for me "just in case"..

By the end of 2004 it was apparent that Lois had very little time left. Indeed, by then she had basically no quality of life. But we had no way of knowing how long she might linger. During the latter part of 2004 I had made reservations for the Stanford trip to Vietnam, Cambodia and Laos. So the question, in light of Mom's condition, was what I should do. I made the decision to go on the trip. Gretchen would be nearby: I had made arrangements with a funeral director to take care of the situation in case she died while I was away, etc. Also, there was nothing I could do by sticking around. I have never regretted the decision to go on the trip.

Lois did die while I was in Thailand. I continued the trip since there was nothing I could do by coming back early. When I returned we made arrangements for a Memorial service at our Church - University Congregational Church. I felt we had a very fine memorial service. Don Mackenzie presided over the service.

I have done a great deal of reflecting over Lois' and my fifty four years plus of marriage. I realize all the time how fortunate I was to have

Lois as my wife. She truly was a wonderful person. And I have always felt that our marriage was about as close to perfect as any marriage can be. We were always very deeply in love. There was a give and take between us which enabled both of us to enjoy life of the fullest. And there was never a time when she did not support me to the full. I have reflected often about her courage in saying without hesitation that yes, we should go west if that is where I wanted for us to live. And in ever so many ways we both just dealt with life as it was given to us. I can hardly imagine being so fortunate. And while we were married for just over 54 years, we really were together for sixty years. From the time I came back to Allegheny after the war and after we started going together, each of us knew that we were made for a life together. And what a life it was!!

25

Seattle 2006-2008

This period in my life, including a portion of 2005, was filled with some very good times, but also with some of the very worst times of my life. One of the worst times came with Lois death in February of 2005, as I noted earlier. Her death was not unexpected. Her health had deteriorated to the point were she had no quality of life. But her death meant the ending of a wonderful marriage and the end of life for my life companion of so many years. It left quite a void in my life. But I knew also with her death that I could not crawl into a hole. I knew I needed to get out and go forward. I knew also from my experience of the last years of Lois' life that living alone was not the lifestyle I would wish.

After Lois' Alzheimer's had progressed to the point that she had to be institutionalized and after she reached the point where we could not communicate well with each other I felt that I would like to get out socially and perhaps see if there was a woman with whom I might be able to spend time. It was not an easy thing to do. Lois had been the only woman in my life for so long that looking for a social relationship with another took a real effort on my part. And I soon learned that while at my age there are a lot more women than men of my age there were not that many whom I felt I wanted to spend much time with.

For I time I spent time with Sara Stoeppel. At first it seemed as if this might develop into a good relationship. After a time it became apparent to me that this would not be a good course. So that came to an end. I knew also that the rest of the family felt it would not be a good idea to continue any relationship with Sara. I have since been told by at least at least one good friend at Church that they were relieved what things with Sara came to an end for me. Then there was Ann Payne, whose physician husband had died a few years earlier. Payne's lived in Blue Ridge. Lois had known Ann quite well and I had known both Tom and Ann reasonably well. She is a very nice woman and we had some good times together. For a variety of reasons, it just did not click.

Another woman at Church whom I had met and seen, generally at or after Church, was Roberta Swenson. Lois had known her through PTA quite a number of years earlier. I noticed that she drove to Church each Sunday as did I, living just two or three blocks from each other. So, nothing ventured, nothing gained. I don't know whether I spoke to her at Church, or phoned her, but in any event I told her that with gas prices being what they were and with all the emphasis on conservation it might make sense for us to travel to Church together. She agreed that made sense and so we started traveling together back and forth to and from Church. That seemed to work out well. Soon I was inviting her to stop and have lunch with me after Church on my deck. Then a little later on I suggested that since we were both cooking our own dinner that it might work out better for both of us if we ate some dinners at her place and some at mine and then each of us would get some relief on the cooking front. That worked out quite well (Roberta says to this day that she had a better deal on the food front when we were doing this than it is since we married.)

After a time I began to think seriously about asking Roberta to marry me. I did so in the fall of 2005. She accepted. We decided that a spring 2006 wedding would be good timing. We spoke to Don Mackenzie. He said he would be pleased but he only had one or two dates open in the spring of 2006 because he would be going on Sabbatical in, I think, May of 2006. So, we set April 22, 2006 as the date

After we became engaged, but before we had set the date, or shortly before the date was set, I did invite Roberta to go with me to Singapore and to spend some time in Bangkok and surroundings in Thailand. She was a little uncertain. She asked her son David what he thought about it, and he said he wouldn't waste heartbeat thinking about it and that she should accept. (Good for David.) We had a great trip. Our good friend Frank Kelsey kidded us and said that we obviously were taking the new modern approach and having the honeymoon before the wedding!!

We decided that we would have a fairly small wedding with family and friends. As the planning progressed the size of the wedding grew and grew. Before we knew it we were at about 200 invitees! So much for the idea of a small wedding!! There was a lot of planning, lots of invitations, etc. etc. Richard would be my best man. Roberta's granddaughter would be her maid of honor. Kirk agreed to be our organist and Kirk's wife Diane was the soloist. Gretchen would manage the guest book at our wedding. Verle Bleese and David Swenson, Roberta's son, would be ushers. Perhaps I haven't included everyone, but I think I have all the parties listed. Then Phillip Rotter, the son of Ruth Marie and Ernie Rotter agreed to handle all the floral arrangements.

Our wedding was a very festive occasion. We invited a lot of our older friends, which was a good portion of the invitees, and they were very pleased to be invited. So many of the occasions for our older friends are memorial services that getting out for this kind of a happy affair is a nice change.

Roberta and I had a honeymoon at Harrison Hot Springs and then returned to the real world. We both began the marriage with the recognition that I am not Ken (her first husband) and she is not Lois. I like to think that we made a good adjustment, although I think we both think that the other is very stubborn on some issues. I think Roberta probably had more adjustments to make than I. After all, she was coming to live in a new house, everything was arranged differently, there were different dishes, different utilities etc. etc.

During 2006 Gretchen continued to deal with some of the side effects of her kidney failure. Kirk's kidney worked well. It's just that there was always the rejection issue looming over everything plus various other side effects. Gretchen also found that she simply did not have the level of energy which she enjoyed before the kidney failure. At this period of time, and for quite some time earlier, Gretchen did volunteer driving, on a program designed to get disabled people to their doctor's appointments, other health care needs, etc. Gretchen continued to so this driving on into the summer of 2007 even though I am certain that as time progressed it became more and more difficult for her to keep up. She was a very determined young lady, and as her doctor said later, she just wanted to keep on "and be just like the rest of the guys" no matter what.

I knew that Gretchen continued to have health problems related to here intestinal functioning. I suggested that she go back to Mayo or Cleveland Clinic for evaluation and such treatments as might be indicated. She was very reluctant to do so and flatly said she did not want to do so. She had confidence in Dr. Tung and wanted to follow her course of treatment and care. By hindsight I wish very much that I had pushed much harder on the subject. Darin has said, though, that he didn't think that Gretchen would have agreed to such a course. Darin encouraged me not to fault myself for not pushing harder to get her to go back for comprehensive evaluation and care.

As 2006 rolled along Roberta and I got out to a number of things, and then in early 2007 made our, or my, usual trip to Singapore. On this trip we took a side trip to Perth, Australia. It was the first trip to Australia for Roberta or me my first trip to Western Australia and we thoroughly enjoyed it.

` During 2006 and on in o 2007 we continued to see Gretchen and Darin although perhaps not as frequently as I had done before Roberta and I were married. Our less frequent trips were basically a result of Roberta and I having a number of people new to me with whom to spend part of our time. By hindsight I wish it had been the other way around and that we had spent more time than ever time with Gretchen and Darin.

Richard and his family spent Christmas with us and at Crystal Mountain as they have done for many years. I have always enjoyed their Christmases with us. This visit with us and the summer visits with us, and of course our annual trip to Singapore have provided us with a wonderful opportunity not just to visit with Richard and his family but to watch Kimberly and Benjamin as they have grown. I have often wished that it would have been possible for Kirk and his family to spend more time here in Seattle.

As the years have gone by my law practice has declined. Clients have died, sold their business, or retired. And it has become ever more apparent that younger people aren't as interested in hiring an older attorney. But I did continue to serve as the attorney for E.K. Riley and also to handle Fourth & Pike business. Changes did occur during 2007 that affected me and both of those clients. E.K. Riley has prospered, its number of offices has expanded greatly, and instead of the dozen or so people around when I started representing it, the total number of persons with the organization had increased to over 100. As the company has grown in size the scope of the legal needs have increased. The work requires a knowledge of more and more legal disciplines. In early 2007 Ed Riley told me he felt the need to hire an attorney with a larger firm to look out for the needs of the company. I agreed that I as a sole practitioner could not provide the level of service needed to meet all the needs of the business. So then in early 2007 the company engaged an attorney with Davis Wright to look out for the needs of the company. I still do an occasional bit of legal work for the company, but not on a regular basis.

Then in 2007 some of my partners in Fourth & Pike became convinced that we should sell the building. As it turned out, after taking into account those who wanted so sell for the sake of selling and those who wanted to sell to diversify their interests, I found myself as the only partner who strongly wanted to keep the building. PREP was engaged to handle the sale of the building. I could see the handwriting on the wall for me and my law practice. My position seemed to remind me Douglas Macarthur's comment that old soldiers never die, they just fade away.

As 2007 progressed Gretchen's health continued to decline. She just did not have the energy to keep going at the pace she had maintained. In late 2006, or early 2007, she changed from a position as floor nurse and took a job, still at Overlake Hospital, in administration. No more long hours standing, no more having to administer all the tests, etc. for the patients. I learned also that by the summer of 2007 she was experiencing swelling in the abdominal area. I wasn't aware of it. Darin told me later, though, that Gretchen shifted to looser fitting clothes that would hide the swelling.

Very suddenly in late August Gretchen called and spoke to Roberta (I was not home), so say that she was going in for surgery. Roberta said that she sounded upbeat and felt that this surgery would resolve a lot of the difficulties she was experiencing.

Gretchen had a very lengthy surgery in which a large part of her small intestines were removed. I began daily trips to the hospital. It took her a long time - two or three days - before she came out of the anesthetic. My concern for her mounted with each day. I observed that after she had come out of surgery that she was eating her meals. About the third day after that, though, I thought to myself that something is not quite right. I think I may have been the only one to notice that something seemed to be going wrong. My suspicion was correct. Something terribly wrong was going on.

Soon Gretchen was not able to breath on her own and she was put on a ventilator. Then we were told that she apparently had developed an infection in the brain. A biopsy would be required. Things just went from bad to worse. She never did recover consciousness. After perhaps nearly a week on ventilator we were advised that Gretchen had suffered a series of strokes, that it was most unlikely that she would in any event recover consciousness, but that even if she did she had lost most of her brain function. Perhaps the toughest decision I was ever called upon to make was to decide whether to remove the life support system. The doctors assured us that Gretchen simply did not have a chance. Darin and I agreed to the removal of life support and within the day Gretchen died - on September 1, 2007.

A part of me died with Gretchen's passing. Without a doubt, it is the very worst thing that has ever happened to me. It all seems so unfair - a young woman, not quite forty four years old who should have been at the peak of her family life, at the peak of her professional career, gone. I am still hardly able to cope with the loss. For months I was not really sleeping well. Today, nearly a year after her death, I can barely cope with the loss. My faith has been badly shattered. For months I declined absolutely to take communion. Today I still avoid it if at all possible. Nothing before in my life has affected me so badly. I don't know how to cope with it and sometimes wonder if anything makes much difference. But I keep trying to deal with the loss and hope that with the passage of time I may recover from this event.

I keep reminding myself that I still have two wonderful sons and their families, a great brother, and a wife who is a comfort. And of course I also have friends to share times and events with. I hope that with the passing of time the impact on me of Gretchen's death will lessen. I do indeed hope so.

Our 2008 trip to Singapore did provide us with an opportunity to get away from the problems in Seattle. But before we did take that trip I had to tend to a medical need which had been impending for some time - cataract surgery. In November 2007 I had the left eye operated on and then a month later, in December, had the right eye done. My vision is vastly improved, although there have been little events in the healing process which reminds one that I'm human. In 2008 our side trip from Singapore was to Penang in Malaysia. We both enjoyed the side junket very much.

In April of 2008 the Fourth & Pike building was sold. We did get a good price for the building. I hope all of my partners are happy about the sale. I continue to feel that it was a tragic mistake to sell the building. Son Richard and I have invested in the new ownership of the building and I have every hope that it will turn out to be a very good investment.

From a personal standpoint, I find my law practice is a part of my past. I am exploring some volunteer possibilities, but whether that will turn in to anything rewarding is an unknown. But Roberta and I do have more time to do some things that we have been talking about.

And so, here I am, eighty two years old and looking forward to more years and also looking back upon a life which I think has been incredibly good to me. As a young boy I could not possibly have imagined all the wonderful experiences and wonderful opportunities which have been afforded to me. Events which have not turned out as well as hoped have been dwarfed by all the wonderful good things that I have experience. I am indeed blessed.

When I get to this point in life I wonder whether I should write my some of my reflections. I should wonder whether I should write about some of my reflections and wonderings about what might have happened if I or we had made some different decisions at certain critical points in my life. Perhaps I should let that alone. I have been so fortunate and dame Fortune has smiled on me so many times that it might be best just to keep such thoughts to myself. But we shall see. We're well along in 2008 and perhaps the best thing to do is just to savor what has been and to look forward to the future - a future which I think will be bright and rewarding.